W9-BGO-815

KEVIN

Steve Delaney

KEVIN

The Last Invisible Vermonter

Steve Delaney

PLAIDSWEDE PUBLISHING
Concord, New Hampshire

Copyright © 2009, by Steve Delaney

All rights reserved. No part of this work may be used or reproduced in any manner whatsoever without written permission from the publisher, except in the case of brief quotations embodied in critical articles and reviews.

Kevin: The Last Invisible Vermonter is a work of fiction. Any resemblance between the characters in this book and actual people, living or dead, is coincidental.

Designed and composed at Hobblebush Books, Brookline, New Hampshire (www.hobblebush.com)

Printed in the United States of America

Publisher's Cataloging-In-Publication Data
(Prepared by The Donohue Group, Inc.)

Delaney, Steve.
　Kevin : the last invisible Vermonter / Steve Delaney.

　　p. ; cm.

　　ISBN: 978-0-9840650-0-4

1. Vermont—Fiction. 2. Government, Resistance to—Vermont—Fiction. 3. Fear—Fiction. 4. Man-woman relationships—Fiction. I. Title.

PS3604.E53 K48 2009
813.6   2009930903

Published by:

PLAIDSWEDE PUBLISHING
P.O. Box 269 · Concord, New Hampshire 03302-0269
www.plaidswede.com

*The late Charlie Cole of Milton, Vermont was
not Kevin by any means, but I did borrow the
old bike and the green clothes.*

*This is for Charlie and the countless men like
him who spent their lives proving that they
knew how to work.*

ACKNOWLEDGMENTS

Orphans are orphans because they lack support systems, those clutches of people who are there when needed.

My story makes an orphan of the young Kevin Beaujolais, but he was never without the help of people who cared about him.

Nor was I, in trying to pin down a story driven by both fear and love.

Frank Dobisky was always there, to read and to cheerlead. Ruth MacDougall scraped amateurism out of the text. John Cushing helped make some of the descriptive passages real. The Iron Skillet and Michelle's Short Stop are fictional, and so is Nilesburgh, and yet the Vermonters who thrive in the real counterparts of those places populate the world in which Kevin and Maureen live, and this is their monument as well. That's because, as a Recovering Flatlander, I've discovered that it's a pretty nice world here.

Chapters and People

Foreword

Kevin Beaujolais is nobody. Nobody I know, although there are echoes of real Vermonters in him.

Kevin is an heir to two centuries of Vermont independence; an embodiment of the same self-reliance that led the 14th state to be an independent nation for fourteen years after the American Revolution.

Kevin is also a victim of the Vermont mythology of stand-alone freedom; the same impulse that keeps many rural Vermonters from asking for help, or accepting it when it's offered.

In that fading subculture there is no expectation of prosperity. Reality is centered on survival. The best response to "How ya doin'? is "Gettn' by."

The only other response is "Not too bad," the stoic's version of "Not too good."

In an earlier book I wrote that Vermonters speak North American English, almost. In fact, we speak two dialects of our language; the one that reflects the speech of classrooms and newscasts, and the one that lingers from an era in which the ear, not the eye, was the teacher of language. It is nuanced, but in its simplest form the speech of old rural Vermont adds an "O" sound to those words which contain a long "I." Thus, Oy, moight, roight, and foind, among others, flavor the words of those more influenced by the family than by the classroom.

A generation ago, the nooks and crannies of Vermont held a scattering of people, many of them farmhands, who lived invisible to the authorities.

In this age of mandatory social security numbers and an obsession with security, it's probably not possible to live that way any more. If that's true, then Kevin is a transitional figure, struggling with both the world that formed him and the world that beckons.

AUTHOR'S NOTE

There's a silly notion that ideas flash into the mind full-grown.

Cartoonists have watered that illusion by drawing lightbulbs in bubbles over the heads of the suddenly-enlightened.

Ideas that want to be books don't emerge like Venus on the half-shell.

They're more likely to struggle to the light from a seed planted in the muck of the mind.

This one traces to a casual conversation with a man whose name I didn't know. He told me of the recent death of an old man in a nearby town, a man who had led a secretive and officially invisible life.

That little seed germinated fifteen years later as a series of questions. Can a man live that way these days? And if so, what sort of man must he be? What must he fear and how does that fear drive his decisions?

The answers, as I imagine them, emerge unfettered by the constraints of reality. "It could have been that way," is a far easier standard than "These are the facts," and generates a much more fertile garden for writers.

What grew there surprised the gardener.

Happy harvest.

Steve Delaney
Milton, Vermont
July, 2009

KEVIN

Prologue

Francis X. Forgan was looking at a brochure of Atlantic City, New Jersey when the phone rang, and so he ignored the phone. The Democrats were going to hold their nominating convention there in August, and Frankie was hoping to be named a Lyndon Johnson delegate from Vermont, or at least an alternate.

An assistant clerk in the vital records office did not have much clout, but Frankie had labored in the Democratic vineyard for years, driving voters to the polls, mailing and posting flyers, making phone calls; the works. *It ain't like they owe me, but maybe I'll call that young Phil Hoff down in the Governor's office. Bein' a Democrat sure is more fun since he got elected.*

When the party had picked the young John Kennedy, rest his soul, last time in California, Frankie Forgan had celebrated from afar by taking his round red face down to the bar behind the Courthouse and drinking himself silly. For once, the binge tasted of celebration rather than of misery.

Frankie's Mondays had been turning into Tuesdays lately. *I gotta stop callin' in sick on Mondays, cause it might hurt my chances.*

The phone didn't stop, so he picked it up, his focus on the Marlborough-Blenheim Hotel on the Boardwalk. Chamber music during high tea in the afternoons, the brochure said. *How many real Democrats would rather do tea and chamber music than talk politics in a real bar? There must be one around there somewhere.*

"Hello, Vital Records, Forgan here."

"Frankie, hey ya musta been on the potty again. It's Shirley over in Nilesburgh."

3

"Hey Shirley. *She's a Republican, like most of them people over there, but maybe she'll come over in the November vote.* Didja pop out another little Nilesbugger?"

"Yup, little boy. Took a long time, the mom was thin and not very strong. And it's Niles*burgher*, Frankie. Ready for the info?"

Frankie Forgan took a yellow form out of his desk and reluctantly placed it on top of the Marlborough-Blenheim. *Wonder if Winston Churchill owns that hotel?*

"Okay, Shirley, let's have it. Name first."

"Calvin Franklin Beaujolais. White male. Seven pounds, four ounces. Nineteen inches long, good health as far as I could tell. Parents: Rejean Beaujolais and Lisette Paquette Beaujolais, husband and wife, I seen the certificate, they was married the year Eisenhower was re-elected, 1956. *I know the old lush counts everything in four-year cycles.* Good Republican, Eisenhower."

"Shirley," he spluttered. "I tolja Ike wasn't no real partisan, not like yer freakin' Goldwater. Ike was a unity figure."

"Frankie, we shouldn't talk politics. You tease too easy. You got all you need about this new boy-baby?"

"Yup. I'll get it into the record in the next hour. Oh, what was the time of birth this morning?"

"Four seventeen, but it was yesterday morning. I slept a little." She didn't quite yawn, but he could hear the fatigue in her voice. She'd once told him that all the difficult births took all night, and that the easy ones were done before supper.

Frankie put down the phone and reached for his coffee. *Geez, I really need it this morning. Gotta find a better brand of gin.* His hand tipped the cup, and about four ounces of black coffee ran all over the birth certificate work sheet, and worse, the brochure under it. Frankie snatched the yellow form aside and mopped angrily at the slick paper with his hanky. *Better get it dry before the sugar sticks everything together. Shit shit shit!*

It was a few minutes before he got back to the birthing form. *Shit. The freakin' coffee ruined it. I can't read the name. Let's see, Calvin. We had a Vermont President named Calvin. Freakin' Republican. And what was next? Roosevelt. Okay, and one of them French names. Bo-somethin'. Bodette? No, three syllables. Bo-re-mi? Come on, Frankie. Bo Del Air, that's it. Do the French spelling.*

Ten minutes later the official record in the County Courthouse listed the following newly arrived Vermonter:

BAUDELAIRE, CALVIN ROOSEVELT, white male, May 6, 1964.
7lbs. 19 in. and sound, born at home in Nilesburgh, to
Ray John Baudelaire and Lisa Parquet, husband and wife.

A carbon copy went into a cubbyhole where the lady from the weekly newspaper would find it, along with the week's harvest of death certificates and marriage licenses. Frankie sat back in his creaky old chair and allowed himself a small smile. The paperwork was right, and orderly paperwork was the key to success as a civil servant. The job was easy, the paychecks always came in on time, and best of all, the politics. There was always something bubbling. Like this year.

Let's see, now. Hot-lannic City in August. Surely there will be good Democratic ladies in there for the convention, ladies who'll be charmed by the fine story-telling skills of a handsome fella with a Vermont accent, and just a trace of the Irish.

The opening skirmish in a one-sided war began on a sunny Tuesday in August, six years later. The winners never even knew there was such a struggle, but it still shaped the losers. It was Beaujolais vs. Bureaucracy, and it would go on for decades, mostly underground.

"Hello, Calvin, I'm Mrs. Mathis."

She got a steady, measuring stare, but no response.

"Right. Now, Mrs. Beaujolais, because Calvin didn't attend kindergarten last year, we don't have his records. Before we can register him for first grade, we need his birth certificate and immunization records."

Mrs. Mathis put her elbows on the once-glossy desktop, steepled her fingers and tried to look as if she were being very patient. There were several other children to be processed, and there was a trickle of perspiration running down her back inside the plus-sized flowered dress.

"Calvin ain't got them things. He was birthed at home on May 5, 1964. Six years ago. I remember, because it was the day my cousin

Jules and his wife got caught up in the rioting in Quebec over gettin' outa Canada. Shirley Cota, the birthin' woman, she was there, and she musta called it in, but we ain't never got no paper from the county." *Damn woman wants all the papers in order. You gotta have order in your life to do that, and there ain't none in mine, thanks to these government people and what they done to Rejean, and now they're tryin' to screw over poor Calvin too.*

"Shirley Cota's dead, Mrs. Beaujolais."

"Well, Calvin ain't dead, look at him."

Mrs. Mathis looked, and her mouth tightened into a thin line that ruined her projection of professional calm. *Why does there always have to be one like this in every new class? It slows the process so much, I'll be late leaving again. Why can't these people get anything right the first time?*

Calvin sat in a chair that kept his feet off the floor. He was wearing the new shoes, the ones the Keeper of the Poor had signed off on. There would be an entry in the Poor Account in the Nilesburgh Town Report next spring: "Shoes for the Beaujolais boy: $2.67."

The shoes were stiff and squeaky, and this was the first time Calvin had been allowed to wear them indoors. The room smelled like floor wax and lavender. *Pee-youie! If this is what a school smells like, I ain't gonna like it when it gets cold and they close them windows.*

"What about his pediatrics records? Those should show what shots he's had." Mrs. Mathis was getting brusque. *Don't these people have any respect for the proper procedures?*

"Needles?" Lisette Beaujolais shuddered, while her son watched, and learned a response to the word. "He never!"

"But we must have proof that every child has been immunized against dangerous diseases. And you can't prove anything. You don't even have papers showing that he was born."

"I ain't gotta prove nothin', lady. You're lookin' at the proof, right in that chair. What we got here is a six year-old boy that needs schoolin' and you gotta take him. *You old witch. I bet you don't treat the Elm Street families like this.* But I know he's had chicken pox and measles. I took him to play with Missy Bonette's kids when they caught all that stuff. Maybe mumps too."

6

Mrs. Mathis allowed a little empathy to slip through the condescension that she wore almost unconsciously when dealing with these welfare women and their half-wild kids. "Look, Mrs. Beaujolais, this is not about measles and mumps. It's about diphtheria and tetanus, you know, lockjaw, and it's about smallpox too. They're dangerous diseases, and one case could infect an entire school, and even kill students. You have to get him inoculated. He's a bright-looking boy *actually looks a bit like a rodent with those eyes and that sharp nose* and we'll be glad to welcome him, but not without his shots. We just can't do it, it's not fair to the other children."

"We can't afford no doctor," Lisette said in low tones, and Mrs. Mathis sat up straighter in her chair. *I know how much it hurts her to say she can't do this independently.* "And no innocu-you-know-what, either."

Calvin saw Mrs. Mathis reach into a drawer for a blue paper, write on it, and hand it to his mother.

"Take this to Doctor Tulley on Main Street. The School District will pay him."

Calvin sniffed up the fresh rich scents of the late summer air as they walked away from the school, a heavy clot of red bricks with multi-paned eyes on two floors, and "ANNO 1912" cut in gray granite over the door.

That night he got a thorough scrubbing, even though it was only Tuesday. The next morning they walked to the end of Poor Farm Road, and turned right toward the village.

Lisette and Calvin seldom completed that walk. Someone usually stopped to offer a ride to the thin woman and her son.

This time it was Ed Millette, who thought it was a little odd to take a truckload of hay to a former dairy farm that now boarded horses. But if the new people allowed their horses to track all over their hayfields, well, hay was money. Calvin sat in the back, looking for clover leaves in the bales.

Hay sure smells better before it's been through a cow, or horse either.

A lotta people must live here.

The boy knew how much space it took for him and Mom to live

in what the landlord called a mobile home. It was about as mobile as a tree, a wheel-less 2-bedroom house trailer, propped up on concrete blocks and poorly insulated.

This house was huge, three floors tall, and with a little tower thing like a pointed cap over its highest window. There was a wide porch around two sides of it, and they stepped up onto it, near the door marked *Clinic*.

He could feel his mother tensing up as she waited for someone to answer the bell, and so he felt apprehensive too.

Thomas Tulley, M.D. opened the door himself. "Ah, the young man the school sent over. Come in." His voice was deep and rumbly. *Mike the butcher wears a white coat just like that one, but this one ain't got no blood on it. It's got stuff sticking out of the pockets. I don't like the mustache. That man that treated Mom so bad had a big one just like that, only brown.*

The doctor led them into his examining room, where there was a small desk, a short bed with one end tipped up, and shelves full of medical stuff.

It stinks in here. He couldn't separate the odors of disinfectant, liniment, mercurochrome and maybe a little ether, but he would always connect that aroma to the world of medicine, and he would never feel at ease with it in his nose.

"Up you go, onto the table." *I coulda got up by myself.* The doctor sat at the desk and motioned Lisette to a small chair beside it. He pulled a form out of his desk.

"Now, then, young man, what's your name?" He looked over his glasses and tapped his pencil.

"Calvin," said Calvin, who had yet to master the letter **L**.

Dr. Tulley wrote what he heard. And he didn't hear very well any more. People muttered so. Kevin, he wrote. "Right, and how do you spell the last name?" Tommy Tulley had been the seventh of nine children growing up in the Charlestown Irish enclave surrounding Boston's Bunker Hill monument, and knew no French.

"It's Beaujolais." Lisette said.

"I asked you how you spell it." The doctor wasn't quite glaring over those glasses, but the woman was already intimidated by the white coat as well as the big house. *Ain't no neutral ground here, where a person could catch a break. So doctors is part of Them, just like teachers.*

"B-e-a-u," she began. "You pronounce that Bo?" he asked. "Yes. Then j-o-l-a-i-s."

"And what does that mean in English?" the doctor asked.

She looked even more uncomfortable. *It means my name, and Calvin's too.* "Beau means beautiful," she said. "But I don't know about the rest. Someone told me it's a French wine."

"Just out of curiosity, would your husband know?"

"He might, but I ain't seen him in five years. He's in Waterbury."

The doctor tried to soften his voice. "You mean the state hospital, don't you?"

"Yes," she said, looking straight at him. "Something happened to his head back in the war, and it just kept getting worse. I don't wanta talk about it just now," with a head nod toward the boy, who was listening intently. "The VA was involved." *Another clutch of weasels.*

Calvin/Kevin didn't cry when the doctor injected his arm. *Hurts a lot, but if I cry, Mom will too, and she cries too much anyways.*

Tough little kid. He's scared of me but he won't show it. Just stares bullets.

Sometimes it was hard for Tulley to justify the time he devoted to chasing into the odd corners of knowledge where his curiosity took him. This time it took only a glance into an encyclopedia to learn that Beaujolais was once a mini-province in east central France, a ten-by-forty mile stretch of Rhone River valley centered on the remnant of the village of Beaujeu, which meant, more or less, beautiful play or beautiful game. *I should order some of that wine.*

The I-G-A store was dark and cool, and had its own smells. It sold food and stuff that working families needed. Boots and gloves and denim clothes, and kitchen things. They went there for a treat after the shots. *Five cents. I can get a lotta hard candy for five cents, or a big chocolate bar that won't last nearly as long.* Calvin stared so hard at the display that he began drooling, and finally picked the brown-wrapped bar with almonds.

Outside, he stripped the wrapper and gave his mother half. She gave him back half of her half, and they walked home through the late summer dust, a lady on welfare and a little boy with a sore arm. He took his mother's hand and felt the comfort in it. *Maybe her next boyfriend will be nicer. Maybe I can get out before supper. Old Man Ellis said he was gonna show me how to find animal trails in the woods. He told me there's eighteen different kinds of trees out there. I'm still missin' a few.*

On the last day of August, 1970, TIME magazine reported that an energy shortage was getting worse, that Black Panther activist Angela Davis was on the run, and that Vice President Spiro Agnew was off to Southeast Asia to try to talk Thailand into putting its soldiers into a widening war.

At the micro end of that day's news a little boy stood in the morning light, watching a breeze tousle a few newly turned maple leaves, and waiting for the yellow bus with a bag lunch in his hand. It was hard climbing up because the steps were so high, but coming down was just a series of hops to the ground.

"All right, children! First graders over here, everybody else go find your classrooms, your names will be posted by the grade numbers on the doors."

This ain't so bad. Some of 'em look scareder'n me. Like that kid with the dark smudges under his eyes.

"All right, students, follow me inside."

Inside was bright with last year's art-work, still clinging to the hallway walls. There was a desk outside a door marked 1.

"Line up here, please, and have your medical forms ready." She smiled at their response. *Not bad. Sometimes you have to teach them how to line up.* The teacher took each form, copied down the name, and passed it to an aide who made out name tags to be pinned onto shirts and dresses. Alice. Jerry. George. Kevin. Lisa. Arnold. Malcolm, who wanted to be called Macky.

"All right, everyone. I'm Miss Ronan. Welcome to your first year at Nilesburgh Elementary. We'll learn a lot in the next nine months."

Binky

The Winnebago's hazard lights were flashing, and it listed to the right on a dirt road where sunlight slanted through maples. It had Ohio plates.

A woman was fluttering behind her husband as he examined the flat right front tire. She was in her fifties, and dressing younger made her look older. He was older, and looked frustrated.

A small cinnamon-colored dog with fuzzy hair danced and yapped at the end of a retractable leash, sparked by three dimly curious Holstein heifers ambling toward the Winnebago in an adjacent pasture.

"Binky, shut up!" the man snapped. His glasses slid down his nose.

"What's wrong, dear?" she asked, leaning over his shoulder.

"What's wrong?" he echoed bitterly. "Well for one thing the goddam rental people didn't put a goddam jack in this goddam tank!"

"It's not a tank George, it's a camper deluxe, and you loved it until five minutes ago. And besides, Dr. Miles said whenever you say three goddams in one breath, you need to take one of those red pills, the ones that calm you down."

"I AM CALM, Gladys. I am calm. And I'd be a lot calmer if a hawk would pounce on your fuzzy goddam rat-dog and carry it off! And if I could fix the goddam tire, and if we could get the hell out of Ethan Allen's goddam armpit. Where the hell are we anyway? Back roads are best for Vermont's peak foliage, you say. Back roads, my ass."

The little dog yapped again, more urgently.

"Shut up, Binky!"

"It koinda sets yer teeth on edge, don't it?"

George looked up from the flat tire. Bicycle wheel. Work boot, somewhat scuffed. Green denim pants, not new, not dirty. Black and green plaid shirt under a sleeveless down vest. Red Sox baseball cap, quite faded. And a weathered face with sunken cheeks surrounding a friendly smile.

George had to smile back. "Gladys says it's a dog. Maybe so. Best day the little bastard ever had, he still pissed on the sofa."

The man had an easy laugh, and even Gladys smiled. Binky produced a sustained growl that sounded like an old mixmaster on slow.

"Well now," the man said, laying his bike down. "Let's see what else is screwin' up yer day."

George told him, with only a few goddams, that the rental people had sent them off without a jack.

"Ya gotta spare mounted on the back. Can ya get it off?"

"Yes, but if I can't get the flat one off…"

"Oh, we'll manage that. It'll take a few minutes. Let's see, Sunday morning, Aaron'll be at church. Otter be able to get the wrecker, Oy know where he keeps the key."

"Wrecker? Does it have to be towed?" George asked.

"Nah, we just gotta pick up the front end a bit." He stood up and dug a flat metal can out of a pocket, and tucked a pinch of its contents in behind his lower lip.

"Chewing tobacco?" Gladys asked. She'd never seen anyone do that.

"Nah, snuff. Dippin' tobacco." *Jeezum, flatlanders don't know shit.*

Gladys tried not to make a face. *Snuff! Do people still do that?*

"Now," the man said as he swung a leg over his bike. "Oy'm goin' ta get some help. Be back in about twenty minutes. Just rest easy, and if Oy was you, Oy'd tie the little fucker's mouth shut." Binky was barking again, straining at his leash and showing a lot of sharp little teeth. "Ya best put him insoide, cause if he gets any a them teeth inta me, he's dead." And the man rode away.

"George, that was a threat!" Gladys was indignant.

"I don't think it was a threat at all," he said. "No more than if he had said it'll get dark when the sun goes down. I think he meant every word of it. *If I'm really lucky Binky will try to bite that guy. If not, I could always kill the little turd myself.* Put Binky in the shower, so when he shits it'll be easier to clean up."

"Do you think he'll come back, that odd little man?"

"He said he would. Now why don't you get out a lawn chair and look at some of those leaves we came all this way to see, while you're waiting?"

In twenty minutes an enormous white wrecker went by blasting its air horn and sending the little dog into trembling hysterics. It turned around somewhere out of sight and came back to park just in front of the Winnebago. The driver climbed down, and George noted it took him three steps to reach the ground.

"Too big ta turn around in the road," the man in green said, doing things with straps and cables in the back.

"How are you going to do this?" George asked.

"Drop two sections of foire hose off the hook with these rings, that's ta keep the cable from scratchin' the bumper, and then we use the hooks on the other end ta catch the tow-points on the camper," he said, doing it as he said it.

"I never saw anything like that," Gladys said.

"Well missus, Aaron's in business ta move anything that's got wheels, and this ain't much of a challenge."

"Does he know you've got his truck?" George wanted to know.

"Pretty much. Left moy boike there, so he'll know who's got it. Anyways, we moight get it back before he gets home from church."

He went to the controls. The truck took a couple of deep diesel breaths and lifted the front of the camper clear of the ground.

"Get in an' romp down on the brakes just in case the wheels don't hold still."

George got into the camper, and there came a metallic chattering, then silence, then more noises, and finally he saw the man lowering the camper back to the ground. He climbed out.

"That was quick," he said. "What was all that racket?"

Man could be a danger to his own self. How'd he get so old, knowing

13

so little? "Aaron keeps a compressor on the truck, to droive the lug wrench. Makes the job go quicker. You'll be foine now, welcome to Noilesburgh."

He climbed back into the truck, which belched black smoke and moved off.

Gladys let the dog out and he piddled on the spare tire. George lifted the flat one into the camper, and pulled back onto the road.

"Who was that man?" she wondered.

"He didn't say. Maybe it was Sam. Yeah, let's call him Sam."

"Sam? Why Sam?"

"For Good Samaritan," he said. "He sure did us a big favor."

A few miles later they drove into Nilesburgh and gassed up at a combination gas station and grocery/deli. The overhead sign said *Michelle's.*

A handwritten notice by the door said *No shirts, no shoes, no service.*

"Welcome to Noilesburgh," the pretty young cashier said. She had short dark hair, an infectious grin that revealed slightly crooked white teeth, and, George thought on glancing down, excellent posture.

The girl examined her newest customers. *They got that on-the-road look, for sure. We been gettin' a lotta these Flatlanders lately. Must be a pretty good leaf season. Anyways, Michelle says they all bring money.*

"Thanks for the greeting," said George. "That's the second time I've heard that in the past few minutes. The first time was a man who changed a flat tire for us."

He described the man, and how he had gone for a wrecker. "I feel like one of those guys at the end of a Lone Ranger episode, asking, 'Who was that man?'"

The Lone Ranger reference went over the girl's head, but George's description must have been accurate.

"That's Kevin. Green clothes, green bike, used face. Oy seen him go by in Aaron's wrecker a few minutes ago."

"Won't this man Aaron be angry when he finds it's been used? And the man, Kevin, you say, didn't stay long enough for us to pay him."

"Well, loike Kevin don't take money on Sundays. And anyways, if he hadn't gone out there, Aaron would have to, and Aaron's woife found Jesus, and so it's easier for him at home if he don't loike get a call during church."

"But I have to find this Kevin and reward him."

"It'll be $45.50 for the gas, mister. And you can't foind him. Nobody foinds Kevin unless he wants them to."

"You mean he just disappears?"

"Yup. *Ain't never tried explainin' Kevin to folks from Away. Ain't even tried explainin' Kevin to myself. He just sorta is.* Do you want some hot goulash while you're here? Only takes a minute to heat it up. Just move that thing off the pump and pull it over by the shed."

She served them at a small tired table that had plastic doilies, paper napkins, and cheap knives and forks. There were mismatched pieces of dusty dining room furniture piled in a corner, with a For Sale sign on top of them.

At a nearby table, a man in work clothes sat hunched over a paper cup of coffee. He stared into the brown surface as if it were a window to a distant and better place. He did not look up at the newcomers.

George looked around at the weathered beams under the roof. *They look like they used to hold up a barn somewhere. Part gas station, part deli, part grocery, I wonder what else?*

"Miss, what do you call this place?"

"Michelle's," she said. "She's the owner, and Oy'm her daughter's step-daughter. Moy name is Lena."

No, what I meant was, what do you call this type of store?"

"Oh, short stop, quick stop, one stop, there's lots of names. Oy guess downcountry you'd call it a convenience store. You can return bottles for a nickel, buy gas for a penny less, buy a sandwich for two dollars, buy beer and woine and cigarettes, snuff too, and you can even buy real food if you don't moind a little dust on the cans."

She came out from behind a glass-fronted deli counter and turned down the radio, muffling Loretta Lynn's warning to her man, not to come home a-drinkin' with lovin' on his mind.

Coffeeman stirred himself. "Hey Lena, Oy can't hear the radio!"

Gladys made a show of placing her napkin. "Listen, miss, Lena, is it? You can turn that back up if you want to."

"Well Oy don't. Oy'm a Trisha Yearwood fan, and Oy don't much loike them old-toimey singers. Too whoiney. Besoides, old Carl's been sittin' here since about sunroise, nursin' that cuppa cold coffee. He gets a little spooky after a few hours." She bustled around the table, whisking invisible crumbs off the checkerboard tablecloth with a napkin.

"Cream with your coffee? And you'll want some salt and pepper."

"How do you know that?" Gladys wondered.

"Cause Oy know who cooked it. And Claire never puts no seasoning in the food. She figures folks will fix it to their own taste."

"So tell me about this Kevin," George prompted. She stared at the ceiling for a moment, as if trying to decide how to answer.

"Well, Kevin is loike, country. He's a bit of a town character and very independent. He owes nobody, he takes crap from nobody, and most everybody loikes him. You can see for yourself he's a koind-hearted man. *Kevin must be in a good mood today. I don't ever recall a story about him lending a hand to Flatlanders before.* And when you droive outa here, you can be proud that Kevin Beaujolais took a loikin' to you."

"He didn't like our dog," the wife said. Some of the sunshine left the girl's face.

"Kevin and dogs is a tricky thing," she said. "He gets along foine with the big old ball-chaser dogs, like retrievers and labs, but it's loike the little snarly ones, loike they don't take to him so much. He's had his ankles nipped quite a lot roidin' on that boike. What kind of dog have you got?"

George laughed out loud. "Perfect match," he said. "Dog's name is Binky, and looks like a fuzzy rat. Her dog," he said, gesturing broadly with a thumb. *Don't want this pretty girl thinking I'd have a dog like that.*

Gladys ignored him. "How much do you think we should pay him?" she asked. The girl scratched on a piece of paper.

"Aaron would probably charge you, loike twenty for the road service, twenty for Sunday and ten to do the toire. So, loike fifty."

"Okay," said George. "If we can't find him, as you say, will you hold the money until you see him?"

"No."

"Why not?"

"Because you don't know me well enough to trust me, and you'll never know whether Kevin gets the money or whether Oy keep it." She looked as if fifty dollars would be a real windfall.

"But," she went on. "When you droive down the road, you'll pass the Iron Skillet doiner. He's there as often as he's anywhere, and they take loike messages and stuff for him. Just wrap a ten and two Jacksons in a paper napkin, and leave it with Suzie. Oh, she won't be there today, you know, loike the best waitresses never work on Sunday, cause they do so good on Saturday. So Laura will be there, and you can trust her to put the money away where Kevin will get it next toime he's in there. Or, you don't have to do nothing, cause he didn't ask for any money, did he?"

"Well, we do have to," George said. "It's the right thing to do."

The Iron Skillet was easy to find, and George was conscious that he and Gladys changed its atmosphere just by walking in.

Chatter slowed or stopped at a row of tables for four that had been shoved together in the middle of the room. Middle-aged men and their women sat over coffee at those tables, planing the surfaces of old stories and searching for gobbets of new gossip.

"Flatlanders on deck," muttered a man who had been in the Navy, and had loved it enough to bring bits of sea-slang home with him. Those who had their backs to the door simply turned around and stared for a few seconds, not with hostility, just looking over the couple and dismissing them as people from Away. After a moment, their coffee and their suspended conversations became more important.

George, who was not easily intimidated, walked right up to the man who had stared the hardest.

"I'm looking for a man named Kevin Beaujolais," he said.

"Don't know him," said the coffee sipper, a round-faced man in an Australian cowboy hat that looked even more out of place than he and Gladys did. *Ain't givin' Kevin away to no stranger. How'd they ever get his name?*

"He ain't here," said a woman in the next chair. *Let's see what they want.* She wore dangly earrings, pink-rimmed glasses, and several metallic bracelets that chinged as she gestured.

"What do you want him for?" asked a friendly-faced woman farther down the table. George zeroed in on her.

"Well, ma'am, he helped us out on the road back there, but he left before we could do anything for him."

"Ya mean loike pay him?" It was Outback Hat's question.

"Well, we'd like to try, or at least say thank you."

"Kevin don't take money on Sundays," said Bracelet Woman. "And anyways, he don't need much."

"Well, he didn't look rich to me," said George.

"Kevin measures rich by his own scale," said Friendly Woman, "and if you think the way he does, he's quite a wealthy man."

George looked puzzled. *I wish one of them would ask me to sit down, but I don't think that's going to happen. And I can understand the words they're saying, but the meaning isn't clear. Maybe I can prompt them a bit.*

"The more I hear about this man," he said, "the more interesting he gets. The girl at the gas station, Michelle's I think it was, she said we should feel really honored that this Kevin Beaujolais took a liking to us."

"You should," said Bracelet Woman. "That'll be Lena, and she's got her own reasons for saying that. But she's roight. Mosta the toime when Kevin meets folks from Away, he just walks away."

This isn't getting anywhere.

Gladys tried. "Look, we just want to do something nice for a man who did something nice for us."

"Well, if you put it that way," said Outback Hat. George and Gladys waited for him to go on, but he just leaned back and folded his hands over an ample lap.

"Look, folks," said a man who dressed like he'd been to church. "Kevin is sort of a local treasure…."

"Now don't you go too far with that!" Bracelet Woman's arms were chingling. "He ain't no freakin' saint, ya know."

"Mister," said Friendly Woman. "It would take a real long toime to explain Kevin to you, and then Oy'm not sure you'd get it. He looks out for some old folks and for some people down on their luck, but he does it his way. And so folks around here look out after him too."

"The girl, Lena, said he just disappears," said Gladys.

"He does. And the reason nobody can find him is, is that nobody knows where to look. A whoile back one of the listers troied to foind him, and troied hard, but she had to give it up."

"Can you be invisible in this day and age?" George asked, unwilling to show that that he didn't know what a lister was.

"I don't know," said Church Man. "But Kevin's been doin' it all his loife, so far."

"Anyway the girl said we could leave some money for him here, and that he'd get it."

"That's roight," said Bracelet Woman. "Hey, Laura!" The waitress came over. "More coffee, Alice?"

"Laura, these folks wanta leave somethin' for Kevin."

George held out an envelope, and Laura wrote *Kevin* on it with the stubby pencil she used to take menu orders. "Who do Oy say it comes from?"

"The Winnebago people," said Gladys. "The ones with the fuzzy rat," said George. "He'll understand."

Ruby

The word *feist* describes a certain kind of small dog. He is inquisitive, energetic and tenacious. He has short wiry hair, mostly white, and he carries himself with confidence.

If Ruby Mongeon had two more legs she would be a feist. Ruby was one of those concerned citizens who step forward in every northern New England town to do the community's civic business. Ruby was hyper-concerned.

She was on the library board, the Historical Society's steering committee, and ran the Altar and Rosary Society at St. Gabriel's Church.

She belonged to the Nilesburgh Senior Center, the Grange and the Democratic Party.

For a while Ruby was also an elected Lister, one of three people who set tax valuations on property. Back when the town had a poll tax, she had to get all the voters to sign a registration form, and take a dog census at the same time.

"I went to every house," she said in a Mission Accomplished voice. Ruby crackled a bit when she spoke, and crackled a lot when she was feeling proud of herself.

"It took me nine months and more, mostly cause I couldn't find Kevin Beaujolais," she told the Town Clerk. "Oh, I'd see him around all the time riding that old green bike, but I couldn't find his house. Kevin didn't have an address," she said, as if that were a civic mortal sin. The Clerk, who knew exactly where Kevin lived, made sympathetic clucking noises.

Ruby's pursuit of Kevin Beaujolais became a running joke down at the Iron Skillet, where working men gathered early for breakfast and gossip.

Jeffrey Adams was the worst.

"Oh, Rooby," he'd sing. "Don't chase old Kevin down."

Ruby was about sixty at the time, and Kevin's elusiveness had stretched all the elastic out of her sense of humor.

"You must want a date pretty bad, to go harin' around after Kevin, he can get roight whiffy sometimes," Jeffrey teased. "Here, ask Leo."

Leo heard his name and grinned. Scrambled egg fell out of his mouth, and his wife patiently forked it back in.

Leo had been a pretty good roofer until he fell off the gable end of a shed and landed badly.

Albie Jackson got the guys at the Skillet to chip in for a lawyer, to see if there was any way Leo's wife could collect disability or some other kind of compensation. The lawyer came back and said there were difficulties.

That lawyer had a practice confined to title searches in real estate sales.

"Hey, Leo," Jeffrey called out. "You'll go out with Ruby, won't you?"

Leo drooled. Ruby lifted a red-tipped finger and showed it to Jeffrey. And Charlie O'Malley choked on his coffee. Charlie was the laugh barometer for the plumbers and excavators and welders who "owned" the diner during breakfast hours.

Charlie thought almost everything was funny, and the sight of little Ruby giving big old Jeffrey the finger struck him as absurd, just as he was trying to swallow. Coffee came out his nose and mouth and tears came out his eyes.

It was Jim Shipley who broke up the diner by slapping Charlie on the back and asking, "You all right, Leo?"

Ruby was still mad. "You better watch yourself, Jeffy Adams. I whupped you in third grade and I can still do it."

"Ruby you were in seventh, and besoides, you had a baseball bat."

"Did not, it was just a stick. Anyways, have you seen Kevin?"

"Sure," Charlie said. "About twenty minutes ago. Had a omelet, didn't he Suzie?"

"Cheese and onion," Suzie said. "He loves them onions."

If Suzie said cheese and onions, then it was cheese and onions. She was legendary for saying things like, "We ain't got that, and you don't want it anyways." Suzie's outfits all showed some cleavage, because she thought it brought in bigger tips, especially after she went to the tanning salon. She had a toddler, a boyfriend in prison and a "friend" who slept in. She seldom smiled, even for Jeffrey.

"He was talkin' about whether there's any day-work at the sawmill," she told Ruby, and Ruby left without seeing an old green bike tucked in behind the diner's dumpsters.

Suzie walked over to the men's restroom and knocked. "You can come out now, Kevin. She's gone."

"Yeah, get out of there, Kevin, I gotta pee. And I guess Charlie does too, hell, he's leakin' from everywheres else!" Jeffrey Adams hopped around his table in a wide-bodied parody of a small boy in the most urgent stage of "gotta go now!"

Kevin came out grinning. "Sounds like Oy missed all the fun."

"Well, you started it. You seen Ruby comin' and run loike a rat for your hoidey-hole. So then Jeffy says she was pretty hard up for a date, chasin' after you, and she could maybe get a date with Leo, and she give him the finger, and then Oy lost it with coffee in my mouth. She just looked so damn fierce," and he started laughing again. The guys agreed it was a pretty good morning at the Skillet.

"Kevin, why don't you loike Ruby?" Leo's wife asked.

"It ain't Ruby, it's what she's about. Oy don't want the government in moy business."

"But it's just updating the Grand List, we've all done it. Oy even soigned up Leo here."

"It's a tax, and it ain't fair and Oy ain't payin' it."

Kevin moved to the coffee pot that Suzie kept filled. The men wouldn't let Suzie pour coffee at their tables any more.

That happened when some wild kid who worked for a concrete company tried playing with Suzie's ass one morning. Suzie emptied her coffeepot in his lap. "If you ever touch me again, I'll cut your pecker off!" She yelled over his groans.

22

Albie Jackson took hold of the kid's arm and stood him up. The kid didn't want to stand, but there he was.

"You're leavin', Fartsniffer."

"You can't make me," the kid squawked, trying to hold his boiled nuts with one hand and to wriggle loose from Albie with his other hand. He was learning that all the new man-strength he was so proud of wasn't going to help him here. He couldn't shake the man's grip.

Albie wasn't as tall as the kid, but he was wide and he was solid. He'd spent most of his life squeezing hammers and cow teats, and his hands were immensely strong. What Albie laid hold of stayed held until Albie decided to let go, and just then he was deciding to clamp down harder.

"Listen, chickenfucker. I can make you, and I will make you, and I don't much care whether you go screamin', or go quiet, you're goin'."

"Hey Albie, can Oy whack him?"

"Nah, Charlie, just open the door."

When they got to the kid's truck, Albie smacked his head on the doorpost, just to get his attention.

"You listen good, peckerhead. Don't come back here, ever. And if I hear of any vandalism here, or if Suzie gets bothered, by anybody, I will find you, and I will squeeze your balls until you squeak like a bat."

For three days the kid couldn't lift his left arm, and for two weeks he had vivid bruises in the shape of fingers on his bicep.

After that, the morning crowd all poured their own coffee, and if anybody touched Suzie's ass, it was an accident, and nobody made jokes about it.

Charlie and Jim Shipley wondered out loud for a few days whether Suzie had done Albie an intimate personal favor in return for the assist, but Jeffrey Adams told them they were being 7th-grade snarky, and they dropped the notion when they couldn't detect any change in behavior between the contractor and the waitress.

"Hey, Suzie," Kevin said quietly on the day Ruby was hunting for him. "Oy've got Leo's breakfast, and Emma's too."

"Can you afford that?"

"Sure, Oy worked yesterday, and Oy'm workin' again today. Besides, Oy ain't got much expenses, you know."

She knew. They all knew. Officially, Kevin didn't exist. There was no record of him anywhere. They envied him for simplifying his life. They liked Ruby too, or they wouldn't have teased her, but if Kevin wanted to live invisible to the government, they weren't going to stand in his way. Not the diner crowd, who had all seen his small kindnesses, and not the Town Clerk, who had seen some big ones.

Uncle

In a few barns and garages around Nilesburgh, and here and there downcellar, there are faded signboards that say *"Vote Billy In."* They're plywood nailed to oak stakes, hand-painted by the Brophys.

There are a lot of Brophys, and Billy is the youngest. He was just out of school when the old Clerk-Treasurer retired, and his deputy thought she would succeed him. Billy Brophy won that election, largely because he had cut grass or baled hay or picked apples or bagged groceries for almost everybody in town. He went to those people and asked them to hire him.

He had a fresh face and a no-nonsense 1967 buzzcut, and he said he would work hard.

That was the last contested election for Clerk/Treasurer. Billy holds the town record for winning consecutive elections, and maybe by now the state record too. When old people came in to say they were having trouble paying their land taxes, Billy would take them into his cluttered little office, and if any tears flowed, he never said so.

Billy Brophy had only been clerking for a few years when young Kevin Beaujolais came to see him one spring day in the middle of the Reagan years.

"How ya doin', Billy?"

"Gettn' by, Kevin. And you?"

"Not too bad. Hey Billy, Oy gotta talk to ya."

Billy opened the locked door that kept the public away from the tax rolls and the deed books and the vault.

"Oy don't much loike bein' locked in."

"Think of it as the rest of 'em bein' locked out," said Billy. *Poor bastard's got a right to be spooky about locks. That last police chief made it a personal mission to lock him up for vagrancy, and before that it was truancy from school, quite a lot of it.*

The Clerk's workspace was an old, heavily scratched desk that had been in service in the office since good handwriting was a necessity. Billy was glad that wasn't true any more. He shoved some papers aside.

"Anyways," Kevin was saying. "It's about Uncle Gormley. Oy been sugarin' with him, ya know."

Billy knew. Emil Gormley had no children, but so many nephews that almost everybody got to calling him Uncle. It had been Uncle Emil for a while, but after a few kids got beaten up for changing that to Uncle Evil, it became Uncle Gormley. After a while, Uncle became his first name.

"Well, Uncle and Hannah have got it rough this year. He has to hoire help because of his back, mostly me, and milk proices are down again. Oy troied to get outa takin' his money, but he's too proud ta let me."

Billy knew about that kind of pride. It undid as many stubbornly independent Vermonters as it ennobled. He'd seen broken men try to stand up straight while paying their land taxes with the wife's egg money and insisting that all was well.

"Uncle ain't got any money, but Oy do, and mostly it came from him. What's his taxes?"

"That's his business, Kevin."

"Yeah, and he'd be madder'n a wet cat for me to know, but ain't it public record?"

"You know, for a man who tries so hard to keep the government out of his business, you sure know a lot about how it works. Wait here a minute."

Billy went to the files and came back with a copy of the three-part tax bill. The idea was to encourage people to pay in three installments, but since the taxes weren't overdue until after the middle of May, most people paid as late as possible, and so the town always had to borrow money against that anticipated revenue.

"All right, the total is public record, and it's one thousand seven hundred and forty two dollars, and some change. What's not public, and I'll deny I ever told you this, is what's been paid on it. A hundred and eighty dollars in September, and forty three in December."

Kevin looked thoughtful. "Oy'd say September was money they got for hay, and December was most of a Christmas check they got from young Molly, downcountry." Molly was the only niece among all those nephews.

"Other words," said Billy. "They're strapped."

"Toighter'n a wind-row hay bale. That's where Oy come in. Here."

The money came out of all of Kevin's pockets. Crumpled fives shedding sawdust, tens with hay chaff in their folds, quite a few greasy twenties, and ones, lots of ones, and seven crisp fifties. Plus, eighteen silver dollars and a half-eagle gold piece that had to be worth much more.

"Wait a minute," said Billy. I got to call a guy." He dialed from memory.

"Hey Jim, it's Billy Brophy. How ya doin?" He twirled the coin, making it spin on his desk, and watching the glow flash from each side as it rotated and then crashed into a stack of papers.

"Not too bad, Jim. Lissen, another one just come in for taxes, and I need to value it. 1909 half-eagle piece, a little wear but not much. Has a nice clink when you drop it on the desk. That much? Okay, thanks, Jim. I'll get it over there today." He twirled the coin again and looked up at Kevin. "He said three fifty. Three hundred and fifty."

"That's more'n Oy thought," said Kevin. "And he counted it for foive dollars when he paid me."

"Kevin, there's nine hundred dollars and more here."

"Noine fourteen seventy foive," said Kevin, "if Oy remembered all moy pockets, and counting the gold for three fifty. Put it against Uncle's taxes."

"I can't do that, and if I could, how would I explain it to them? They got their tax bill last fall."

"You're the smart guy, Billy, you figure it out. Sure you can do it, Jeezum Crow, why do you think folks keep votin' you back in? They trust you. Uncle and Hannah, they trust you. Just say when you were lookin' things over, you found somethin'. Don't gotta be a mistake, just you found somethin', and their balance is what, six hundred and foive dollars?"

Billy punched some buttons on his calculator and it burped.

"$604.25. Kevin, for a guy who started shaving your second year in fourth grade, you do pretty good with the numbers."

"Numbers is easy, it's letters that always got me. Ya know, a big K looks loike a K, but in handwriting a little k looks loike a pinched h. Anyways, thanks for helpin' out, and don't say nothin' about me."

Billy was left shaking dust out of Kevin's money, and shaking his head as chaff rained lightly on his desk. Kevin had refused a receipt. "If you wroite one, you'll keep a copy of it, and there moy name will be on a government paper. Oy ain't havin' it. Besoides, Billy, Oy trust you too."

The Gormleys came in ten days before the tax deadline, and Billy Brophy trotted out the line he'd been rehearsing, about a non-specific "something" in the tax records.

Uncle didn't even let him finish.

"That flea-scratchin' little woodchuck done this, didney."

"Did what, Uncle?"

"Jeezum Crow, boy, Oy ain't stupid. Oy know how much my taxes was, and it's near a thousand dollars over what you got showin' on that bill. Freakin' Kevin done it, and he run you in on it too." Uncle's outstretched index finger had a big blue spot under the nail, where he'd missed with a hammer.

Billy tried a diversion. "Uncle, did you ever ask for help on this?"

"No Oy never. And Oy never would. Billy, a man otter pay his taxes, and it ain't nobody else's business." Uncle's face reddened, even above the hat line, where it was white and bare. Billy read that as embarrassment.

Hannah just sat there quietly, twisting her plain gold wedding band around her thin finger. She always brought him a baked treat, and for a while he had taken them over to the Senior Center. That stopped after Hannah and Uncle had lunch at the center one day and she recognized her apple pie.

She had made Uncle drive her straight to Town Hall.

"That was from me to you, Billy, not to be spread around among all them old people. You don't know what a gift is, so you won't be getting' no more."

It had taken her six years to get over it. Now she brought cookies, mostly chocolate chips, figuring that if Billy was going to give them away, at least the cookies wouldn't have to be sliced up.

"Uncle, you didn't ask Molly for a check last Christmas, did you. But you cashed it, right?"

"How'd you know about that? Aha!" The blue-nailed finger rose again.

"That shit-lickin' Kevin! Sorry, Hannah. Oy promised Hannah Oy wouldn't say shit, and now look what you made me do."

Billy tried again. "Uncle, if a man held a door open for you, would you refuse to walk through it?"

"No, but that's different."

"No, it ain't. Just in the details. And anyways, you didn't ask. That's the important part, right?"

"Well…"

"By the way, how was your sugar this year?" Billy knew when the point had been made.

"Me'n Kevin made about 240 gallons, a lot of fancy grade early, and then pretty good darker stuff. Been sellin' pretty good too."

The Gormleys had one of those small Vermont Maple Syrup signs in their dooryard. Once in a while, tourists and even locals would turn in to buy.

They'd leave with a rectangular tin container that bore images of horses in the snow, sap buckets and a steamy sugarhouse. The dooryard price was usually twenty dollars a gallon.

Billy said he was having trouble with his syrup filtration system, and Hannah suggested adding a few layers of diaper material to the felt.

Billy stopped himself from saying he didn't have any diaper material, because he knew that would start Hannah on another round of match-making. She'd been trying to get him married off ever since he was first elected, and her taste in prospective brides was nowhere near his.

By then Uncle was over being mad that part of his taxes had been paid for him, and took out his checkbook to pay the balance.

"I can put a stamp where it says, 'Pay to the order of...'" said Billy.

"Thanks. Here you go." The check was number 143, drawn on a bank that had been merged into another bank. Billy would have to walk it into the successor bank to get it negotiated. Last year, he had asked Uncle Gormley why he didn't get new checks. He should have known better.

"What the hell for? They charge for them things. And anyways, the name's roight, the address is roight, and the phone number's roight. Besoides, Oy still got near a whole box of 'em."

Kevin was at the Iron Skillet when Uncle and Hannah found him. That's where most people found him, if they were patient.

In those days Tough Thelma ran the place. She was little and stringy, and somewhere past 60. She wore bright lipstick and bright orange smudges on her cheeks.

She never wrote anything down, she never got anything wrong, and she never insulted first-time patrons. Kevin was fair game.

"Hey, it's Bozo Beaujolais, Oy thought Oy smelled somethin'. When's the last toime you had a bath?"

"Long toime after you last had a date, Tough. When was that, 1946?"

That settled the niceties of protocol, but Thelma wouldn't let it go.

"Not 1946, Bucko. Oy had a better year in '46 than yer freaking Red Sox, losin' the Series to them birds from away downcountry."

Tough Thelma knew them birds were called Cardinals, but she couldn't say the word. She knew what a Cardinal was. It wore red robes and lived in Boston, and preached against most of the pleasures she enjoyed. She buttoned the shapeless sweater she wore, and went on the attack.

"Besoides, all them boys was just home from the war an' somebody hadda make 'em feel welcome. Jeezum Crow, Oy sure done moy share. Hey, maybe one of 'em was yer daddy. Sumbitch, Kevin, Oy moighta been yer mama! Now watcha want fer breakfast?"

Kevin looked decidedly unhungry. "Just coffee, Tough. Oy feel a little sick right now."

A fat guy stopped abusing his chair, and got up to leave. "Jeezum, Thelma, Oy'd feel sick too if Oy had to think about you bein' my mama."

"Out, you frickitty basketball! And next time, see if you can taste the rat poison in yer eggs."

Uncle and Hannah paid no attention. There were always loud voices in the diner, sometimes because the older patrons didn't hear well, but more often because Tough Thelma had found a chink in somebody's armor, and was pouring on the acid. They sat down at Kevin's table.

"What's wrong with you?" Hannah was not subtle.

"Tough Thelma just hinted that she screwed my old man when he got home from the war. Said she coulda been my mama." He was almost shuddering.

"Hell, boy, Thelma screwed everybody in them days," Uncle said. "They didn't call her the Noilesburgh Open for nothin', ya know."

Kevin chuckled. He'd never heard that title, though there were plenty of Tough Thelma stories going around.

Hannah was not amused. "You too, smiley boy?"

Uncle stalled. "Kevin, pass the sugar. No, not me, dear. Oy was bloind except for you, everybody knows that." Kevin raised his eyes to the ceiling.

"Look at her," Hannah muttered. "She moighta turned heads in 1946, but she turns stomachs now, don't she Kevin?"

Kevin thought anything he might say would just encourage her, so he made a production out of stirring his coffee.

"We been lookin' for ya, Kevin," Uncle said in a low voice.

"Yeah, what's wrong?"

"Ain't nothing wrong, exactly," Hannah said.

"What is it, then?"

"It's what you went and done behoind our backs," Uncle said, waving his finger in Kevin's face and trying to look fierce, without effect.

"Oy don't get it."

"Yeah, you get it all roight, you sneaky little pissant. Who gave you the roight to pay down on moy taxes?"

"Uncle," Kevin said. "If Oy asked you, you would say no, and yer taxes would be delinquent." Kevin tried to avoid suit-wearers' words, but he knew all about "delinquent," having been declared one a time or two.

"But you been pokin' around in moy business," Uncle Gormley grumbled.

"All right, Emil, that's enough." Hannah was glaring at her husband, and Kevin took note. *Ain't seen that before. Jeezum, she's pretty good at it.* Uncle sat back in the booth and wrapped his hands around the suspender snaps on his overalls. The case for a pair of eyeglasses peeked out of one of the front pockets, and the glasses themselves nestled in another.

"Now Kevin," she went on, folding her hands on the tabletop. She had a salt shaker trapped between her palms, and was spinning it slowly with her thumbs. Kevin felt a burst of sympathy for that salt shaker. *She's got me trapped too. Can't just get up and walk out.*

"You've put us in an awkward position, young man." Hannah was a minister's daughter, and could get preacherly. "We owe you, and we don't loike bein' beholden."

"Oy was just tryin' to help."

"Ya did help, and that's the frickin' trouble." Uncle had been trying to keep quiet and let Hannah do this, but it was too hard. "Now we gotta help you." He looked glum, and the sun-reddened skin on his face went purple in the fluorescent lights.

"Oy don't need no help," Kevin protested.

"Kevin, where do you live?" Hannah's voice had a snap to it that hadn't been there before.

"Oh, here and there." There wasn't a good answer to that one. Kevin squirmed in his seat, not looking her in the eye.

"Nonsense, young man. Don't be thinkin' that a slow body houses a slow moind. Fact is, you ain't got no place to sleep, unless it's somebody's barn, or a hunting camp. We're gonna fix that."

"We are?"

"We are," Uncle affirmed. "Now shut up and lissen."

Hannah was twisting that salt shaker again. "You know where Alan Chartier used to live?"

Kevin nodded, having been told to shut up.

"Well, it's empty since the last hoired man left. How would you loike to live there, for no rent?"

Kevin had been inside that house, and he'd gone to school on old man Chartier, who could do anything with tools and animals, but nothing with people. The house had never been painted, its vertical hemlock siding had silvered with time on the north side. The south side was darker and pitted where the sun had been at it.

"How can you do a no-rent deal?" Kevin didn't want to give away the little ping of hope that her words had launched.

"Well, when the Soliere farm went to auction a few years back, we bought forty acres that backs up on our land, and the house came with it."

"Well, Oy can't take it for no rent."

"Don't you be as stubborn as Emil!" Hannah was twisting the lid off the salt shaker, and Kevin thought she'd prefer to be twisting his neck.

"No money changes hands," Uncle said. "But if we need help…" he hung the thought out to dry.

"All roight," Kevin said. "But you have to call."

"Ain't no phone there. You just come by every couple days, and we'll see how it goes."

Two years later Emil Gormley sold his herd and most of his machinery, and retired from dairying. After a month without milking, he got up in the middle of the night, and dropped dead of a heart attack in the kitchen. The glass of orange juice he had poured stayed on the counter until after the funeral, when Kevin poured it down the sink.

"Kevin, nothing changes," Hannah said, dropping ungracefully into the worn and creaky kitchen chair her body had been training for decades. "You'll do the sugarin' again in the spring, and cut some hay just like always. And I might need some help doin' chores that Emil used to do."

33

He drove her to see the Town Clerk, and a few days later to a lawyer. There were several trips to the lawyer, but Kevin didn't think much about it. He didn't get to drive very often, not having a car or a license, and was enjoying Uncle's old Buick too much to wonder about the errands.

It was during sweet-corn season in that rainy year that Hannah made supper one night out of all the pills in the house. Kevin found her a day later. Natural causes, they said. She had thrown away all the pill bottles the week before, and made sure Kevin took that load of garbage to the town dump. He thought she died of emptiness, lost without Emil, even though he had discovered that she was the stronger of the two.

It's like losin' my parents all over again. I ain't ready for this. At least this time I'm not a lost half-grown boy. If Uncle and Hannah hadn't stepped up when Mom got taken away, where would I be now?

She had left an envelope on the kitchen table. "Deliver to Billy Brophy" was written on it, and so he did.

The envelope contained the harvest of Hannah's trips to the lawyer. It was a will directing that the farm be sold, except for twenty acres of woods with a brook along one side, and the Chartier house. There was a trust that would pay the taxes and upkeep on it, with a provision that any extra go to the school for a remedial reading program. Billy Brophy was to be executor.

Because of that, Kevin lived on in the secluded house in the woods.

His name appeared on no document. Even in the will he was just "present tenant" and was not to be evicted. And nobody knew any of that except Billy and the lawyer, whose practice was two towns away.

All eleven of the nephews and Molly the niece were in the will for ten thousand dollars each. Some of them came sniffing around, thinking there must be more, but Billy sent them to the lawyer. He showed them a document Hannah had signed, assigning funds to the remedial reading program, and they went away grumbling.

Ralph

K evin didn't know he had an Irish name until he was into his thirties. When he found out the original Kevin was a saint to boot, he just let out that dry little chuckle and tucked a pinch in behind his lip.

"Saint, you say. Well, Mama always called me Calvin, but she coulda called me Adolph."

At the time, Kevin had a girlfriend, one of the Brendas. Kevin collected Brendas. When Ralph told him Brenda was named after another Irish saint, Brendan the Navigator, Kevin had a swallowing accident. When he recovered he said, "That's wrong too. Only place Brenda can navigate to is K-Mart."

It took Ralph a long time to figure out how very different he and Kevin were.

Ralph was Randolph E. Montgomery the Third. He'd always thought that his father and grandfather had been criminally unimaginative in naming their sons, but when he thought about it, Ralph III was a much better sounding name than Kevin Beaujolais. Ralph's sense of order rebelled at the ethnic mix-n-match. It was like calling someone Yitzhak O'Reilly, or Antoinette Bogarovski, or Svein Ghadallah. Unseemly.

Ralph asked his son if there were any Beaujolais kids in the school, and Eldon said no.

Ralph and Kevin met during the winter of Ralph and Helene's first year in Nilesburgh.

"Dad, there's a man at the door," Eldon said.

Ralph went to the front door and saw no one.

"Garage door, Dad."

Small man. Checkered wool shirt, green and black. Fleece vest, no sleeves. Red Sox cap with the blue faded to a purple-gray uncolor. Big nose. Sunken cheeks. Stooped shoulders. Sun-rutted skin, mostly laugh lines. Small blue eyes.

"Seen ya woodpile. Ain't much left. Yawnt smore?"

"I beg your pardon?"

Jeezum Crow, another one. The man tried again.

"Look, you gotta woodstove, roight? How much ya burn so far?"

"Well, we bought three cords in October, and there's maybe half left."

"Ya bought green, and ya got a third left, and it ain't yet past January. You gonna be cold, come sugarin' time."

How does he know all this? Ralph asserted himself. "Sir, the man said it was seasoned, but it smokes a lot and it doesn't split well."

Baby. The man's a frickin' baby. "It don't split because it's fulla elm, and elm don't split, least not for you. Plus it ain't seasoned, none of it. Oy'll say it was cut two days, maybe three, before you bought it. You order this stuff?"

"No the man came to the door, just like you." *Funny, he used the garage door too. These people don't seem to believe in entrances.*

"Big red truck? Big red face? Thought so. Yain't been long in Vemawnt, have ya?

"Well, we came here in August."

Puppies. Jeezum Crow, the woods is fulla puppies. "Well, ya got screwed. Ain't yer fault, ya just walk around lookin' like a target. Come up here to weed ya life, didnya?"

Why do I feel defensive? Who is this guy? "It's beautiful here," said Ralph, waving an arm toward the ridge.

"Not up there, it ain't. Nothin' but ledge."

"Anyway," Ralph struggled on, uncertain what a ledge was locally, and unwilling to ask. "While we can't live off the grid, we can at least use renewable resources for a lot of our energy."

"Off the grid, what's that?"

"You know, no electricity from the power company, CVPS."

"Oh." *If I tell this turd-licker I never been on no grid, he won't believe me and I don't feel like explainin'.*

"Let's get back to the firewood," Ralph said.

Kevin did some math on his fingers. "Oy can get you three cords, seasoned, No elm. Foive hundred dollars."

"That's a lot of money."

"Ya got somethin' against whoite oak and rock maple? No elm."

"Four hundred and fifty dollars."

Knew the dickhead would try that.

"Hey, where are you going? We're negotiating here."

"No we ain't," said Kevin, who would have settled for four hundred if the man hadn't been so hard to talk to. "Oy named my proice and you didn't meet it. So be cold in March."

"Wait. What's your name?"

"Kevin," said Kevin. "What's yours?"

"Ralph. Randolph Montgomery the Third."

Aw Jeez. No wonder the poor fart-sniffer's so confused. Named after two Vermont towns and don't even know who he is. "Okay, Ralph. Foive hundred, and if you're lucky moine will last you, and you won't hafta burn any more of that crap ya got out back."

"All right, when can you deliver?"

Kevin tucked a pinch in behind his lip and thought. "Some toime after dinner and before milkin'."

What the Hell does that mean?

"I see,' said Ralph, who didn't.

"He means after one o'clock and before four," said Eldon.

How does he know that?

"Helene!" Ralph called out. "Bring the checkbook."

She came out of the kitchen. Kevin took off his faded Red Sox cap, and blushed to the roots of his untended hair.

"Hi, I'm Helene," said Helene.

"Kevin," said Kevin. "No checks."

"What's that?"

"Oy don't do checks. Oy do cash."

What do you mean, you don't do checks?

"Kevin, I don't have five hundred dollars in cash just lying around the house."

"That's okay, Oy ain't got three cords a hardwood, but Oy will tomorra. Ain't askin ya ta pay until delivery."

Kevin walked out of the garage favoring one leg, got on a bike that was old when Schwinns were in, and rode off down the driveway with a wave and a little ringle on the bike's bell.

"Eldon, how did you know what time he meant?"

"Well my friend Eddie is a dairy kid, and they call lunch dinner, and the second milking is around four thirty."

Helene was still watching Kevin pedal away. "If he's got that bike, how is he going to bring the wood?"

Ralph went to the Nilesburgh branch of the North Country Bank the next morning and sought out the friendliest of the tellers.

"Do you know if a man named Kevin Beaujolais has an account here?"

"Mr. Montgomery, we can't give out that information." She cashed the check. "What is Kevin doing for you?"

"What do you mean?"

"Well, it's easy enough to figure out," the girl said with a smile. "You come in and ask about Kevin, and you cash a big check like you haven't done before, and so Oy figure Kevin's doing some work for you and, as usual, wants his pay in cash. Here, he loikes twenties."

"How do you know that?" Ralph was slack-jawed.

"Mr. Montgomery, everybody knows Kevin. Besoides, he's my step-mother's first cousin. Tell him Judy says hello."

That afternoon Kevin showed up with a load of wood. The big red face driving the big red truck didn't seem at all embarrassed that he had sold Ralph green wood for a premium price three months earlier.

Michelle

Half the women in Vermont are named Jennifer. Half the rest are Michelles, and one of them owns a short stop called Michelle's.

It's a matriarchy. Michelle staffs it with daughters, and with some single moms who got too pretty too young and are now raising the harvests of their failed romances. Body art is in.

Michelle's has a comfortable old shoe air about it and could use a makeover, just like its owner.

She's a widow, with hints of Shelley Winters. She's got French Canadian roots, like almost half the people around here.

Ralph had learned that when you wanted to find out something about the town, you asked Michelle. He found her behind the deli counter, and nodded to a morose-looking man studying a cup of coffee at one of the tables that seemed to stay intact mostly out of habit. The man ignored him, and did not look up when Ralph asked her about Kevin.

"Oh, he's always been around. You can see him roidin' that old boike even in the snow. Goes up and down by here most every day. But he don't react much when folks wave and call out."

She stopped talking, but it was a soap bubble of a pause, and it broke quickly. Ralph had never heard a circular saw shriek through a 2 by 6, so he didn't know how to describe Michelle's voice.

"Oy think the kids, the boys, used to tease him when he rode by, and it's got to where he pretends they ain't there. Mostly they ain't, because that crowd's up and gone but he remembers too close. Oy told him to let go of all that and wave back when folks call out to him, but Oy think he'll never do it. He don't do much of what Oy tell him."

She replaced the straw in her coffee cup; it had begun to wilt. The straws lasted longer as the coffee cooled. "Well Oy do it cause Oy got to loikin' iced coffee that way years ago, and Oy ain't never seen a reason to give 'em up. Now, about Kevin," she re-aimed her words.

"You know about radar, roight? You floy along and the radar signal bounces back and can tell where you are, maybe even what you are, big plane or a little one, you know?" She paused until Ralph nodded that he did indeed know about radar.

"But if you floy too low, my grandson told me this, the one that went to the Air Force, yeah Marvin. Well Marvin said if you floy close to the ground the radar can't foind you cause of what they call ground clutter. You know, ridges, and radio towers and tall buildings and stuff like that. Well, Kevin don't show up on the radar, cause the rest of us are his ground clutter. Kevin's about thirty-five years old, Oy guess, and he's the only man Oy know that the Government doesn't know he exists."

Ralph was astonished. The government, or part of it anyway, knew almost everything about his life. "You can't do that these days."

"Yes you can do that, mister, cause Oy been watchin' Kevin do it all his life. He don't droive, he don't pay taxes on what work he does, and he don't own nothin'."

Ralph was gassing up his car at Michelle's short stop one morning when Kevin rode by, head down and legs pumping. Ralph waved. Kevin didn't.

What's wrong with him?

Ralph paid up and soon passed the bike. He pulled into the Grange parking lot and waved Kevin down.

"How are you today?" Ralph asked.

"Not too bad." Ralph was beginning to recognize that as the standard answer. "Not too bad" actually meant "All is well," but Ralph figured Kevin, as a native Vermonter, wouldn't put it that way. Optimistic pessimism. Could be better, but could be a lot worse too. Not bad enough to mention.

"I waved at you, back at Michelle's."

"Oy seen ya, and Oy nodded back. Yever seen that blacktop around Michelle's? Probly not, in a big car. But on a boike it's bumpier'n a case of hoives. Michelle thinks Oy don't wave cause the kids usta yell at me along here. But the truth is, Oy let go them handlebars, Oy moight go asshole over applecart, and Oy hate wearin' gravel in moy face." Kevin scratched, and tucked a pinch in behind his lip. "Ya didn' flag me down just to say howdy, didja."

"No," said Ralph. "I've got this tree that's dying, and I want it cut down before it falls on my house."

Kevin squinted into his memory. "Seen the tree, it's a white ash. They make baseball bats out of 'em. Burn pretty good too. Yawnt me to cut it?"

"Well, yes, if you can fell it safely."

"Tell you what. You hammer a stake in the ground where you want that tree ta fall, and Oy'll droive the stake with it. Ya gotta chain saw?"

"Why no, I've never needed one."

"Ya mean ya never used one, roight?"

Why do I let this guy make me feel defensive? "No, but I could learn."

"You go to Jim Shipley down at the Noilesburgh Rent-all, and if he ain't there ask fer Eddie. Tell 'em you want a Husky, a big one. They'll know, and if they troy ta teach ya ta use it, tell 'em it's fer me."

"Husky. You mean that plastic molding place over in Milton? They make chain saws?"

Baby. He really don't know shit. "Nah, it's Husky-varna, Oy think. Ain't no Americans to speak of in the chainsaw business, except maybe McCulloch, and their good ones are small. This one's Swedish or somethin' like that."

Jim Shipley explained that the best heavy-duty chain saws were Scandinavian and German, and that Kevin was a good man with a saw.

"Then why doesn't he have one of his own?" Ralph wondered.

"Mister, Kevin Beaujolais has got his life weeded down to what's important to him. He don't need to own stuff, if he knows how to get ahold of it, and he's good at that. Here, it's sixty dollars fer the week, and I tossed in some chain oil. You got gasoline?"

Ralph said he did, and then wondered some more about Kevin, and the evident simplicity of his life.

"I've known him a long time," Jim Shipley said. "Kevin don't count his yesterdays and he don't fear his tomorras. He's pretty much of a right-now fella. When he cuts down your tree, he ain't doin' nothin' else, he ain't thinkin' about nothin' else, and that's just what you want. By the way, he'll ask for payment in cash, and he likes twenties."

Ralph already knew that.

The tinny bell on the green bike rang at about 7:30 the next morning.

Jim Shipley had warned Ralph that Kevin would be early, and so the coffee was ready.

"Just black," Kevin said, examining the chain saw. "Thanks."

"You know, we never did come to an agreement on how much you're going to charge for this."

"Couldn't say till Oy seen it." He tucked a pinch in behind his lip, and studied the tree. "Gotta stake?"

Ralph produced a two-by-four about four feet long. Kevin started the saw with one pull, and got it settled down to burping. He cut the stake in half and sharpened one end of it, all with quick, efficient strokes of the saw. *He handles that thing like it's a scalpel.*

"Where ya want it ta fall?"

Ralph hesitated. "Well, I don't want it too close to the house."

He ain't looked at the tree. He don't know what it wants to do.

"Well," Kevin said. "Tree leans this way, wind blows that way, ground slopes another way. Droive the stake out that way about fifteen feet. No, fifteen. Six more. Now a bit to the north. *Ah Jeez. How'd he ever live long enough to grow up?* The other way. There."

Ralph drove the stake in about six inches.

"Little more," said Kevin. That left about fourteen inches of stake above the ground.

"Too bad it's dying," said Ralph.

"Somethin's been getting after ashes these days, some koinda bug, they say. They don't live as long as they usta, and they don't get so big. Okay old tree, let's do this noice and easy."

"Do you think the tree can hear you?" Ralph asked, and instantly regretted the question. Kevin stared hard at him before answering.

"Look, mister, Oy don't know if trees got ears. But Oy know when they're hurtin', just like Oy know when an old dog or an old horse is hurtin', and needs to be put down. So Oy talk to 'em."

He walked around it with the saw muttering in his hand. He stepped back to where the stake stuck out of the grass. Ralph thought the saw sounded like a small motorcycle when Kevin revved it up.

With the saw howling, Kevin cut a neat incision in the tree, a horizontal line just under halfway through the trunk. Then an angled cut downward to the first one, and out came a neat wedge of tree, looking as if it had been cut off a wheel of cheese.

Kevin went to the other side of the tree, and made his felling cut with a long burst, coarse sawdust flying. The tree trembled. Kevin paused, then cut a little deeper, and withdrew the saw.

There was a crack, and the tree fell, landing with a great thump that shook the earth under Ralph's feet.

"Ya wouldn' wanna be under that." Kevin said, reaching for his tobacco.

"I certainly wouldn't," Ralph said. "I can't believe you dropped it right on that stake."

"Well it don't always happen," Kevin said around his chaw. "But ya gotta have an aimin' point, just like when yer huntin' Ya do hunt, don'tcha?"

Ralph didn't answer. He was married to a woman who thought hunting amounted to murdering Bambi, and he didn't own a gun. He only told Kevin that last part.

Jeezum, the more I learn about this man, the stranger he gets.

"But everybody got a gun. Shotgun for critters and birds, pistol for thieves, and rifle for huntin' deer."

He talks as if he has an arsenal. I don't think Helene would go for that.

"Oy usta take folks from Away out huntin' for a week at a toime," Kevin was saying. "But Oy don't do that no more. Few years back one of 'em shot what he thought was a deer, and turned out it was a man from here in Noilesburgh. So Oy quit guidin' and now Oy just shoot enough for moyself." He didn't say a bit of that shooting was done way out of season, and he knew Ralph wouldn't ask.

Maureen

Maureen McGuckin was smart and pretty, and twenty-five years old when she took a job at the Nilesburgh branch bank. She'd just been through teller training, and believed she was on track to become a personal banker, or even a loan officer.

College hadn't happened for Maureen O'Rourke, but Gene McGuckin had, and so last summer there had been a huge Irish wedding in Philadelphia. Maureen's father had petitioned the Archbishop to allow a wedding in the family's old parish church, which had been closed for lack of interest after the immigrant generation left or died. Maureen's great grandfather Dermot O'Rourke had been a plumber in County Cork before immigrating to Philadelphia in the 1870s.

There were lots of McGuckins at the wedding and lots of O'Rourkes, and a scattering of O'Haras and Doyles and McQuades as well, including the priest cousin who presided over the exchange of vows.

Maureen thought he was a pompous prig, but Gene didn't care who conducted the wedding, and Maureen's mom said it would be offensive to all the McQuades and some Doyles too, if Father Denis got by-passed.

Maureen and Gene moved north to his job at IBM, near Burlington, and now she was working too, learning from a tutor-teller not much older than herself. Maureen thought she and Judy could become good friends, but for the giggle. Judy's laugh covered nervousness, and sounded to Maureen like an Irish step-dancer trying out new shoes. A lot of sharp noises, closely spaced. She wasn't surprised that Judy was no longer married.

When the man came into the bank, Judy was helping an old lady decipher her monthly statement.

"Now how many checks did you write after the last one on the statement? See? It cleared on the tenth."

The man stood quietly behind the fake velvet rope, waiting.

"It's gonna be a few minutes, Kevin," Judy called out to him. Mrs. Averill turned far enough to see who was there, and sniffed loudly.

Kevin winked, and she made a show of turning her back on him. "Now, dear," she said. "Teach me again about putting in the deposits. I think I've almost got it."

Sure you do. That's why we go over this every month. You're so awful to people that the only way you can socialize is to come in here and pretend you're stupid. Besides, lose that snotty English accent, lady, you've been living here for more than forty years.

"Good morning, Mrs. Averill." Kevin's voice was cheerful and loud, as if he suspected the old lady was hard of hearing. She ignored him.

I didn't want the new girl to get stuck with her, but now here's Kevin, and I'm not sure she's ready for him either.

"I can help you over here, sir," said Maureen, right out of the training manual.

"Waitin' fer Judy." Kevin said it with a little squinty grin, to take the edge off what was essentially a "no thanks."

"I think it'll be a few minutes before she's free," Maureen tried again. *Is it me, or do they just like Judy? The only time anyone comes to my window is if she's busy, and this one won't even do that.*

"Ma'am, Oy ain't in a hurry."

"Kevin, for heaven's sake," Judy said, and Mrs. Averill turned around to give him a glare.

"Well, you know moy business, and she don't need to," Kevin countered, and then gave it up. After all, the girl was pretty, and he liked the way she kept flipping her bangs out of her face, bringing light to a short Celtic nose dusted in freckles. He moved to her window.

"Good morning, sir, my name is Maureen," said Maureen.

"Kevin," said Kevin. *Marine? Odd name for a pretty girl. Don't look like no Marine I ever seen.*

"Now, what can I do for you?" Brisk but friendly, the trainers had said.

"Change some cash," Kevin said.

"Sir, do you have an account here?" Maureen was still in the tellers' manual.

"Nope."

"Well, then, I'm afraid we can't cash your check." Maureen had been taught how to look firmly sorrowful.

"What check? I ain't got no check. I don't do checks."

Frickin' flatlanders is takin' over. This one don't even lissen, cute or not. Ain't this town got enough folks to run a bank without havin' to run downcountry for help?

Judy was deep into fourth grade arithmetic with Mrs. Averill, who was prolonging the "I-don't-get-it" phase of her visit.

Wish I'd had a chance to explain Kevin to Maureen, but who ever knows when he'll come in, and I can't just let Mrs. A stand here to go all snitty while I deal with him, and if I do that, then Maureen will think I don't have any confidence in her. What a morning, and it's still early.

"All right then, Kevin," Maureen was saying. *I got that psychology training, let's see if it's worth anything.* "I know Judy would love to help you, but you can see she's not free just now. I'm pretty good at problem-solving, let me try."

The door opened and two large women came in, talking in toxic terms about the school board.

Kevin sidled up to the counter and spoke softly. "Oy wanta change some money."

"Oh, then I have some good news for you. Canadian is down a bit today, and so is the Euro. I can get you pretty good exchanges on both," she smiled and brushed a bit of hair aside.

Jeezum Crow, how can I make it any plainer?

"Not Canadian, American." Kevin was almost whispering, but the waiting women were ripping the skin off the school superintendent, and paying no attention to him. "Look." And he pulled out a thick roll of bills, holding them so no one else could see.

Maureen opened the roll, noting that each was a twenty dollar bill, that Andrew Jackson's face was never upside down, and that a lot of the bills were the older, pre-color ones. She counted them twice, and looked up to see Kevin holding a finger over his lips.

"Oy know how much," he said. "Fifties for them twenties, please."

Kevin wasn't quite why he'd said please, but then she did have a nice smile.

This is the strangest man I ever met. Why is he so secretive? Maureen took a closer look while she counted out fourteen fifty-dollar bills, twice. *He's not very big, his skin is awfully weathered, he needs a haircut, and he's rough-dressed. But there's pride in him too.* "Here you go, sir," she said.

"Kevin," said Kevin.

"All right, Kevin." There was that nice smile again. Kevin had grown up among bad teeth, and admired Maureen's perfect white grin. That would have pleased her father, who had spent several thousand dollars on the braces that had perfected that smile for a man like Eugene McGuckin of the Philadelphia McGuckins, a man far from Kevin's world. "I'd be happy to help you change cash any time you come in," she said.

As Kevin left, she noted an acrid whiffy smell in his wake. She knew it wasn't stale sweat, but she couldn't name it. Judy could.

"Kevin," she called. "Next time don't wear your barn boots in here."

He grinned and waved, holding the door for Mrs. Averill, who turned sharply and went out the opposite door.

Well, that was hateful.

Maureen and Judy dealt with the education reformers and then the bank was empty again.

"Well," Maureen said, launching Judy's giggle. Gene had heard it one day when he'd come in to take her to lunch, and said Judy sounded like a neurotic Uzi. He'd had to explain that Uzis were small Israeli machine-guns with a rapid rate of fire.

"What," Maureen's eyebrows lifted into her bangs, "was that?"

Judy giggled. "Which one?"

"Okay, let's begin with that horrid old woman." Maureen shoved her lower jaw out to mimic Mrs. Averill, and glared toward the fake velvet rope.

Judy fired about half a clip of giggle, and wiped her eyes. "Mrs. Averill is the saddest person in town. She hates everybody, she's mean to kids, and there's a rumor she poisons animals."

Maureen had a sudden mental picture of Judy posing for a mug shot photo, with a signboard around her neck reading RUMORMONGER. "Oh, how awful! What made her that way?"

"Well," Judy rubbed her hands together and got into full gossip mode.

"She married a man from here and came home with him after the war. She's English, you know, and apparently her family had money. My mom says she pissed on everything in soight when she got here, not literally, of course." Giggle, giggle.

"Well, I'm sure it was different here for her," said Maureen, who was mentally comparing northern Vermont and eastern Pennsylvania.

"Different! She didn't loike cold weather, she didn't loike cows or maple syrup, or snow, she didn't loike old Jeremy's family and friends, and pretty soon it was clear she didn't loike him either."

"Then why didn't she leave him and go home?" Maureen asked.

"Well," and Judy lowered her voice to conspirator level. "You didn't know old Henry Mayo, of course; he doied. Noice man. Well, Henry was the Postmaster here for years, and the way it sugars off is that Henry Mayo told my mother's best friend that Mrs. A never got a letter from England."

"Sugars off? What's that mean?" Maureen interrupted.

"Oh, it's an old way of saying getting to the bottom of things. Comes from boiling maple sap down into syrup. Anyways, she used to write over there every month or so for the first few years, but she never got a letter back, not ever, so after a while she quit writing and just turned sour, even more than before. And she blames that man Kevin who was in here, for her husband being killed. He was shot in a hunting accident by a man Kevin was guiding. Anyways, since then she's just been impossible."

"How sad," Maureen said, thinking about being a woman in a

strange environment with no links to home. At least she could call and get a mommy-fix when she needed one. Not that she and Gene were having trouble, far from it. *I'll try extra hard to be nice to her the next time she comes in.* "Okay then, what about that strange man?"

"Kevin? Oh, everybody knows Kevin," Judy said, and giggled again.

That could get really annoying.

"Well, I don't," Maureen said, somewhat sharply. "Why does he act the way he does?" The question dangled unanswered for a while, as customers came in, making deposits or cashing checks, or asking about the rates for certificates of deposit.

"Imagine," said Judy when the bank was empty again, "being somebody who doesn't trust institutions, and obsessing about avoiding them, especially the ones with links to the government. That's Kevin."

"But why," asked Maureen. "What triggered that kind of aversion reflex?"

"That what?" Judy asked.

"Aversion reflex. It's a phrase I learned in training. It means instinctively running away from something that scares you. So, what scares this Kevin?"

Judy wasn't giggling. "My step-mom Janice, she's his first cousin, well she talked about it once when Kevin had done something or other that was really weird, you know? And she said it's because of his parents. The Veterans' Administration put his father into the state hospital when Kevin was little, and then his mom fought with all the bureaucracies, and the schools, and the welfare, until she got TB, and the government put her away too when Kevin was a young teenager. Both his parents doied in government care before he was sixteen."

"Oh, how sad," Maureen said.

Judy wasn't finished. "So now he tries to stay away from any level of government. He doesn't even have a checking account, cause he thinks banks keep too many records, and they'll foind him, and do something bad to him. I never said it was logical, it's just Kevin."

"But what about his paychecks? They must take out taxes for Social Security and the IRS."

"Kevin just told you, he doesn't do checks. He does cash, and when he gets a big wad o' them twenties, he comes in here and changes them for fifties. I asked him about hundreds once, and he said they're too hard to break."

"What about real estate taxes?" Maureen asked. She and Gene had just gotten their tax bill, and the numbers were disturbingly high.

"Kevin doesn't own anything, especially not any land. If he did, then the government would know he exists, and he can do without that."

"But why? It's so sad that he feels compelled to hide!"

"Maureen, he's not hoiding, you can see him around every day, and if you didn't know better, he'd be just loike everyone else. But he's way different, isn't he?"

Jeremy

One sunny Friday early in November of the year between 9-11 and shock and awe in Baghdad, Henry M. Jordan loaded three rifles into his SUV along with some cold-weather clothing and an orange vest, and drove north out of New Jersey.

"Hey, Bennie," he yelled into his cell phone on the Garden State Parkway. "It's Harry. I'm on my way and I'll be there in six or seven hours." Bennie Morris was one of the three Princeton classmates who would spend a week with Harry at a hunting camp in northern Vermont.

Harry drove into Nilesburgh about an hour before dark. *This is a pissy little place. Wow! One traffic light.* He didn't notice that except for a McDonald's and the gas stations with their brightly lit logos, the small businesses of Nilesburgh were all independent. There were no chain stores, and there were no vacant storefronts on the main drag, Riverside Road. He followed Bennie's directions to the camp.

The last turn took him off a dirt road and onto a faint track where grass grew between the ruts. It was Harry's first trip, and as he shut off his car, he redefined his image of "camp." There was nothing grand or pretentious about this one, more shack than lodge.

There was a porch he thought would look good on a hillbilly cabin, a big woodpile, smoke coming out of the chimney, and an old green bike leaning against a tree.

As Harry was removing his gun cases from the car, a man came down from the porch.

"Oy'll take them guns for ya," the man said.

"It's all right, I've got 'em, Harry answered.

"It ain't all right, mister. Oy check all the guns that go insoide."

Harry was getting annoyed. "Are you the guide?"

"Yup."

"Well, they're not loaded."

"They're loaded until Oy see 'em empty, and Oy can't see 'em in them leather coats."

"Do you know who I am?" Harry used his best intimidation voice, the one that worked so well on headwaiters and other low-lifes back in New Jersey. The bluster didn't seem to travel well.

"You're one a them downcountry fellas Oy'm supposed to look after this week. Don't much give a shit which one."

"I'm Henry M. Jordan of Bergen, New Jersey."

"Kevin," said Kevin.

Harry looked him over. The man was small and had weathered skin and blue eyes. *He doesn't blink very much.* Green work pants, old and worn, and good boots. Orange vest over a green plaid shirt. Boston baseball cap. *I may not tell this yokel I'm a Yankee fan.*

Kevin noticed a price tag on one of the rifle cases. "You foire these weapons much, mister?"

"Well these two are brand new, bought for this trip. This one I've had out to a range behind the Legion Hall back home."

Jeezum. Most a these Jersey guys ain't so bad, but where the hell did they find this one? Frickin' flatlander's gonna shoot first and look second, unless I keep a real good eye on him.

Another car rolled up while Kevin was having unkind thoughts.

"Hey, Bennie, this so-called guide of yours won't let me take my guns in the house, if that's what you call it."

"Right, and he's still alive. Good to see you, Kevin." Bennie walked up and held out his hand. To Harry's surprise, Kevin shook it warmly.

"Nice ta see ya. How many more, two?"

"Yeah, Andy Halvorsen and Max Rooney, same as last year."

"Big bald guy and a funny little Oirish fella?"

"That's them. Harry, give the rifles to Kevin. No weapon goes inside until he's personally certain it's not loaded."

"He doesn't trust us," Harry said, looking truculent.

"Harry, settle down. Kevin says half the hunting accidents in deer season occur when someone fires a round inside the camp. He's just making sure that can't happen here. Now come on, let's get inside."

Jeezum, are we gonna hafta explain common sense to this asshole?

Harry felt better when he got inside, where the air was warm and smelled of stew and wet wool. He was still annoyed at that rube Bennie seemed to like, but he was sure he could make the guy shape up later.

Meanwhile, the place looked better inside than outside. There was a real poker table with eight sides, and cup-holders on the rim.

There were four bunk beds, two over two on the long wall opposite the door, and windows flanking the fireplace on one end. At the opposite end a second door led to the outhouse and one corner was set up for cooking on a propane-fired stove.

A gun rack took up space on the front wall, while a heavy clothes-line stretched from side to side not far from the fireplace.

"How did we get stuck with this yokel?" Harry muttered to Bennie while Kevin was busy in the "kitchen."

"Hey, try to leave your Jersey in Jersey. This 'yokel' knows more about the woods, about deer and about how to find them than anybody who lives in that last town you drove through. And they all know a lot more than we do. Relax, man, you're in the hands of a master."

The hell I am. And I'm not going to let a smart-ass bumpkin order me around for a week. I'll have to teach him who he's dealing with.

The door slapped the wall as a huge man pushed hard to open it.

"Kevin!" he yelled, filling the doorway with body and the air with noise. "I want at least a six pointer this year." Lost behind him was a man of about Kevin's size.

"Good thing it's not bear season, Andy, or you'd be a rug before the week's out. Kevin, how much would you charge to skin a carcass this size?"

"More'n you could sell it for," Kevin grinned. "How ya doin', Max?"

"What is it you guys say here? 'Not too bad'?"

Kevin laughed and Harry Jordan wondered why his classmates were so cozy with the man. He watched as Kevin went out onto the rickety porch and came back with two rifles that he hung on pegs in the wall.

"All safe," he said. "Now you fellas can drink and play cards all you want, and if you fall out over somethin' it'll just be bruises. At worst."

Bennie Morris looked curious. "Kevin, have you ever had trouble with your clients?"

"Just once. Fella from Albany pulled a knoife on me the first year Oy did this work, and Oy got his friends to take him home. Didn't earn nothin' that year." He shook his head and grinned.

"Whattaya mean pulled a knife? What happened?" Harry Jordan demanded.

Kevin looked him over for a few seconds before answering. "Well, his arm got broke, and then he didn't want to cut me no more. Wasn't but a minute. Now you fellas decide who's gonna clean up tonoight, and who's gonna get up and feed the foire. Be ready to go when Oy get back here an hour before dayloight. Should be around 4:30."

"Wait a minute," Harry objected. "How are we supposed to play poker with just four of us?"

"Play bridge then. Look, mister, Oy don't shit where Oy eat, Oy don't sleep where Oy work, and Oy don't play cards with hunters. That Albany fella, he objected to how the cards fell. If Oy beat you, you'll be pissed, and if you beat me, you won't lissen to me in the woods. It's better this way."

Kevin was out the door before Harry could say anything.

"You guys believe that little shit?"

Bennie Morris had had about enough. "What's your problem with him, anyway?"

"He's a backwoods smartass, and he doesn't know who he's dealing with. Imagine ordering me around. Me! And besides, he's a liar."

"What do you mean?" asked Max, who was not smiling.

"All that bullshit about a knife."

Andy Halvorsen pulled out a chair and told Harry to sit in it.

"Hear me good, Harry. We invited you up here cause we thought it would be fun for you, and you'd be good company for us. So far, you're not."

"Harry," said Max. "Me and Andy, we've been here five times before this, and Kevin Beaujolais is a good a man as you'll ever find. But he is different. He's so not impressed with you, that he won't even call you by name. That's cause you've been obnoxious from the beginning. And as for the knife, there's a long scar on his chest, where the guy got a slice out of him before Kevin broke his arm. Don't even think about challenging him physically, and for your own sake, pay close attention when you go into the woods tomorrow. He knows his business."

Harry Jordan slept badly. There were too many strange smells and noises. Slowly he identified the sounds coming from the fireplace, and the good smell of the applewood Max had used to bed down the fire.

The wind blew through cracks around the windows and doors, and it whistled. There were soft pattering sounds too, and Harry was glad he'd drawn an upper bunk. And finally, Max snored. Harry finally dozed off, telling himself he'd get the first and biggest deer in the morning. He wasn't quite sure how that was going to happen, but after all, he had the best weapons and the most competitive spirit. The guys had been a bit cool since they got here, but he was sure they'd come around after he scored big.

"All right, mighty hunters, rise and shine!" Max did the four AM wake-up call with malicious glee.

I'm gonna sit on his skinny ass and fart. Andy Halvorsen was not a morning guy. He was the last one up, and slowly started pulling on longjohns, red ones. So did the others.

"Harry, where's yours?" Bennie Morris asked as Harry began putting on camouflage pants over his skivvies.

"I don't have any," he said. "Besides, it won't be that cold."

"You don't know that," said Bennie. "You're going to be in the woods for hours, and you can't step inside to warm up. Here, you're about my size, wear these. Didn't you ever hear that layering up is the secret to staying warm in cold weather?"

"Thanks," said Harry. *They're overdoing this thing about cold.*

Max was cleaning up after a quick breakfast of fried eggs and bacon when Kevin came through the door. He had zipped the sleeves into his down vest, and over that wore a thinner vest of what Harry thought of as Coast Guard orange. There was a matching hat.

Looks like an orange snowman on toothpicks.

"Lookin' good, fellas, everybody's got their oyes open. Okay now, checklist. Lemme see yer orange. Good. Water, everybody should carry two a them plastic bottles, and bring the bottles back. Don't be droppin' em in the woods." *I don't wanna go bottle-pickin' when they leave this time.* "Samwidges, two each."

"Workin' on 'em," said Andy.

"Weapons. Get 'em down, check that they're unloaded. Keep your loads in your left front pockets till we get where we're goin'. Mister Jordan, please take the roifle that you've foired. Oy'll be happy to zero in the others when we get back."

"But I paid eight hundred dollars for that one, just for this trip!"

"Mister, till you get it soighted in, you got no idea where that bullet's goin, and Oy ain't havin' no virgin roifles on moy hunt. Bad enough havin' virgin hunters."

"You can't order me around, nobody orders me around. Who the hell do you think you are?"

"Mister, Oy know who Oy am, Oy don't know who you are, and like Oy said last night, Oy don't much give a shit, but these fellas are good guys, and Oy wanta keep 'em aloive through this week."

Harry felt other eyes on him, and started to speak, but the little yokel wasn't finished.

"Now, Oy ain't gonna foight you over every safety decision Oy make. Oy don't give a rat's ass whether you go huntin' or go home, but you make up yer moind roight now. Oy can take three as well as four."

Harry glared at him, but the man locked his eyes on Harry's and did not blink.

"All right, I'll go along."

"And you'll do what he tells you," said Andy Halvorsen. "Or I'll sit on you and fart."

An hour later, Harry was grateful for the borrowed longjohns. Every part of him hurt because of the cold. It had never been so cold in New Jersey, where he didn't have to get out in it much. This was way different. The sun wasn't up yet, and the gray light of pre-dawn was just beginning to break up the solid black of night.

He'd just heard about wind direction and clumps of brush and south-facing slopes and a number of other common-sense tips on finding deer, that he never would have thought of, and allowed himself a little grudging respect for the yokel. Those kind thoughts wore off quickly once he was assigned to a tree stand.

Harry was alone ten feet up in an old beech tree, sitting on the rough board platform of the shooting stand, waiting, listening, looking, fuming.

That little cocksucker! How dare he assign me to a tree stand! All the others are out there stalking and I'm sitting here like a damn trapdoor spider.

Wait! What's that? Fuckin' antlers, is what. Hot damn, let's see now, eighteen inches under the antlers and twelve inches behind. There!

BAM! *He's down!* "Hot damn! I got me one, and a big one, too!"

"Stay up in yer stand!" It was that little asshole Kevin, and reluctantly, Harry stayed.

Kevin moved into the brush where Harry had fired.

"Shit!"

A man lay bleeding, a gaping hole in his back, where the bullet had come out.

"Jeremy?" Kevin touched him lightly.

"I just couldn't stand her any more," the man gasped, his eyes unfocused. "Lose the antlers. I looked for the greenest of your guys, and I guess I found him."

"Jeremy, yer bleedin' out and Oy can't do nothing for ya."

"It's okay. Suicide by hunter," he whispered, and stopped breathing.

Kevin untied the antlers from Jeremy Averill's head and tossed them deeper into the bushes just before Andy and Max showed up.

"There's been an accident. You two take Jordan back to the camp and stay there till Oy get there. Don't let him clean his weapon, if he knows how. Now doial 911 and gimme yer cell phone."

Arnold Jacobs had been a Nilesburgh police officer for ten years and a sergeant for three. This was his first hunting fatality, but he knew there would be lots of attention drawn by the case, and he wanted to be careful. The newspaper guys always made a big deal out of dead hunters, and the TV people were even worse.

He told the guys from the funeral home to stay off to the side while he examined the body and the scene. He found the victim's tracks leading into the brush, and saw Kevin's tracks over them. Kevin showed him where the tree stand was, and he figured the entry and exit wounds were consistent with a shot from above.

"Hey Cooney, Oy wanta show you where the other two guys came in, and where they and the shooter went back to camp."

"Kevin, try not to call me Cooney in front of folks."

"Well, you still got them black smudges under yer eyes, just like in first grade. And anyways, it was Charlie that started callin' you Raccoon, not me."

"Tell me about Averill. Did he say anything?"

"Nothin' much. Oy think he knew me, but he was tryin' pretty hard to breathe. That woife's gonna take this pretty hard."

"I ain't so sure, Kevin. We got a file, and they ain't been real nice to each other, specially her. She's a bit of a wacko, but you never heard me say that."

"Oy know her a little," said Kevin.

"Now, tell me about the shooter, before we get back to the camp."

"Well, he's from Away. New Jersey. All of 'em are on this trip. The rest of 'em didn't see nothing cause they was all up over the ridge. Oy come back to check on this Jordan cause he was so green and so hard-headed."

"Whattaya mean, hard-headed?" Jacobs wasn't taking notes, but he was listening intently.

"Well, he didn't take much to the safety stuff. Didn't loike lettin' me safe his weapons. Didn't loike it when I wouldn't let him use a roifle he's never foired. Still got the proice tag on it. Pretty fulla hisself overall. He's just about sure to say he seen antlers and knew he was shooting at a deer."

"Funny thing though," the cop said. "Did you notice how the victim was dressed? No orange. In fact, he wore drab colors that made him blend in instead of stand out. And what the hell was he doin' wanderin' around in the woods in rifle season anyways?"

"It's his woods, Cooney. Old Man Averill owns about 300 acres out here, includin' that camp where Oy sent my hunters. He gets a piece of my guide fees. Or, Oy otter say, he did."

Harry Jordan was in a vile mood when Kevin and the cop got there.

"When can I get the hell outa here?" he demanded.

"Settle down, Richard," the cop said.

"My name's not Richard, it's Harry. Why did you call me that?"

"Because you're a dickhead, mister, and I don't know you well enough to call you Dick. Now, as to you leavin', we gotta get through whether, before we get to when."

"Whattaya mean, whether? You can't hold me, I'll get a lawyer and be outa here so fast you'll hardly see the dust."

Jacobs was a patient man, but the hunter annoyed him.

"Listen to me. You just killed a man. Has that sunk in yet? You just killed a man. Don't you bluster me about what you can do, or we'll finish this chat with you in handcuffs. Now tell me what happened, Richard."

"Well this asshole stuck me up in this tree and said wait, and the deer will come, and it was fuckin' cold, man, and then just after daylight, one did come, and I saw the antlers, big ones, with lotsa points, and I figured where the heart should be and I fired. And then this asshole comes runnin' up and says stay in the tree, and goes into the brush. Then he says there's been an accident, and I shot a man, and then these other two come and got me back here. That one came back later. They didn't see anything."

"Mister Jordan, 'this asshole', as you call him, is trying to get your sorry ass off. He says it was an accident and maybe it was. But we don't like it around here when folks from Away come in and shoot our citizens."

Jacobs moved to the stove and helped himself to a cup of coffee. The circles under his eyes looked darker than ever, and he was getting angry. The coffee helped a little.

"Look, it would help a little if there were just a trace of remorse, Mister. But I don't think you've got it in you. In fact, you're just about the most selfish prick I ever saw, and it's a mystery to me what justifies you thinkin' you're so special, or why any sane person would want to spend a week in your company. Now, I'll need the rifle and I'll need to get your formal statement. Kevin, I'll need yours too."

"Oy ain't so good at that."

"Just tell it, and we'll get Brenda to type it up. Nothin' to it."

Kevin looked uncertain. "Brenda? Which Brenda? Oy know some Brendas."

Cooney Jacobs laughed. "This ain't one of yours, Kevin. She's way past sixty, and she's a widowed grandma."

"Hey, what about me?" Jordan demanded.

"We'll decide what to do about you. Personally I'd like to clap you in the slammer, but the evidence won't let me. Chances are you'll walk away from this, but not yet. As for the rest of you, I'm afraid this hunting trip is over. Your guide's gonna be busy for the next few days. Mr. Jordan, you're gonna check into the Village Inn. You can't leave town, but I'm not going to lock you up. Much as I'd like to, I'm tryin' to keep this from gettin' personal, Richard."

The hunters began packing up and Jacobs told Kevin to put his bike in the police SUV.

"Who's tellin' Mrs. Averill?" Kevin asked on the way to town.

"Chief's doin' it, and takin' Shirley with him. Kevin, have I got the whole story here?"

"Is somethin' missin'?" Kevin didn't answer directly and Jacobs noticed.

"What's missin,'" Jacobs said, "is the Why of all this. It don't make any sense on its own, so I think there's something important that I don't know, and you do."

If I tell Cooney, I'll be named in his report. But then I'll be in it anyways cause I found the body. Damn.

"Cooney, Jeremy was wearing antlers and rustling around in the brush when the man shot him. He said to me, 'Oy just couldn't stand her no more', and asked me to lose the antlers. He said 'suicoide by hunter' just before he doied. We can go back fer the antlers if you want."

Sergeant Jacobs thought for a long minute as the car kept moving toward the village center. "Why didn't you tell me this back there?"

"Jeezum, Cooney, them undertaker guys was hangin' around with their ears all proimed for juicy stuff. You know how them guys gossip, and yain't sposed ta speak ill of the dead, roight?"

Jacobs drove in silence for another minute.

"Kevin, I think what we've got here is a tragic hunting accident. If it gets to be something more than that we'll have the goddam press all over it forever, and that old lady's life will be ruined as well. I think your instinct was right, but I needed to know the rest of it."

"What about Jordan?"

"That snot-gobbet! Let him stew for a couple of days, it'll be good for him. But we can't charge him with bein' fooled by Old Man Averill."

Cooney is a smart guy and a good cop. Too bad that makes him a government man.

Gene

Maureen was attracting her own customer base at the bank. *It's because I'm good at what I do, not what Gene says.* What Gene said was that she should do a gender count among her regulars, and they'd be mostly men. *Even Judy thinks that, and everything Judy thinks comes out in words. Everything.*

"I think Kevin's got a crush on you," Judy half-sang one morning after the shy little man came in to change twenties to fifties. And then, of course, that annoying giggle followed.

"Judy! He does not."

"Does too. He never even looks over here any more. And he comes in more than he used to."

"Oh, you're imagining things." *Is that true? He hardly speaks, and it's not like he leers or anything. That Judy! If I tell her the Green Mountains are being dyed blue next week, she'll have half the town believing it by dark.*

Maureen and her husband were finding friends in town, some among his IBM colleagues, and some from their neighborhood. Maureen wanted them to be known as Gene and Maureen McGuckin, but people wouldn't say that. It was always Maureen and Gene, and eventually she gave up trying to change it.

"Gene, do we know them well enough for this?" Maureen was having second thoughts about their invitation from the neighbors.

"Honey, it's just an outing on the lake. Lunch at some place that's supposed to have great sandwiches, and then some island-hopping in the afternoon. Make sure you pack us some sun block."

Maureen had already thought of that. He had orange hair, while Maureen's was black against what was usually very white skin. She and Gene had been paying for their pale Irish complexions all their lives. *I think I'll lie out in the sun a few minutes every day this week and try to build up a little base tan so I won't burn on the boat.* They'd met at an outing to the Jersey shore, where they were the two reddest people on the beach. Maureen's face got even redder when two of the girls in the group took off their tops to sunbathe. *Not doing that, I'd fry, and besides I don't want this nice man to think I'm a tart.*

That nice man had seemed to enjoy the scenery without drooling or making any smarty remarks, and proved to be good company. *McGuckin.*

His great grandfather was an immigrant teamster. Mine was a plumber.

On a Saturday morning that promised a hot afternoon in Nileburgh they walked next door with a cooler full of ice and snack food. "Don't buy any beer," he'd said. "I'm sure he'll have some with lunch, but I don't want to ride around with a half-drunk boat driver." Gene had already noticed that Danny Macon's hand seemed custom-designed to hold a beer can, and often did. Danny's waist line had gone missing, especially in front.

The boat was up on its trailer, and looked small to Maureen. Danny was standing in it, stowing things for the ride to the launching ramp. Gene passed the cooler up as Marie came out of the garage with another. He lifted that one too as Maureen waited to hand him a case of cola. She glanced once or twice at Marie's choice of boatwear. *That halter top looks like it's right out of the hippie Sixties. If I wore something like that, I'd probably fall out of it and embarrass myself. Wonder if it's comfortable.*

"Let's see, you're Mary Ann from Gilligan's Island," Gene said, noting Marie's short shorts. *Skinny legs, skinny everything, pretty much.*

Danny laughed. "Well, if that's true then Maureen is Ginger." Maureen's shorts were longer, but her legs were too. And her white polo shirt hinted that the blue-and-green bikini top under it was full.

On the drive to the lake Gene discovered that Danny knew a lot about the Red Sox, and next to nothing about the Phillies, except that the Red Sox manager had once managed in Philadelphia. Maureen learned that Marie bought supermarket check-out line newspapers that saw angels in tree stumps and Elvis on Mars.

Gene admired the skill Danny displayed in backing the trailer down the ramp. He stood on the adjacent dock with a boat-hook and a mooring line, and secured the boat while Danny put the SUV and trailer in the parking area.

The big inboard-outboard burbled quietly as Danny nosed away from the dock, and Gene gave him points for keeping the boat at low speed until they were well away from the ramp.

There was a hinged center section in the windshield, and Danny closed it after the wives opted for seats in the bow.

He pushed forward on the chrome-plated throttle, and the boat surged ahead, coming up on plane as it reached its cruising speed.

"Wow! How fast are we going?"

"About thirty five knots, maybe forty miles an hour." The boat's wake cut a wide curve as Danny headed north a few hundred yards offshore.

"How wide is it here, and how deep?" Suddenly Gene was full of questions about this new experience.

"About a mile and a quarter to Savage Island, over there to port, that's left, and maybe another mile beyond that to the Grand Isle shore. Here, you can read the depth off the fish-finder on the console. Sixty feet here, but we'll cross a hundred and sixty in the trench where those guys are trolling for lake trout and landlocked salmon in the deep water."

Up front, the breeze was whipping past the girls as the shoreline receded.

"This is wonderful!" Maureen exclaimed.

"Yeah, can you feel the sun?" Marie asked. "If your husband weren't here I'd have this top off by now."

"You wouldn't!"

"Sure I would. We're a mile offshore and more than that from any other boats. Look." She lifted one side of the halter top. "See? No tan lines. The lake is the greatest place for sunning, you should try it."

"With my skin? I don't think so. I'd be a lobster in an hour. I don't think I want to burn my tender bits. By the way, what's this place we're heading for?" Maureen thought a change of subject would keep her from sounding more defensive. *I might flash a little for Gene, but damned if I'm showing anything to that Danny.*

"Well, Eats 'n' Cleats is a general store with marina attached. It serves tourists in cars, and tent campers on the islands who come in by boat. And the food is delicious. They've got picnic tables overlooking the harbor, and some of those tables have umbrellas over them for shade. I think you'll want one of those."

During lunch they watched the boat traffic to and from the Eats 'n' Cleats dock, noting how some boaters were really good at docking and trying off their boats, while others bumped into the dock, and seemed to think that the more line they wrapped around the cleats, the better their boats would hold. Fortunately, wind was not a factor.

By day's end, they'd circled the Knight Island State Park, and had a swim off a beach on the Woods Island State Park. Marie whispered that sometimes you could see nudies running around the beaches of Knight Island, but they saw no one at all.

"The water off the south end of Knight Island is really shallow for a long way out, so we need to be careful here, especially in August, when the water is lower." Danny also mentioned low-water hazards off both ends of Savage Island and in the channel between Burton Island and the mainland.

"What did you think?" Maureen asked when they got home.

"Magic," he said. "We have to get a boat, so we can explore on our own."

"Do you know that Marie wanted to take her top off right out the middle of the lake? Apparently she does it all the time."

"Honey, I'm not sure I want to know those people all that well, and I'm not up for giving Danny any free peeks at you. He might have run us aground."

"I think we got past it, but I agree that we ought to try to get our own boat."

A month later, an eighteen-foot trailered open cruiser came to live beside the garage, and Gene practiced backing it up into a simulated launch ramp.

Gordie

On mornings when he felt restless, Ralph Montgomery would get up early and drive into the village for coffee and gossip at Michelle's and to run errands. So he was the first one to drive the West Bend Road after sunrise.

Damn people just toss trash out on the road, won't spend money to take it to the dump. Hey, that's not trash.

Thirty second later, he was on his cell phone, dialing 911.

"I need an ambulance and the cops on the West Bend Road, about five miles out of the village. Yes, there's an unconscious teenager lying in the middle of the road, and it looks as if he's been badly beaten. No, I'll wait, and I'll divert the traffic. I damn near ran over him. No I don't have an I-D yet, do you have any kids missing? Hold on, I'll check… yeah, Gordon Paul Willard. Yes, I'll stay with him, I already said I would."

He could hear the sirens from a long way off, and wondered whether the ambulance or the police would arrive first.

Sergeant Arnold Jacobs jumped out of his police SUV quickly. "Pulse?"

"Fairly strong, but he's bled a lot."

"How did you find him?"

"Just as he is, I haven't touched him except to check that he's alive, and get his I-D for the 911 operator. I tried not to walk around too much."

Jacobs was back on the radio quickly. "Dispatch, 204."

"Go, 4."

"Julie, get one of the guys to bring out the camera, some of that

68

casting plaster, and some traffic cones. I'm shutting the West Bend Road down to one lane, probably for several hours."

"10-4."

"And call the Willards, and tell them we've got their boy, looks like some lacerations and a broken arm. He'll be in the hospital in St. Albans in about a half hour."

"Anything I can do?" Ralph asked. *This cop knows what he's doing.*

"Yes sir, just wait till we get this kid on his way, and then I want to go over exactly what you saw and did."

The crew in the boxy, orange-trimmed "Nilesburgh Rescue" vehicle didn't look much like TV medics in their dark gray jumpsuits, but they were quick and gentle, and their siren soon faded in the distance.

The sergeant went over to where the boy had been, and squatted, looking at the ground. He moved around without scuffing up the marks on the dirt road, and then went to where Ralph was sitting in his car.

"I know most of the people around here, but not you. Do you live in town?"

Ralph grinned. "I haven't made it a priority to get noticed by the police," he said, and the cop's eyes squinched up a little. "Here's my license. I'm Ralph Montgomery, and I live on Grist Mill Road."

"Is that the new house on the left about a half-mile down?"

"Yes. Look, Sergeant, you saw that kid. This was brutal, not just a kid-fight. Somebody really worked him over. What's going on here?"

Jacobs looked him over. *This is a pretty bright guy, and he did do the right things when he found the kid.* "I'll tell you what I know, and then what I think, keeping in mind that those are two different things."

Ralph nodded, half thanks and half understanding of the distinction Jacobs was making.

"Over there, we've got heavy footprints. Looks like somebody got out of a vehicle, walked to the back of it, and then walked back, and got in again. We've got some blood in the road, where the kid's head was, and some impact marks. You have to discount the marks the Rescue guys made. Now, it looks to me as if he was rolled out of the vehicle, which is probably a truck by the tire marks, and just left here." Jacobs made a chopping motion with his hand, as if to fence off fact from speculation. "Now, as to what I think. I think we'll be able to I-D the tire type, and the kind of truck that tire goes with. I think we'll find the beating took place somewhere else, and that the victim was brought out here. I think we won't get much help from the victim in identifying his assailant, because this smells like an intimidation, an object lesson. And finally, because the victim is a teen, we'll be looking for a drug connection of some kind. I don't know what we'll find." He looked up. "Those young guys really like to hear their sirens," he said, as another police car rolled dust over them as it lurched to a stop. "Thanks for your help, Mr. Montgomery, I'll call you if we need any more information from you."

"Will you call me if you find out anything certain? I mean, I sort of have a personal interest in this, after finding the boy. I've got a son of my own not much younger than this victim, and I'm feeling a little uneasy about him right now."

Jacobs studied the man some more. "Yes, I'll call you, unofficially of course, cause it's police business."

"Thanks Sergeant, but I think something like this is everybody's business."

When Eldon Montgomery got home from school that afternoon, his father pounced. "Do you know a kid named Gordie Willard?"

"Yeah, he's older than me, I think he runs on the track team. I didn't see him today. What's up with him?"

"I saw him this morning, unconscious on the road. Somebody had beaten the crap out of him. What's going on in your school?"

"Dad, I haven't heard anything. But my friend Dennis has an older brother, I'll call him."

It took forty-five minutes, but that wasn't much longer than most of Eldon's conversations. He found his father trimming bushes.

"Dad, you're not going to like this. Dennis says his brother

70

thinks the kid got beat up, beaten up, because he owed money to a drug dealer."

"Eldon, one of the reasons we moved here was to get away from that stuff. What do you mean drug dealer?"

"There's this big guy who used to go to school here, and he hangs around at those plaza stores, and kids buy stuff from him. Either Dennis didn't know his name or he wouldn't tell me. But I think he's a scary guy, from the way Dennis was talking."

"Somebody who would beat a kid half to death and leave him senseless on a country road?"

"Yeah, maybe." Eldon looked relieved when the interrogation ended.

It didn't end, it just shifted to the Town Clerk's office.

"Mister Brophy, I want to ask you about this problem I've got."

"Look, call me Billy. When I hear 'Mister Brophy' I start lookin' around for my dad, and he's ten years dead." *Wonder what this guy wants.*

"You may know that I found a kid on the road yesterday, a kid named Gordie Willard."

"I heard," said Billy.

"I heard," said Ralph, "that he was attacked because he owed money to a guy, some big guy who used to go to school here. *I'm not going to mention the drug angle.* We're new here, and my son is fitting into the school pretty well. But we don't know the town well enough for me to warn him off hanging around with anyone who might be dangerous. Now, does that description mean anything to you?"

This guy's pretty smooth. He wants me to tell him what he didn't ask.

"Any time younger kids hang around with older ones," Billy began.

"That's way too general for me, Billy. If I'm going to tell Eldon how to avoid trouble, he has to know where trouble is, and who. And he doesn't have to know where I found out, or does anybody else," Ralph finished with a direct stare at the Clerk.

"All right, and you didn't hear it here. The cops are going to ask the Willard kid who beat him up, and he won't say because the point of the beating was to scare him. But I hear there were other kids around. Having witnesses was part of the intimidation. And the whispers are that a real thug named Archie Tourangeau, old Nilesburgh family, all of 'em in trouble most of the time, that he's the one. He's big and not very smart, but crafty. And he's mean enough to attack anybody, especially a soft target like a young kid. The Willard kid's probably a hundred pounds lighter than this Archie, and six inches shorter. Chances are it was pretty one-sided."

Ralph was getting agitated, and Billy noticed.

"If you go back and ask Cooney Jacobs, scuse me, I mean Sergeant Jacobs, he don't like the nickname, he'll say they're tryin' hard to get enough evidence on this guy to put him away. Maybe they'll do it this time."

Cooney

"Gordie, do you want a coke or some ginger ale?" Kevin asked the bandaged boy in the hospital bed.

He mumbled something that Kevin took to be "Yes."

"Judy, would you take care of that?" Kevin asked his cousin's step-daughter. He wanted a few minutes alone with her nephew, who had been so badly beaten. A turban-like bandage covered the scalp injury, swollen bruises appeared on each side of his face and his left arm was in a sling, newly splinted.

"Okay, Gordie, who done this?"

The kid closed his eyes.

Kevin had been in the bank when Judy's older sister called to say her 16 year-old son had been found unconscious on a dirt road out west of town. He'd gone with Judy to the hospital in St. Albans, and now he repeated his question.

"Who beat you up, son?"

"Can't say….threatened Mom…"

"Okay then, how many guys beat you up?"

Gordie stirred, hurting through the sedatives. "One. I fought, Kevin, but I don't think I hurt him."

"Was it another kid or an older guy."

"Older. Had a club."

"Can you tell me why?"

The boy shifted again, small in the tilted bed. "I owed him."

"You owed him money and you couldn't pay, so he did this? How much?"

"Hundred dollars."

"Jeezum, Gordie, was it drugs?"

"Can't say," he whispered.

Kevin leaned in and grabbed his good arm. "The hell you can't. Pills or weed?"

"Pills. Uppers. But don't tell Mom or Judy."

"Okay, where were you when you got beat up?"

"Back side of the plaza. I don't wanna talk no more, Kevin."

"Just one more. What koind of car did this guy droive?"

"Kevin, please. I can't tell ya. I'm really scared." He turned his face away.

"Gordie, this can't stand. If it ain't stopped, it'll get worse. Now Oy can't do nothin' if Oy don't know nothin'."

"You can't fight him. He's too big and too mean. He'll hurt you, Kevin, or maybe worse. Besides the cops are on it."

"Yeah, and you didn't tell 'em nothin' they can use. And so the sloimy fuck gets away with assault, and everybody pretends nothin' happened. Bullshit, boy, in this family we keep score. Now, what did he droive?"

"Dodge Ram, white."

Judy came back with a ginger ale, and a nurse chased them away, saying the patient needed rest.

"Judy," Kevin said, "can you bring me back here tomorrow after the bank closes?"

"Sure, I was coming anyways. And Joyce will be here with Leonard, I'm sure."

Gordie Willard leaned back on his pillows and sipped his drink. *Well, I always thought Kevin was just an odd little guy out on the edge of the family. But he sure looked grim goin' out of here. I hope he'll be okay.* The fog of medication drifted over him, and he slept.

Cooney Jacobs' police suv was parked in front of Michelle's when they drove back into Nilesburgh.

"Drop me off here, Judy, and Oy'll walk back to the bank for moy boike."

"Kevin!"

Somebody's always yellin' my name whenever I walk into a place. Wonder why they do that? "Keepin' busy, Cooney?"

"Kevin, I been askin' ya to call me Arnold in front of folks."

There was no remorse in Kevin's grin. "Jeezum, Cooney, ain't no folks here excep' Michelle, and she knows ya better'n Oy do." Sergeant Jacobs had once been married for a wonderful month and a terrible year, to one of Michelle's daughters. No children, no rancor, healed emotional bruises.

"Hey, Kevin," Michelle said. "Cooney, let me ask you if there's an ordinance that will keep weird people outa here?" She was looking at Kevin, her eyes twinkling. Jacobs let out a hearty laugh.

"Jeezum, Michelle, look at who comes in here every day. If you ban weird people, you won't have any customers at all." He gestured toward Kevin and then toward an old man sitting motionless over a cold cup of coffee.

Kevin grinned around the lip of a coke bottle. "Anyways, Oy gotta talk to ya, Sergeant, Sir," and he nodded toward the door.

Jacobs was working on a big ham and cheese sandwich, and brought it out to stand between the gas pumps. "What's up, Kevin?"

"Well, ya know Oy get by the Skillet off and on, and Oy hear you guys is keepin' a lookout out for a whoite Ford 150, regardin' that kid that got beat up."

"Kevin, that's police business, and I can't tell ya."

"Well, Cooney, Oy been tempted lately, to talk about that Averill shootin', remember that? Tragic accident, it was called at the toime. Be a shame if it comes out the cops didn't get that one roight."

"Are you threatening me, you little shit-hook?"

"Cooney, how can you say that? All Oy done was ask about a white truck, and you go all official on me. Sorta tells me the Skillet guys was roight about that Ford bein' a druggie-mobile."

"Well, who was talkin'?"

"Jeezum, Cooney, Oy don't know. They was over by the wall and my back was to 'em. Besides, Oy lost my good hearin'. Too many chainsaws, and not enough ear plugs."

Jacobs took a big bite of sandwich and talked around it. "Don't bullshit me, Kevin, you hear better than a deer. Besides, it's a Dodge Ram."

"Oh. See, them fellas can't get nothin' roight. Wish Oy knew who said that so's Oy could straighten him out."

Jacobs had been listening to truth shaders and outright liars for a decade. He gave Kevin his best "I don't believe you" stare, and chewed methodically.

"So, Cooney, if Oy see that Dodge Ram, Oy call you, roight, and you get the arrest."

"Stay out of it Kevin, these are not nice people."

"Aha! So you know whose truck it is. Grab the fuck."

"It ain't that simple, Kevin, there's a thing called evidence. We hafta catch him either dealin' or in possession, and so far, we ain't. And we can't make assault stick in court without testimony from the victim, and we won't get that unless he's sure we can put this prick on ice for a long time."

"Okay, who is this guy?"

"Have a good day, Kevin. Nice to see you again, and I like your memory just where it is. Don't sharpen it on my account."

The next afternoon, Kevin rode his bike to the bank, and when it closed he and Judy went back to the hospital.

"Oy'll be there in a minute, Judy. Gotta make a stop first."

Kevin found the business office and walked in.

"Can I help you, sir?"

"If you got a boss, you can find him for me."

Oh no, another case of bill-bitching. And this one looks like he won't settle for "he's in a meeting." "May I tell him who's here?"

"Sure, go ahead, it's okay with me."

"What's your name, sir?" The voice was decidedly colder.

Kevin told her. "You got a sorta nephew of moine in here, and Oy'm here to see his mama don't get no bill. Now, who do Oy see about that?"

"One moment please, sir."

Two minutes later Kevin was looking across a glass-topped desk that was too clean to be a work space, at the hospital's business manager. *A soft man. No color to his skin. No strength in his handshake. And he ain't lookin' at me, everywheres but.* "You got a Gordon Willard in here, gettin' over bein' beat up by a drug thug. Oy'm here to see that his mama don't get no bill for what it takes to fix him."

"Well, sir, there have to be charges. After all, he's receiving treatment and using bed-space."

Jeezum, how do places like this run with assholes in charge? "You ain't listenin', mister. Oy said his mama don't get no bill. Oy never said there should be no bill. Oy'm here to pay it."

"Well, we don't know what it's going to be yet. There are fees to be allocated."

Kevin went into his pockets and began pulling out fifty-dollar bills, until he'd made a tidy stack on the super-clean desk. *The man looks like he never seen cash before.* "Now, here's the deal. You're gonna release him today, and you know how much he's run up since he got here. Print out a bill, and leave off all that shit about eight dollars for a box of Kleenex, and show me the total. Oy'll pay it, but no frills, no extras that you can't explain. And then you won't hafta deal with insurances and billing and all that shit. Oy'll wait." And he settled back in a chair that was way less comfortable than the manager's.

Ten minutes later he was examining a lengthy document that stated Gordie's injuries in dollar terms, lots of dollars.

Well, well. If I stand up and lean over this turd's desk, he gets nervous. Let's see what happens if I do that and talk louder too.

"Twenty dollars for a discharge fee? That's the koind of bullshit charge Oy told you to leave off."

Two minutes after that, most of the pile of fifties was in the manager's hands, and Kevin had a doctor-signed discharge slip.

He showed it to the nurse on duty, and told Gordie's parents to pack him up.

"But we ain't settled up," Leonard Willard said. "That's gonna be tough cause we ain't got no insurance on him. I mean I got some from work, but it don't cover family."

"They ain't gonna bill ya," Kevin said firmly.

"How do you know that?" Joyce Willard asked, holding her son's hand.

Kevin lied. "Oy been down there and seen the guy in charge, and Oy told him to wait till the cops catch the guy who done this to Gordie, and then bill him. After all, it ain't Gordie's fault that he's here."

The Willards seemed to hear only the last part of what he said.

"It was so his fault," said the angry father. "He was out there hangin' around with them low-lifes, and it was his fault he got into that thug for a hundred dollars and didn't say nothin' to his parents, and he'll answer for that for a long time."

Good. They bought the billing part.

Ten minutes later, Gordie was wheeled out the door and bundled into the Willard family car. Judy and Kevin followed them back toward Nilesburgh.

"All right, Kevin, it's truth toime," Judy said.

"What do you mean?"

"You know perfectly well what Oy mean. If Joyce and Leonard hadn't been so upset they never would have believed you. Send the bill to the beater, indeed. How many of your fifty dollar bills did it cost you to get Gordie out of there?"

"Twenty-noine."

"Jeezum, Kevin, that's almost fifteen hundred dollars! You don't have that much money."

"Judy, you don't know everything about me. Mosta that money came through your hands, either you or that other teller, Marine. Do you want me to go back and kill the deal, and have them people hounded for money they ain't got? Works better this way."

Judy drove in silence. *Every time I think I've got Kevin figured out, he does something that doesn't fit what I think about him. How did he get through that mess with his family, and come out so kind-hearted?*

Slicer

*A*rchie Tourangeau. *I shoulda known.*

He was huddled in a grove of young trees that grew between a medical clinic and the rear of a small block of businesses that included a hair salon, a chiropractor's office and a carryout pizza place. The paved parking lot included rear access doors to those businesses, but it was not lit, and generally not well kept. No sign identified the little shopping strip as the plaza, but that's how it was known.

People in search of supper came to the front of the plaza, paid for their purchases and drove away.

People in search of other consumables came to the back more furtively, paid for their purchases, and drove away.

Kevin had been watching the cars circulating through the lot, drifting past the ugly backsides of the commercial strip. Most of the cars, he saw, were driven by kids, but not all.

The Dodge Ram acted like all the others. It made a slow pass around the building and then parked in the front lot. A cluster of kids moved in to talk to the man who got out of the truck.

That sumbitch was a bully in high school and now look at him. A no-class lumpa pig-shit.

Archie Tourangeau towered over his potential customers. At six feet two and two hundred forty, he had six inches and eighty pounds on Kevin.

Eventually, Tourangeau got back in his truck and drove around to the darkened back side. One by one, three cars pulled up beside the truck. Arms reached out and drew back, and then the cars moved away. So did the truck.

They wasn't just shakin' hands. I couldn't see plastic bags bein' swapped for money, but I'm pretty sure that's what was goin' on.

A day later, Kevin's old bike was parked for a while beside the police station, and he had Arnold Jacobs' ear.

"Oy know what the chicken-fucker done and where he done it, and when he done it."

"Which chicken-fucker, Kevin?"

"Come on, Cooney, it's that damn Archie, and you know it. Oy can tell ya how to catch him."

"We catch him all the time, Kevin. We take him to jail charged with possession with intent to sell. About two hours later he's out on bail, and after a while his lawyer bargains the charge down to a misdemeanor, and he gets a small fine and a suspended sentence, and he's back in business."

Sgt. Jacobs managed to look angry and resigned at the same time.

"What about all them lives he screws up, Cooney? What about that kid he beat half to death last weekend. You seen that kid, you know what he done."

"Well, Kevin, we don't know he was the one that done it. The kid won't talk and nobody else will either."

"Bullshit, Cooney. Oy bet you could foind that kid's blood on Archie's truck."

Jacobs leaned back and fiddled with the equipment clipped to his shiny uniform belt. "What's your interest in all this, anyways? You're not a guy that goes around bleedin' over other folks's troubles."

I guess he don't know me like he thinks he does. But if he's fishin', I ain't bitin'. My link to Gordie is pretty thin, and nobody knows I got family anyways. "Look, Oy know you cops think Oy'm the next thing to a vagrant, but Oy still got a sense of roight and wrong, and that big wormshit fits inta wrong, Cooney. And a court system that lets him fuck up kids' loives is wrong too."

"We do what we can, Kevin. It's not the cops that make the laws.

In fact we got so many assholes locked up that the prosecutors are under pressure to cut deals, cause the state can't afford to keep everybody in jail who oughta be there."

The following Friday night Archie Tourangeau made his usual recon sweep around the back side of the plaza, then stopped in the front parking area to hold court.

"Oxycontin's a special order, kid. Oy get money this week, you get hoigh next week. Okay, let's see. One special order, two bags of grass, one bag of uppers. Oy'll see you in the dispensary out back."

He drove slowly around the building.

Pretty good night so far…. Aw, shit. Shit!

Two police cars blocked his way, and two more pulled up behind him.

That asshole Jacobs has his gun out. Okay, Archie, don't panic, and don't do nothing that gives 'em an excuse to whack you.

"Hands up, cocksucker. Put 'em where we can see 'em, and outa the truck now, on the ground!"

When the cuffs went on, he knew they'd found the stuff.

"Looka here, Sarge. Controlled substances. Tucked in where the passenger-side airbag oughta be. Except the Dodge Ram don't have passenger-side airbags. You push on that panel and lookie what pops out."

"You have the right to remain silent…."

Shit…gettin' caught on a Friday night puts me outa business for the whole weekend, and them downtown guys are gonna move in on me. Kids ain't got no loyalty, they just go where they can get it. Hope this ain't about the one I beat up, but he won't talk, and the rest of 'em will swear they weren't there, after they seen what happened. Punishment is better when they can see it and get the word out. I got 'em scared shitless right now, but I gotta be on the street to keep 'em that way.

An hour later he was making his one permitted phone call.

"Hello, Dad? Archie. Oy'm in St. Albans. Yeah. Possession with intent, just loike always. Not tonoight, they ain't gonna call no judge to bail my ass out, not tomorrow either. But call the damn lawyer. Then go in the hoidey-hole and get out three thousand dollars, for bail on Monday. Oy think they'll set it at 25 thousand, because of the priors, and we'll need ten percent. And have Jimmy droive my other truck up here, cause the fuckers impounded the Ram."

Late on Monday morning Archie Tourangeau walked out of the Franklin County courthouse. His lawyer had whittled the prosecutor's request for a hundred thousand dollars in bail down to twenty five thousand, arguing that Archie was not a threat to flee, had never done any extended time in prison, and promised to be a good boy until his trial five months later.

That afternoon he drove a blue Chevy pickup truck to Burlington and restocked, including the special order for oxycontin. Then he drifted through the high school parking lot to get the word around that the business was shifting to the deep rear parking area behind a health club not far from the shopping plaza, and quite close to the high school. From there, he could crash through some brush to another street if he needed to close up shop quickly.

It was well after dark that night when the phone rang at the Tourangeau house.

"Hello, this is a message for Archie. Gordie Willard will be on the high school track at twelve o'clock, with money."

Inside the chain-link fence around the track, there's a freestanding wooden wall built to the dimensions of a soccer net. Young players use it to sharpen their shot-making skills. Tennis players find it handy too, for solo practices.

A few minutes before midnight a large man moved cautiously along one side of the wall, taking comfort in the pistol tucked into the back of his belt, and trying not to walk in harm's way.

On the other side of the wall, harm waited.

Archie Tourangeau was trying to persuade himself that he wasn't just a little nervous making this meeting.

I never beat a hundred dollars out of anybody before. I wonder if the kid has friends waiting to jump me. Nah, I scared all of 'em pretty bad, but it woulda been easier to meet someplace else, like behind the health club.

As he passed the end of the soccer-net wall, a baseball bat snaked out and smashed into his shins. Tourangeau bellowed and doubled over in pain, and the bat struck again, a rising blow to the throat. He forgot about trying to reach for the pistol.

Can't breathe. Ah, shit!

The bat wielder swung again, a stunning blow to the head, and he rolled over on his back, only semi-conscious. There was a savage strike to each side of his face, and he was dimly aware of being dragged to the fence, where his hands were bound to the links, as far apart as they could get.

He opened his mouth to scream for help, but a dirty cloth was pushed in, and the gag secured by a strip of duct tape that went all the way around his head.

Who the fuck…Shit, it's just one guy. Can't see his face, and he ain't said nothin'.

The attacker wore a dark hooded sweatshirt, but had it on backwards. He'd cut eyeholes in the back of the hood, and the fingernail moon didn't cast enough light to see any details.

Tourangeau tried to scream when he saw the knife, but only a muffled squeal came through the tape.

My ear! Oh, shit, my ear!

Then it was quiet on the track except for his ragged breathing, and some scuffling as he tried without success to get to his feet. His wrists were bleeding from the effort, as the plastic ties cut into the skin. His scalp was bleeding, and his head hurt horribly. And the blood ran down his check from where his left ear used to be. Finally, he sank down in as much comfort as he could manage, and endured.

Andy

A few minutes before six, as the gray light was brightening into silver ahead of the dawn, Rufus Vickery bounced out of a car and trotted toward the track for his morning run. Suddenly, he stopped, sniffed and stared.

"Rufus, what's the matter?" Ellen Vickery asked. Rufus was a young golden retriever, and he didn't like anything his nose and eyes were telling him. Keeping Ellen behind him, he started a furious, urgent barking, with a few growls thrown in for emphasis.

"Rufus, stop it. What in the world are you….. Oh, my God!"

Quickly she brought out her cell phone, the one Henry had told never to leave home without, dog or no dog.

"Hello, 911? Yes, I need the police at the high school. Ellen Vickery. Yes, I'll tell you all that later, but I think you need an ambulance too.

"Rufus, quiet, here boy! What's that? Well, there's a man here on the ground thrashing and moaning, and his hands are tied to the fence, and he's gagged and bleeding, and there's something terribly wrong with his ear. Oh my God, oh my God, it's been cut off! The poor man! What's that? Are you kidding me, I'm not going anywhere near him! Yes, I can hear the siren. Tell them I'm on the track just past the parking lot. Yes, I'll wait here."

Andy Benoit had been headed for the cop shop when he got the call, ten minutes before his shift ended. He was new, but not too new to recognize the urgency in the dispatcher's voice. *So much for getting off on time. This midnight shift really sucks. Something always happens at the last minute.*

84

Here we are. Okay lady you can stop waving, I see you.

"Dispatch, 216."

"Go, 216."

"Julie, I got that blue truck we've been looking for. Chevy, Vermont plates 8934-JXT. Could you run that plate while I see what we got here? And call Jacobs, he's the one that put out the alert on the truck."

He walked through a gate in the fence, and saw the woman trying to control her dog, and still holding her cell phone.

"Mrs. Vickery, could you put the dog in the car, please? Thanks. Now let's see." He turned to the fence.

Archie was writhing against the plastic cuffs. *Shit, I'm glad to see him, but I ain't. He'll find my stash for sure. But wait a minute, I'm the victim here.* "Mmmmmph. Uhmm!"

"216, Dispatch."

"Go, Dispatch."

"Andy, that plate comes back registered to Walter Tourangeau on Blue Mountain Road, and it's under suspicion in the Archie Tourangeau drug case."

"Well Julie, what we got here is Archie himself, or most of him, gagged and staked out on the fence, and somebody has sliced off his ear, in addition to working him over pretty good. Keep the ambulance coming, and get the day shift to bring the camera. We're going to be here a while."

"All right. When I told Jacobs about the truck he said he'd be right there."

More sirens. When the Rescue crew cut Archie loose from the fence, Officer Benoit cuffed each of his hands to the gurney. He didn't know why Jacobs wanted this guy, but he wasn't going to fight a man the size of Archie and get mud stains all over his uniform.

"Hey, Sarge, looky here. Old Archie was gagged with a pair of dirty underpants, tidy whiteys. I think he done the damage to his wrists by himself, but somebody split open his scalp, whacked him on each cheek bone, and of course took off his ear."

Jacobs leaned over the man as the ambulance crew started to

load him into their vehicle. "You wanta tell me what happened, Archie, or do I get to make it up?"

"Fuck you, Jacobs."

"Sorry, asshole, it's you that's gonna get screwed this time. We found the Willard kid's blood in the back of the Ram, from when you hauled him out on the West Bend road, and we found the Ram's tire prints there too, along with some boot prints that look like they'll match the ones you're wearin'. There's a concealed weapon that violates all kinds of statutes. Andy says there's more dope in the Chevy. You are goin' away this time, cocksucker, that sleaze lawyer can't bargain down aggravated assault to a misdemeanor, not this time."

"But somebody tried to kill me! Oy'm the victim here!"

"Lissen, peckerhead. If whoever done this had meant to leave you dead, you'd *be* dead, you dumb fuck. This was done so's we'd find you, and thanks to that nice lady and her dog, we did. Suppose you'd still be lyin' here when the school buses comes in, and all those kids you've scared to death come out and see your sorry ass all trussed up, helpless and earless. That's what the intent was. Humiliation. Do you even know what that is, you shit-licker?"

"You can't talk to me like that. If Oy'm under arrest Oy want my lawyer."

"Harmon, you go with him to the hospital, stay with him until the docs are finished, and then take him to jail. I'll know what to charge him with by then. And don't give him a chance to run, or to swing at you."

The ambulance moved off, light and siren opening a way through the crowd of arriving high schoolers.

"Andy, I've got some of that Police Line tape in the SUV. Let's get this area roped off and see if we can figure out what happened here."

Ten minutes later they were squatting on their heels, looking at marks in the soft earth. "What do you think, Sarge?" Andy Benoit could see the marks, but he wasn't sure how to interpret them.

"Well, these big boots is Archie, comin' along the wall. Whoever got him, waited on the other side. See, there's no clear marks, Andy. What we got here is the cross-hatch pattern made by a burlap bag.

That means it's pre-meditated. Somebody covered his shoes, and I'll bet there's not a print to he found anywhere around here.

"So then here's where Archie fell to his knees, and I think turned over on his back or was rolled over. That's not clear. But the rest of the beating happened here, cause there's blood splatters, not just drip-stains, on the grass where his head would be.

"And then he got dragged to the fence and zip-locked into it. See, more blood, that's where he lost his ear. There's also a little blood under each of those plastic cuffs, where he tried to get himself loose. I'm guessing he was there for five or six hours."

Andy was impressed. It was all there, if you knew how to look at it. Maybe some day…

"Sarge, he says he don't know who did this to him, that he couldn't see a face. Do you think some of his druggie pals were tryin' to teach him something?"

"Could be, Andy, that would make sense. Although there's something about the pattern of damage that's familiar, naggin' at the edge of my mind."

They spent an hour taking pictures, shooing kids away and getting Aaron Ormond to come and tow the truck away.

Ralph Montgomery sat up straight when the story hit the TV news that evening.

The reporter, microphone in hand, was standing where the camera could show both the wooden wall and the fence, while she described the savage attack on a Nilesburgh resident.

"… and the most bizarre injury, of course, is that Tourangeau's left ear was sliced off with a sharp instrument. Police chief Gerald Harrison spoke to reporters this afternoon."

I know Jerry Harrison. He hates this kind of thing.

"Chief, what can you tell us about the victim in this beating?" "Archie Tourangeau is a 24 year-old resident of Nilesburgh, and is known to the police. He has a scalp laceration, bruises to both sides of his face and to his shins, and of course the ear. None of those is considered life-threatening."

"Where is he? Can we talk to him?"

"He's in jail in St. Albans, and no, you can't talk to him unless he makes bail, and I don't think that's going to happen. And even if he does, I don't think he'll talk to you guys."

"Chief, you said he was known to the police. Does that mean Tourangeau is a person of interest, or a suspect in an ongoing police investigation?"

Jeezum, the kid from the local paper has a pretty good source somewhere.

"Mister Tourangeau is in custody for possession of controlled substances, possession of an unregistered weapon, and for violating the provisions of a bail agreement made last week on similar charges."

The kid was persistent. "Do you have a motive for this attack?"

Screw that. "Well, Tommy, I'm afraid you'll just have to make a living on what I've already said. At this time, I'm not prepared to go any further than the facts I've given you. A discussion of motivation would be purely speculative, and I'm not going to do it."

There was more talk, but Ralph noticed there was no more information. Just the reporter and her anchorman mulling over the savagery of a vicious assault in quiet little Nilesburgh.

They don't know very much and, and Harrison's not fueling a feeding frenzy. He knows more than he's saying, or at least he suspects more. I wish I knew more about where their investigation is going.

Chief

Chief Jerry Harrison had once seen a movie in which Town Marshall Glenn Ford had done his best thinking with his feet propped up on a desk. He looked between his boots at Sergeant Jacobs and Officer Benoit, and opened the after-action analysis.

"Okay guys. What we got here is an upgrade in violence. The attacker was ruthless and efficient, and what he did was premeditated. You know very well that when we get beatings it's almost always booze or a broad, or both, and it's spontaneous."

Jacobs shifted in his chair and Harrison noticed.

"Cooney, whattaya think?"

"Well Chief, I told Andy when we went over the ground out there, that something was on the edge of my mind, something unusual about the beating. And now I know what it was. Archie's injuries were exactly the same as that Willard kid's. Bruises to both sides of the face and a split scalp. Only difference is, the doer swapped a broken arm for an ear. Arms heal, ears don't. Now we got evidence, circumstantial, but evidence still, that Archie beat up that kid, for some reason, maybe a drug debt. So now somebody whacks Archie the same way, and the ear is the escalation. Somebody's trying to teach that fuck a lesson."

"But that's a huge guy, and a known fighter and bully," said Benoit. "When I was askin' around at the school I got a feelin' that they're all scared of him. So my question is, is who would take him on like that?"

Harrison swung his legs to the floor. He hadn't become chief by letting his mind sleep through his years in uniform. "The kid told us he didn't know who beat him up. But he told somebody, cause a week later Archie gets the same beating. Andy, go back to the high school, and have another go at those kids, the ones that hang out at the plaza. I think at least some of them saw the Willard kid get hurt, and now that Archie's been stripped of his big bad wolf label, maybe their memories will improve. Cooney, you know the ones to ask, don't you."

"Yeah, there's about four that may not be so scared of him any more."

"Okay," and the feet went back up again. "What else do we know?"

"Chief, let's follow this notion of a link between the two beatings. A day or so after the first one, a guy comes to me askin' whether there's a connection between a certain truck and the drug trade, and whether we're lookin' for anybody. I don't let on, but he figures out that I got a name in mind. I may have let slip about the Dodge Ram. Few days later he comes back with the info we used to grab Archie behind the plaza. Then Archie makes bail, shifts his office to behind the health club, and is back in business. But only for one night. I think that same guy lured him to the high school track, and beat the shit out of him."

"Maybe," Harrison said. "But who?"

"Kevin."

"Kevin Beaujolais? Yer shittin' me. He ain't half as big as Archie, and he ain't a fighter. Archie would kill him."

"Chief, this was nowhere near a fair fight. From that first whack on the shins, Archie never had a chance. It was cold-blooded punishment."

"Yeah, but Kevin? What's the motive? Kevin's a farm worker, does spot labor at the sawmill, odd jobs and stuff. And he's always smilin' and helpin' folks out. Lotta people think he's a little simple. Are you sure?"

Jacobs looked uncomfortable. "No, I'm not sure, but I'm trackin' what I know, and that leads me to what I think. I don't think the kid's father was the one, and he's the logical suspect. And anyways, I think your man Kevin's a lot smarter and a lot more devious than you think he is."

At the Iron Skillet that Monday, the beating was warmed over so often that it began to taste like the conversational equivalent of old coffee.

It was rehashed whenever a new face sat in, and each time, the story became less tethered to facts. There was little sympathy for the victim.

"The way Oy hear it, the shit-licker got what he deserved."

"Yeah but how'd you like it if somebody carved off your ear? I wouldn't want that guy that done it to get mad at me."

"Well Charlie, you ain't been beatin' up teenagers, have ya?"

"Jeezum, Jim. Yeah, that's me. Or why don't you come right out and say Oy done it. Or maybe that's the wrong tag. Maybe Oy'm the Slicer. Shit, boys, that's about as likely as Leo done it. Yeah, that's it! Leo is the Slicer."

"Kevin! How ya doin?"

Kevin pulled up a chair, poured his coffee, and sat while the buzz swirled around him.

"I don't care whether he deserved it or not," said Jeffrey Adams. "What they done to him was pretty cold."

"Whattaya mean, 'they'?" asked Hatman. "Oy heard it was just one guy done it."

"Well that don't make no sense," Albie Jackson said. "He's too big for one guy to whip."

"Hey Suzie! You knew Archie from high school, right? How was he in them days?"

Suzie had her arms loaded with breakfast plates, and put them down before answering. "He was a jerk. He made me feel dirty when he looked at me. And once I had to knee him in the nuts to get him offa me, right in the hallway. Mister Helprin was right there, and he seen it, but he didn't do nothin'."

"Kevin, did you hear the cops think Archie got it cause he beat up that Willard kid?"

"Ain't heard that. But Oy know the Willard kid a little, and he didn't deserve to get what he got."

"So do you think Archie did?" Jackson asked. "Deserve it, I mean?"

"Jeezum, Albie, Oy ain't got much use for drug sellers. Who done it?"

"Well, that's the question in any mystery, ain't it?" said Jeffrey Adams. "What about the kid's old man?"

"Leonard Willard?" Kevin shrugged dismissively. *They don't know Leonard's fighting cancer, and ain't hardly strong enough to swat a fly.* "Oy don't think he's the sloicer you're talkin' about. He's mad over his kid, but Oy don't think he's a hunter. And Oy hear somebody purely stalked ole Archie and laid him out."

"Well, I think they oughta let the law handle it," said Jim Shipley. "Can't no good come from havin' somebody go around whackin' whoever he don't like."

"Vigilante law, you mean?" asked Adams.

"What's that?" Kevin wanted to know.

"That's when folks take the law into their own hands cause the police either can't act, or won't act," said Adams. "Lots of times in the past, that kind of thing has led to lynchin' and to hangin' the wrong man."

"Anybody think they got the wrong man this toime?" Kevin asked.

Nobody did, and nobody had any solid ideas about who did the damage to Archie Tourangeau. Kevin sat back and enjoyed his coffee and his cheese and onion omelette.

The men talked of starting a betting pool, with the winner to be whoever could guess the Slicer's identity. Kevin noticed that the idea foundered because nobody had any nominations.

The Post Office sells envelopes of various sizes, and some of them have a protective liner of bubble-wrap on the inside. One of those turned up in the morning mail at the Tourangeau house, addressed to Archie. Since Archie was in jail, his father opened it.

Inside was a human left ear, and a note, in block printing on lined paper.

YOU ARE OUT OF BUSINESS.
IF YOU DEAL ANY MORE
YOUR WOODIE IS NEXT.

Walter

Nilesburgh made the transition from agriculture to Burlington suburb without much grace, and with some internal tensions.

For a decade or two, farmers in the town named for Vermont's first Congressman had been selling off part of their holdings, mostly lots that fronted on the roads. Few of their sons or daughters wanted to stay on the farm, and developers were offering good money for land of marginal agricultural value.

That set up a culture clash between Old Nilesburgh and New Nilesburgh.

Old Nilesburgh was made up of long-established and intermarried families who owned the farms and stores, served as the community's tradesmen, and made the speeches at Memorial Day observances held in front of the Civil War monument that listed their ancestors' names.

New Nilesburgh grew as homes appeared on old pastures, and people who worked in Burlington or Essex found the commute to be reasonable in most weather. New Nilesburgh ran the newspaper and voted Democratic and didn't "get" the Grange. Its kids played soccer and lacrosse in high school. Old Nilesburgh ran cafes like the Iron Skillet and voted Republican and didn't "get" organized social services. Its kids played hockey and baseball.

The two sets of residents were not yet formal political factions, and some thoughtful people worked hard at preventing the town from side-slipping into an Us vs Them mentality.

And both sides turned out strongly at the first meeting of the Board of Selectmen after news of the beatings got around.

The current Board consisted of three Olds and two News, including a woman and the Chairman.

Walter Tourangeau was in the audience, looking angry. *Flatlanders and pansies on that Board. Three of 'em I don't know and the other two I don't like. And who are all them people out front?*

Old Nilesburgh also included families that had fallen on hard times, and families that had never known any other kind of times.

Walter Tourangeau headed one of those families. The Tourangeaus had been adrift ever since the market for farm labor eroded in the years after World War Two. They had brought no skills beyond the handling of horses into a changing world, and they foundered there.

Walter Tourangeau was often annoyed at the unfairness of the fact that others had, while he had not. That anger had put him in jail more than once for brawling and for burglary. *None of 'em seem to know how it is with workin' folks.* The fact that he hadn't held a job for more than a year did not dilute his bitterness at the Board.

There was a printed agenda, but none of it seemed to have anything to do with him, or with the reason he was attending his first Selectboard meeting ever. So when the Pledge of Allegiance was over, he stayed on his feet.

"Oy wanna talk about moy boy."

"What's your name, sir?" asked the Chairman, who had lived in Nilesburgh for all of seven years.

"Walter Tourangeau." *Hundred years in this town and this asshole don't know who I am. Well, when I get through suin', he will.* "Yer damn cops got moy boy locked up, and they set the bail too hoigh."

"Mister Tourangeau," said the Chairman. "There's a great deal of interest in the events of the past two weeks, and as I'm sure you've noticed, Item Six on the agenda is a public hearing on those events, and you're welcome to speak then. And as for the bail bond, this Board has no powers in the judicial system."

Fucker makes me feel outa place in my own town. Maybe he thinks everybody can read.

Ralph Montgomery was there, in a row near the front. He was

learning to dress down for these Selectboard meetings, where board members showed up in jeans, or in green denim shirts with their names embroidered on one of the pockets.

I made the right choice. The only necktie in the room is around the Town Manager's neck, if you don't count the three police uniforms.

It did not occur to Ralph that a plaid shirt and fleece vest would have looked more like Nilesburgh than the turtleneck and cardigan sweater that he wore.

"With the Board's consent," the Chairman said, looking left and right, "I'd like to move Item Six forward on the Agenda, because so many people are here tonight about crime and safety issues in Nilesburgh." Getting nods of approval from his colleagues, the Chairman proceeded.

"The public hearing into crime and public safety issues brought to light by the events of the past two weeks, is now open at six forty-seven. Mr. Manager, do you have a presentation?"

"I'll defer to Chief Harrison. Chief?"

Harrison strode to a small podium where he could see the audience to his left, and the Board to his right. Board members sat in comfortable padded chairs that swiveled and tilted. The audience sat on metal folding chairs. Once during a long meeting, a member of the audience had suggested that meetings would be a lot shorter if board members also had to sit in hard chairs.

"Mister Chairman, members of the Board, I'll try to give you a time-line on the events that have brought so many people here tonight.

"As background, we've always had a low-level drug economy here, mostly around the high school and mostly involving small sales of marijuana. In recent months the intensity of that trade, and the potency of the substances involved has accelerated, and has led to violence.

"Twelve days ago a sixteen year-old high school student was severely beaten behind the shopping strip known as the plaza. He was then taken out of the village to a point on West Bend Road, where he was rolled out of the back of a pickup truck and left for dead in the roadway. We believe there were two motives in that case. One, he owed money to a drug dealer. Two, we believe the beating was done in front of other kids, as an object lesson in fear. In other words, this is what happens if you don't pay your dealer. So far, none of those kids has come forward, nor has the victim identified his assailant."

Looking directly at Walter Tourangeau, he continued. "As you know, we have a suspect in custody in that case, and the State's Attorney thinks we have a pretty good case."

"You ain't got nothin'!" Tourangeau yelled. "You can't prove shit!"

Chief Harrison looked at the Chairman, who used his gavel forcefully.

"Mister Tourangeau, I promised you a chance to speak during this hearing, and you will get it. In the meantime, you will be quiet."

"Asshole," Tourangeau muttered, a little too loudly.

Bang, went the gavel again. "Look, mister, you're not helping yourself by being belligerent."

What the fuck does that mean?

"Just save up the things you want to say, and then bring them up when you have your turn. Besides, I didn't hear Chief Harrison mention any names. Go on, Chief."

"Well, Mr. Chairman, you're about to hear a name. Not the victim, because he's under age. But the suspect is this man's son, Archie Tourangeau. You sit still, Walter. Even without witness testimony there is solid evidence that he committed aggravated assault on the young victim.

"Now, to the second case, which is even more troubling. About a week after the first beating, Archie Tourangeau was found by an early-morning dog-walker, tied to a fence at the high school track. He had suffered identical injuries, except that there were no broken bones. Instead, his left ear was cut off. We think that was a revenge beating, and was pre-meditated. We do not have a suspect in that case."

"Oy ever find out who done it, the fucker's dead!"

Bang! "Mister Tourangeau, one more outburst and I'll have you thrown out of here. And by the way, you might want to think about the consequences of threatening to commit murder in front of sixty people. Chief, what else?"

"Well, Walter here provided us with a note to his son that was written when somebody mailed him the lost ear. It's a threat to further personal violence against Archie if he don't get out of the drug business. A little beside the point now, cause it's not likely Archie will be out and about, as the Canadians say, for quite a long time.

"I just want to emphasize to the Board and to the community that my officers are conducting a very active investigation into all this. Sergeant Jacobs and Officer Benoit are both here at my request, in case they're needed to answer questions. And let me say I hope these incidents have a chilling effect on those young people who've been dabbling in drugs. The violence is a new development, and we will move the Earth to get it stopped." Harrison sat down to applause.

"Chief Harrison," one of the Board members called him back. "The papers and the TV guys are calling the person who did the second beating 'The Slicer in the Hoodie.' Can you explain that?"

"Yes sir, the victim told Officer Benoit that he could not see who struck him, because the light was poor and because the assailant was wearing a hooded sweatshirt backwards, with eye holes cut in it. If you'll recall, a guy wearing an outfit like that was involved in some bank robberies down around Burlington a couple of years ago. We do not think that same man was involved in this case, primarily because he's been in prison for the past year, and will be there for a few more years. But clearly, somebody thought that get-up was a pretty good disguise."

"Mister Tourangeau," the Chairman said. "Would you like to speak now?"

"Damn right Oy would. Folks are callin' this Sloicer guy a hero. Truth is, he's a criminal. He ruined moy son's looks and you ain't even arrested nobody."

Arnold Jacobs allowed himself a smile. *Ruined his looks? When they said big is beautiful they weren't lookin' at Archie.*

"Instead you got Archie in jail. What's fair in that?"

This time the Town Manager spoke. "Mister Tourangeau, your son is not in jail for being mutilated. He's there because he's facing some serious felony charges that have nothing to do with the vigilante justice he also received."

"What's that mean?"

"It means that somebody took the law into his own hands."

Cheering broke out in the audience, and Tourangeau got up and glared at the people behind him as the gavel banged again. The Board members took notes on how the wind was blowing.

"We do *not* condone that," the Manager continued. "And as the Chief has said, we're trying hard to find out who did it. And by the way, when we catch him, the courts will deal with him, not you."

Ralph stood up. "Mr. Chairman, may I speak?"

"Yes. State your name for the record please."

"I'm Ralph Montgomery, and I live on Grist Mill Road. It seems to me, Mr. Chairman, that the underlying cause of all the violence you're discussing is the drug trade. What I'd like to know is, what additional steps can this community take to suppress that trade, so we don't have any more incidents like this."

Ralph noticed nods of approval among audience members. Officer Andy Benoit shifted on his feet in the back. *Nobody's gonna say it, but maybe one of those steps has already been taken. The diplomats call it a deterrent when they talk about nuclear war. Don't start something if the consequences are going to be severe.*

"I'd like to inform everyone here," the Chairman said, "that the Town is moving to do some of the things your question is raising. Specifically, we're appropriating money to get street lights installed behind the plaza shopping strip, and in two other badly lighted locations where we know young people gather. We're also increasing and diversifying police patrol patterns in the village and out into the surrounding areas as well. And our legislators have been asked to push for a bill that would give us additional tools to punish drug dealing within a thousand yards of a school or church or youth center, even a daycare center.

"Beyond that, this Board welcomes input from a variety of sources within the community. We're going to ask tonight for people to come forward to serve on a study commission that will help us define the extent of the problem and point us toward additional solutions. If anyone would like to participate, please see the manager after the meeting."

"Mister Chairman." A tall, white-haired man stood in the back of the room. "Yes, sir," the Chairman nodded.

"I'm Howard Eppley, from out on the Sugarbush Road."

Ralph sharpened his attention. *I've heard of this Eppley. The Town Clerk says he used to be a civic powerhouse. Some kind of computer chip consultant, ex-IBM, moved here 20 years ago and just kind of melted into the local community. Wonder why he quit serving on boards.*

"Noice ta see ya, Howard," said one of the board members from Old Nilesburgh.

"Thank you," Eppley said. He turned to face the audience. "I think what we've got here is a scary situation, with escalating violence. Mister Montgomery was right in asking what else we can do to diminish this drug business, and I commend the Chairman for his suggestion of a citizen study committee. I'd be willing to serve on that, if it's broadly representative of the town; that is if it's not just the usual five per cent of civic activists who sign up. I'd be glad to sit down with some folks who know everybody, and make some nominations." He turned back to the board. "We need to harness all the energy that's represented here tonight, and move in a unified direction, or we're wasting our time." He sat down to applause.

Sensing that the tension had drained out of the room, the Chairman closed the public hearing and moved to the other items on the agenda.

After the meeting, Howard Eppley and the Manager decided to ask Jim Shipley the rent-it man, and Billy Brophy the Town Clerk to serve as nominators.

Walter Tourangeau left the meeting feeling that somehow he had been short-changed, or cheated in a way he didn't understand. After all, Archie was still in jail, and it was clear the audience approved of that, and that the Board wasn't going to lift a finger to get him out. *If Archie was loose we could go back to that kid and make him tell us enough to go huntin' on. Or maybe we could lean on some a them other kids. Put the fear into them.* It did not occur to Tourangeau that that was precisely why his son's bail had been set so high.

Alvin

M aureen was so full of the news, and so proud of Gene when she got to the bank, that she almost blurted it out to Judy while customers were there.

"Judy, you won't believe this!" she finally said. "They've got a committee set up to study drugs and violence, and they've asked my Gene to serve on it. Isn't that wonderful? He'll be good, he's thoughtful and fair. I wonder how they knew to pick him?"

"Oh, that's very great!" Judy gushed. "I saw in the paper where they're asking people from all parts of the community to serve, but it didn't give any names. That's wonderful! What does he have to do?"

"I don't know, and he has to clear it with IBM first. So don't say anything until it gets all sugared off. There, did I say that right?"

Judy grinned. "Sweet," she said with a nod.

Four days later Gene McGuckin was in the Town Manager's office.

"I've got a problem, Mr. Kester. My engineering team at IBM has come up with a new chip modification that's got a lot of promise, and now they want me to go around and tutor engineers at our other plants, on how it works. I'll be gone a lot over the next few weeks, and so I've got to decline your invitation."

Alvin Kester was the third Town Manager in five years, and was becoming known for his flexible thinking, and his ability to keep his Selectboard at least loosely tethered to reality. Funny though, how the same old phrases cropped up wherever he worked. "Alvin Kester guards his keester."

"I'm sorry to hear that, Gene," he said. *This is a sharp young guy. How do I keep him interested in civic service? I thought this was pretty good bait, but if he can't do it… wait.* "Gene, doesn't your wife work at the bank? Maureen, right?"

"Yeah, but…"

"You don't mind if I ask her, do you?" And he dialed the bank's number from memory. "Mrs. McGuckin, please. Yes, I'll hold. Hello?

"Yes, this is Alvin Kester at the Town offices. I've got your husband in my office. No, nothing's wrong. He's just told me that job conflicts will keep him off the drug and violence study committee, and I'd like to know if you'd be willing to serve in his place. Of course I'm serious, I don't do practical jokes. Yes, I'll put him on."

"Hi, honey," Gene said. "Well it was a surprise to me too, but it makes sense. They want someone fairly new, and young, and willing to serve, and you fit that as well as I do. Probably better, because you meet more local people through the bank. Yes, I'll tell him. Love you too, bye."

He was grinning as he put the phone down. "She says she has to think it over for a while, but I'm betting she calls you before noon tomorrow to say she's in. Maureen's been talking about putting down roots here, and getting involved is certainly one way to do it. That's why I was interested when you called me." Then, blushing slightly, he added, "And I think a little pillow talk will keep me up to speed on what's going on."

Ralph and Helene began having Saturday morning breakfast at the Iron Skillet a few weeks after Archie Tourangeau was jailed. They got some nods of recognition from the regulars, but no invitations to the coveted central row of tables.

I think those greetings are for Helene, not for me. Somehow I don't think that many five-foot, ten-inch blondes come in here wearing size six in this year's clothes.

Jim Shipley was a friendly face and a cheerful wave. And there was a round-faced man in an Australian hat who usually sat with his back to the door, and then turned and examined everyone who came in. *I don't think I've heard Hatman's name. And why don't they take off their hats when they're eating? Let's see, 5 Boston Red Sox caps, and two for that dead race car driver. Maybe those guys are all bald. Imagine the scolding they'd get for those hats from my grandmother.*

Ralph eavesdropped on the morning gossip, realizing that the pace was slower on the weekends, and that if these tradesmen were working, they weren't starting as early as they would during the week. It wasn't hard to follow their chatter because Jim Shipley didn't hear well, and a semi-retired excavator named Bill-something spent most of the morning with a hand cupped behind his ear and his eyes focused on whoever was speaking. The word was that old Bill used to be quick with the wisecracks, but that was in a time gone by, before he started using dynamite as an excavating tool.

These people have had a lifetime to hone the friendships among them and to build a data-base of memories for the jokes they tell on each other. Data-base of memories. Hmm. I guess you can't do that if you move around all the time.

"Kevin!" a man bellowed and grinned.

"Who's that?" Helene asked.

"I think his name is Charlie," said Ralph.

Kevin took an empty chair across from Shipley and next to Hatman. "Mornin' Ralph," he called across the room. "Mornin' Missus."

"How're you doing, Kevin?"

"Gettn' by."

"He knows my name," she whispered. "Why doesn't he use it?"

"You make him nervous, partly because you're taller than he is, and partly because he thinks you're outrageously gorgeous."

"He does not!"

"Yes he does, that's why he blushes whenever he looks at you. I don't think our man here has much of a track record with ladies. Women, maybe, but not ladies, and he's got you catalogued as a lady, right or wrong."

"He's right, you oaf. You must be suffering from PCB this morning."

"PCB? You mean that cancer-causing stuff, that chemical in electric stuff?"

"No silly, PCB like in pre-coffee blues. Go pour yourself a cup; you'll start seeing the world a little more clearly. I don't make anybody nervous."

When the others drained their coffee cups and left, Kevin brought his ham-and-onion omelet to their booth and settled in beside Ralph, while shooting only the briefest glances at Helene. He had never joined Ralph while Helene was there, and only once when Ralph was alone. *Wonder what's up? This is almost like taming a wild animal. What kind of animal would Kevin be? A small predator, I think. Maybe a badger.*

"What's up, Kevin?"

"Aw, nothin' much." He looked uncomfortable.

"Must be something," Ralph prompted.

Jeezum, any way I say this, it's gonna sound stupid. "Ya know Oy like to keep moy head down, and not draw a lotta attention." Ralph nodded. "Well, there's reasons for that, but now here comes Billy Brophy, and wants me to be on some koind of study group about drugs and violence." Kevin looked uncomfortable. "Oy don't wanta get out front on somethin' loike that, but Billy says Oy know a lot about the town and the people in it, and loike that. Oy don't hold with no drug thugs messin' with kids and screwin' 'em up, but Oy can't see moyself doin' somethin' like this. Oy'd be embarrassed, maybe, or maybe Oy wouldn't have nothin' to add. What do you think?"

I'm flattered he's asking me. "What I think is if you're part of the town and you take an interest in its well-being, then you should do this. You can't treat your town like it's a motel room, you've got a stake in it. It's not official yet, but they asked me too, and I'm going to do it."

Kevin grinned. "Ain't that a kick! Kevin Beaujolais and Randolph Montgomery the… what, Fourth? Third, okay, the Third, servin' together on a committee. What would my mama think?"

He sat there for a moment, absently eating his omelet and imagining conversations that could never be.

Kevin

"Chief, I can't find Kevin Beaujolais."

"Come on, Cooney, we see him almost every day."

"I mean he's not on paper. There's no birth certificate in Vital Records. DMV has nothing. He's not on the tax rolls or the Grand List, meaning he doesn't own any property. He's not registered to vote, and the Clerk doesn't even have an address. The only thing I've got is for a couple of years he was on the Poor list as a kid, and the school has records that he was there. Dropped out of high school. I was in grade school with him, and he's always been around, but I never realized he'd be so hard to pin down."

"You still want him for that Tourangeau beating?"

Jacobs hesitated. "It's not like he's a suspect, and not that we could prove it, but this kinda work teaches you not to believe in coincidences, and the injuries were just too much alike. It smacks of revenge. I did find out that Kevin is supposed to be first cousin to the Willard kid's mom, and that Kevin went to see the kid in the hospital. The administrator there said he also settled the bill, in cash. Fifties, mostly. It's beginning to walk like a duck, Chief."

Harrison had his boots on his desk. "I don't think it's gonna quack for you, though. Where does a guy like Kevin get that kind of money? We got any unsolved break-ins? Does he have an alibi? Can anybody vouch for where he was while Archie Tourangeau was getting a make-over?"

"I haven't pushed that far yet, he's not a suspect. But I do want to talk to him. Besides, if he mailed that ear back to Archie, we got him for the note, and that's as much of a threat as I've ever seen.

But that's only a three-year sentence and there's no way a jury is gonna make Kevin do time for threatening to cut Tourangeau's pecker off if he deals drugs again."

Harrison smiled a little, relishing the memory of the somewhat fastidious female member of the Board turning red when the manager had to explain to her the meaning of the word "woodie." Of course the note contained no prints, and the state police expert said he thought it was written by a person wearing gloves. He had suggested they look for someone who would use "woodie" for penis, considering that there were so many other synonyms.

"Well, stake out the Skillet, and see if those guys know where he is. What do you have on the other one, the Willard kid?"

"First, a stakeout at the Skillet is good for about twenty minutes, and after that he'll know not to go there, cause those guys will tell him. Some of 'em treat Kevin like a mascot or something. As for the Willard kid, he won't say it was Archie, and when Andy went to the high school, several kids told him they knew what happened to young Willard, but that it was some other kid who saw it and told them. And of course, nobody could remember just who it was that told them."

"Jeezum, Cooney. That bastard had them all buffaloed, and still does. They're still afraid he's going to beat the charge and then get out and beat them up too!" Harrison looked at the case file. "I think we've got a case, and so does the state's attorney. Possession with intent, twice, bail violations all over the place, including the concealed weapon, and the kid's blood in the bed of his truck. Plus the cast of his truck tires out on West Bend Road. Too bad we don't have bloodstains from the plaza."

"Okay, if we get a conviction, how much time is it worth? The prosecutor says we don't have enough prior convictions to label Tourangeau a habitual criminal, although he certainly is. And here's the thing, Chief. If we get him into court, that asshole lawyer will put him on the stand as the victim of a vicious assault, and that ear is likely to weigh more with a jury than the kid's broken arm. I think without a talking witness, we may have three to five, and he'll serve about a year. That's not enough to give those kids much courage."

"Jeezum, Cooney, some detectives we are. One case we pretty much know who the Slicer in the hoodie was, and we'll never prove it, and the other case, we can prove it, but we can't get a long sentence and get rid of that bastard once and for all. And the heat is on from the town to do just that, believe me. What a job!"

"I got an idea, Chief. Maybe we make a hero out of the Slicer in the hoodie, and then we can flush him out to take credit for doin' Archie."

"Work on it."

"By the way, you talk to Keester today?"

"Yeah, he wants you to represent the cops on that committee. You okay with that? I didn't promise him."

Jacobs looked sharply at the Chief. "He didn't tell you who else he and Brophy put on it, did he?"

Harrison looked puzzled.

"Freakin' Kevin, that's who!"

"Holy shit! Interestinger and interestinger."

A week later, Kester was in Billy Brophy's office, looking puzzled.

"Billy, I'm trying to send out notices to all the people on the committee, and I've got a problem."

"Yeah?"

"This guy Kevin Beaujolais that you wanted, I don't have an e-mail for him, or a phone number, or an address. It's like he doesn't exist."

Brophy looked up at his office wall, where there was a highly polished and polyurethaned cross-section of a maple tree with a sap spout glued into it. Kevin had given him that after the Gormley will business had settled down.

"Oh, he's real enough, I can tell you. And like I said, if you want a group that represents a broad spectrum of the community, like old Howard said, then Kevin's a good fit. And I'll make sure he knows when and where we're meeting."

Howard

"The first thing to do," Alvin Kester said, "is to elect a Chairman."

"I nominate Howard Eppley," said Billy Brophy, who had done his groundwork.

"Second," said Ruby Mongeon, who'd been prompted by Brophy.

"Are there any other nominations?" the Manager asked twice. "Hearing none, all those in favor of Howard Eppley serving as Chairman of the study committee on drugs and violence in Nilesburgh, please signify by saying 'Aye'."

"Aye," said nine voices. Kester turned to Eppley. "Mister Chairman?"

"Thanks, Alvin. I'd like to go around the table, since I don't think we all know each other, and have everybody say who you are, what you do, how long you've lived in Nilesburgh, you know, the get-acquainted stuff. Let's start here, to my right."

"I'm Billy Brophy, and I'm the Town Clerk and Treasurer. Have been for quite a few years now. I'd like to say I've lived in Nilesburgh all my life, but that's not true, yet. Hope I still got some life left in me."

"I'm Roger Helprin, and I'm a guidance counselor at the high school, here representing the school district. I live in Fairfax, but I've been with the school system here for eighteen years."

"Well, I'm the oldest, that's for sure. I'm Ruby Mongeon, and I've been on things like this before. I used to teach school, among other things, and about thirty years ago I was a Justice of the

Peace here, and later a Lister. I won't say how long I've lived here, because that would tell you how old I am."

"I suppose I'm on the opposite end of that. I think I'm the youngest as well as the newest to live in Nilesburgh. I'm Maureen McGuckin, and I work at the bank. My husband Gene was supposed to be here, but I was asked when his job at IBM got in the way. We came here a year and a half ago from Philadelphia, in Pennsylvania."

"I'm Alvin Kester, the Town Manager for the last two and a half years. I don't think it's good policy for a manager to live where he works, and so I live in St. Albans. Before that, I was a Town Manager in Connecticut."

"Kevin," said Kevin. "Oy been livin' here a long toime, and Oy hafta say Oy ain't never done nothin' loike this before. Oh, Beaujolais. Kevin Beaujolais." *This ain't so bad, so far. Didn't know Marine was gonna be here.*

"Ralph Montgomery, a resident here for less than two years. In fact I think I moved here after Mrs. McGuckin. I do some engineering consultant work, and I think I'm here to represent people who have moved in recently."

"I'm Jim Shipley. I run the Nilesburgh Rent-all out on the highway, and I came here twenty six years ago from the Air Force when I married Amy Magee, who grew up here."

"I guess I'm the last one. I'm Arnold Jacobs, and I'm a sergeant with fourteen years service on the Nilesburgh Police Department, representing them on this committee. I think I know almost everybody here, except Mrs. McGuckin. I met Mr. Montgomery the day he found the Willard boy."

"Maureen," said Maureen with a smile.

"Maureen, then," said Jacobs.

"Ralph," said Ralph.

"All right, some people call me Arnie," he said, looking pointedly at Kevin. *I hope that little shit doesn't go to callin' me Cooney.* Kester saw Billy Brophy and Jim Shipley smile a little at that, and wondered what they knew that he didn't.

"All right then, we've got a good cross-section of the town," Howard Eppley said. "Thank you all for agreeing to serve, and I can promise you we'll be busy. We're all going to spend the next few weeks trying to deal with a high level of anxiety over drugs and violence that was clear to see at the Selectboard meeting the other night. I know you've all got ideas, or at least I hope you do, but I want you to hang onto them for a little bit. Go around the town and talk to the people you know best, and even some you don't know, and listen. If folks think you really want to know, they'll open up, sometimes in surprising ways. Let's meet again in a couple of weeks to compare notes. The 17th all right with everybody?"

Jeezum, they're all pullin' out little calendars and markin in 'em.

They settled for the 19th, and even then Jim Shipley would miss the meeting because of a pre-scheduled vacation.

Warrior

"Billy, Oy don't know what the hell Oy'm doin' on that committee."

"Is there anybody on there that you don't know?"

"Well, Oy know them new folks ta talk to, but not like Cooney or Jim Shipley. And remember when Ruby Mongeon chased me around over the poll tax? And you, and Howard, but not that Manager guy, Keester."

Billy grinned. "Kevin, make sure you say Kester. Keester is a not-so-nice where he comes from, it means ass, so be careful." *Kevin's filing that away, I can see that little crinkle around his eyes. He thinks that's a pretty funny name.* "But just think a minute. You've got nothin' to be ashamed of. You know more different kinds of people here than any of 'em, you get along with everybody, and you keep tryin' to hide how smart you are. You're on this thing because what you bring to it they can't find anywhere else."

Kevin looked uncomfortable. "Jeezum, Billy, stop sendin' me flowers. Oy ain't dead yet!"

Billy Brophy laughed. "Just let 'em see a little humor, and they'll listen when you talk. They know you see a different Nilesburgh than they do."

"Yeah, but is it the real one? You know from what Michelle calls 'under the radar', not pushin' moyself up, stayin' away from government stuff, trying to lay low, and now look what you done. You got that guy Keester-Kester askin' for my e-mail address. Jeezum Crow, Billy, this is squitchy fer me."

"What's that?"

"Well, koinda not so good. Squeezy from all that attention and itchy from not knowin' how to behave. Oy ain't even got one a them cute little calendars they was all readin' the other night."

Billy laughed and reached into his desk. "Here. I get lotsa these every year from people that want to do business with the town. This one oughta fit your pocket. I wear mine opposite my wallet."

It was Kevin's turn to laugh. "Billy, Oy ain't got no wallet. You put yer droiver's loicense in there, and yer credit cards, and yer Social Security card, and yer insurance cards, and alla them things. Oy ain't got none a that, and my money folds inta my front pocket. So Oy got plenty a space fer this thing. But I still ain't sure about all this. Oy get tangle-tongued around them people."

"No, you don't," said Billy. "Just around that girl Maureen. You can't even look at her without blushin' like a teenager."

"Now you shut up, Billy!" *Jeezum, I'm yellin' at him. He must be right. He is right, I'm just a piddly puppy around that girl.*

"Tell you what," said Billy, feeling a little guilty that he had teased such a strong reaction out of the shy Kevin. "You just listen at them meetings, and let Howard Eppley do the leadin'. He's a good man, and so is your friend Ralph Montgomery, for a Flatlander."

"He ain't my friend, he's just a guy Oy know from workin' around his house. He don't know shit about wood, Oy know that, and he don't hunt, and past that, Oy don't know much about him, and nobody else in town does either. He just moves in, builds that big house, and starts pokin' into town business."

"Kevin, we need all the people we can get pokin' into town business. There's hardly enough to do all the work. We've always got vacancies on the library board, we haven't elected a moderator in years, and can't hardly find folks to run for the Selectboard and the School Board, and the ones that do may not always be the best. So if this guy wants to come in here and be part of things, make him welcome. Who knows, he may turn out to be another Howard Eppley."

When Kevin left, Billy Brophy sat at his desk and thought for a few minutes. Then he got up and went down the hall to the police department.

"Hey Jerry, you got a minute?"

"Sure, Billy, what's up?"

Billy lifted an eyebrow toward the Chief's office, and followed Harrison inside.

"Private talk, Billy?"

"Jerry, what do you guys know about this Montgomery that's on the crime study committee."

"Not much. Been here a year or so. Built a house, paid his labor on time, put his kid in the school, you know. Keeps his head down. Cooney didn't even know who he was when he called in finding the Willard kid. Why, does he smell bad to you?"

"Just curious," said Billy. "Here we got this guy on our committee, and we don't know nothin' about him, where he came from, what he did before he got here. It's kinda hard to pigeon-hole a guy if you don't know what kinda pigeon he is."

"Billy, are you askin' for a background check on this fella? Technically you can't do that. You're not in my chain of command. I'd have to go through Kester."

"Jerry, wake up. You're a pretty smart guy for a cop. Do you think I'd come in here askin' a favor if I didn't think you'd say yes?"

"Yeah, what's your leverage?"

"Okay, we're keepin' this real friendly, right? All I can say is my brother's widow seems real happy these days. Of course if I ever found out that you're screwin' her silly, then I'd have to be indignant." He leaned back in his chair. "But since I don't know anything, keep up the good work."

Harrison put his feet up on his desk. "Billy, I was readin' about a civil case the other day, one that got settled. And the story went that the defendant, without admitting any culpability, agreed to pay the plaintiff an undisclosed amount of money." He ventured a wry smile. "I think that's what we got here, Billy. I'll see what we can find out."

Harrison shook all the bushes he could reach, and was surprised at what eventually tumbled out under the heading *Randolph Montgomery III*.

"Cooney, take a look at this, while you're tryin' to find links to the Tourangeau beating."

Sgt. Jacobs read the dossier for what seemed like a long time. "Jeezum, Chief. Maybe we got the wrong doer. This guy certainly looks capable."

"Well, let's see. Forty-three years old, retired Senior Chief in the Coast Guard, attached to their quick response unit since its founding, and an instructor in underwater demolition. Now a consultant to companies that specialize in imploding old buildings, like those ugly public housing units that are always being blown to dust on TV."

"What's the quick response unit, Chief?"

"Good question. I had to talk to some guys to find out. Back when Homeland Security took over the Coast Guard, the Secretary wanted his own private little commando force. So the Coast Guard sifted its guys, and found the real warriors, and put 'em into a couple of company-sized units that flew Blackhawk helicopters armed with heavy machine guns. Those guys secured the Boston and New York harbors during the political conventions back in '04, and began running clandestine anti-drug operations after that. Strange thing, he don't look like a Charles Bronson type," Harrison said.

"You mean all those movies where Bronson was a vigilante and just shot up drug dealers, a few dozen per movie?"

"Yup. Ya never know, Cooney."

"Tell ya one thing, Chief. When he found that kid, he did all the right things and none of the wrong ones. He wasn't scared of the blood, or of me, and he was angry. Billy told me this Ralph was in to see him, tryin' to get information, and Billy gave him Archie's name."

"Holy shit, Cooney. Here we got two guys that are totally opposite. This guy and Kevin. On the surface neither one is likely to be the Slicer, and yet..." he let the thought drift away into the air vents on the office wall.

"Either one of them could be," Jacobs finished, and the two of them sat quietly for a few minutes, thinking about that.

Travis

Travis Mangum was pretty good at video games. He thought that was because he was decisive and acted quickly to adjust to changing situations.

He played for hours, because he wasn't very busy. A succession of bosses had been slow to understand, and slower to accept, that truly bright people like himself should not be shackled to tired old work rules that were all right for ordinary people.

This thing about showing up on time, for example. What kind of order-crazed supervisor would insist on that, when it was often impossible because his alter-self was in crisis mode in some game?

Travis began to think they all had it in for him, these bosses, since they all seemed to want references from former employers, and those reference letters turned out to be full of biases.

He would have been insulted, outraged in fact, to hear someone say that his brain functioned on a primitive level of logic, and that most of its energy was devoted to stoking his own high opinion of himself.

Mr. Mangum was twenty years old and thin, with black hair and blue eyes, and really ordinary-looking at just under six feet, unless you noticed his eyes and his hands. Twitchy hands, always in motion. Twitchy eyes too, eyes that gave him a furtive rodent look. Travis didn't get an original idea very often, but when he did, he chewed on it until all the flavor got sucked out. This last one was pretty tasty.

The reason most bank robbers get caught is cause they're stupid. They stay too long in the bank, or they don't see the person who punches in a silent alarm, or they get too greedy, or they accept bills that have been marked so they can be traced. I don't think they treat all the bills, just the ones they leave around so the robber can get out with loot.

So here are the new rules:

Do it on a Tuesday, when there are fewer bank customers.

Catch an employee shutting down for the day when there's nobody else around.

Fire a shot from a real gun so they know you mean it, and force them to re-open.

Take only what's in the drawers, don't mess with the safe.

Shackle the teller out of reach of any phones, and then just walk out, and spread the spending around.

Don't buy anything big for cash until a month goes by, and then plan the next one.

It all made so much sense that he almost chirped like a songbird.

I can do that! It's just a matter of keeping it simple. Man! No more bosses bitchin' about my work habits. Wonder why more people don't do it?

Travis did a recon or two at the North Country Bank branch in Nilesburgh, first going in to ask for those paper rolls that people shove change into, and then bringing some filled rolls in to change for paper dollars. He'd stolen the coins in those rolls from an MS Walkathon fund-raising jar at Michelle's and at two other quick stops.

There were three counter positions, but only two of them were used. Opposite the center one, a hallway split the building and led to offices, rest rooms and a conference room. He could see out to where cars came to the drive-through window, but that would be low-risk after hours. And there was no view of the bank's interior from the ATM slot on the outside wall.

When I do it, I gotta stay on this side of the counter, cause if I get back there I'd be too far from the door.

He had to be careful about the gun. He hadn't stolen it, and the guy he bought it from said he hadn't either, but Travis was pretty sure it had come out of a burglary in the past few weeks. It was a .45 automatic, like army officers used to wear. Travis had gotten the price down because there was only a half-clip of bullets with it, but then he'd need only one.

One Tuesday evening he rolled into the bank's parking lot just as the last teller was leaving. *Okay, then, this is it! Oh, shit.*

The teller, a pretty young woman, came out and kissed a big red-headed guy who had obviously been waiting for her, and they got into a car and drove off together.

Not today. Patience. A professional has to have patience.

He saw that same car in the lot for the next several days, on the side where the bank staff parked, away from the close-in spots where customers parked.

Tuesday evening came again, with a bank of clouds building in from the west. *Good. No cars in the lot except hers. And no boyfriend.*

He didn't see an old green bike leaning on the bushes.

Kevin had come in to break down a hundred-dollar bill he'd been paid, and had asked to use the rest room.

Maureen had her keys in hand waiting for him to come back, when the man burst in with the gun. He pointed it at the ceiling and fired, blinking at the enormous noise it made. What neither of them knew was that the sudden sharp noise had triggered an alarm at the cop shop a half mile away. Or that a passing driver had heard the shot and called 9-1-1.

"Okay, lady I'm serious," Travis yelled, choking a little on the acrid smell. "Get back behind that counter and start shoving cash into one of them moneybags. Don't do nothin' stupid, like hit no alarms."

Oh my God, that gun looks like a cannon! Let's see, teller training says stay calm. Calm! That thing could blow me in two, and he's really crazed, look at those eyes!

"Sir, my instructions are to cooperate, and **not** resist in any way. And I won't touch anything but the money."

Ohmygod, here comes Kevin, sneaking down the hall with his shoes off! The guy can't see him as long as he's looking at me and the money.

Kevin made a sign with one hand, opening and closing the space between thumb and fingers, and mouthing speech.

He wants me to talk, to keep his attention.

"Sir, do you want the money banded or just loose? I can get some banding papers from the vault, but it'll take a minute or two longer," And she pointed toward the safe, behind yet another set of gates.

The man looked, and his fine plan came apart all at once. Kevin hit him with a flying tackle that crushed his chest into the edge of the counter.

The gun went off again, punching through the drive-through window. Maureen screamed and stomped on the floor-level silent alarm.

When she looked up, the robber was fleeing, and Kevin was getting up off the floor, chasing him outside.

Travis wasn't moving very fast, since there was something wrong with his ribs, and Kevin tackled him again in the parking lot. The two were rolling around and the gun flew away, sliding across the lot.

That's when Ralph Montgomery saw the fight and slammed on his brakes. He jumped out of his car just as Travis got up to run past him.

"Stop him!" Kevin yelled. "He's a bank robber!" Ralph hit him with the flat edge of his hand, and Travis went down again.

Ralph ran across the pavement and grabbed the pistol. "Stop! On the ground!" He yelled again, "Stop!" but Travis was up and running at him again, suddenly holding a hunting knife. Ralph moved in a blur, and Travis went down and stayed down, howling and holding his knee.

Kevin was on his feet again. "I thought you didn't own a gun," he said around the gravel in his face.

"I don't but that doesn't mean I don't know how to use one, especially one of these. It's like an old friend. But still, I'm glad I didn't have to shoot him. It would have made things really complicated."

Suddenly the air was full of sirens, and Maureen came out of the bank dabbing at her eyes. "I'm glad you got him," she said. "He scared me so."

Kevin went over to the suspect. "Oy don't know this guy," he told the cops. "Do you?"

Andy Benoit was trying to remember the sequence of things he should be doing. He called for an ambulance, and for the Chief, who was on his way anyway, ordering more backup. Within minutes all four on-duty officers were milling around in the bank lot.

"Travis Mangum. Does that ring to you, Chief?"

"Nope. Mrs. McGuckin, are you all right?"

She nodded, the scattering of freckles across her nose more prominent on extra pale skin. She'd already called the branch manager. Gene was away on one of his IBM trips.

"Andy, read this perp his rights right now, and then follow him to the hospital. Mrs. McGuckin, can you open the bank again? We have to do some work in there, and I'd like to talk to you and these two men in your conference room."

The cops took pictures of where the two shots had gone, of the money bag on the floor on the tellers' side, and of the marks left where Kevin had slammed the robber into the counter.

Harrison got them all in the conference room. Maureen felt like a foolish hostess among guests she didn't want. *I'll make coffee. I don't want any, but I have to do something to keep my hands from shaking. We could have been killed, all of us. I want to go home, but I don't want to be alone. Damn you, Gene, I need you.*

"Who stopped him?" Harrison asked.

"Kevin did," said Ralph.

"Ralph did," said Kevin.

Harrison sighed and put his feet up on the conference table. "Look, guys, in about ten minutes the F-B-I outa Burlington will be here, and from then on I won't even be able to ask you how you like your coffee. So let's see what we can get done in the next few minutes. Kevin?"

"It was closin' toime, and Oy took in a Franklin that a guy had paid me for cuttin' back some sumac and box elder and junk trees loike that. They been pinchin' his pasture, growin' in from the soides. You know Greg Conrad on Bishop Road? Yeah, his pasture. Yeah, well Oy say to Marine can Oy use the bathroom after she gives me foive Jacksons. Oy'm back there zippin' up when there's this gunshot, heavy pistol, from inside the bank. Marine is koinda squeakin' and that dickhead's holdin' a gun on her and tellin' her to get back insoide the cage and start shovin' money inta bags."

Kevin peeked into his memory, and replayed more of the highlights.

"So Oy sneak down the hall and he's got his back to me, and Oy signal Marine to keep talkin', keep him distracted, and his head turns when she points off toward the safe, and then Oy tackle the prick and smash him inta the counter, and the gun goes off again. Scared me, that's a loud bastard.

"So now we're both down, but he's up faster and out the door. Me, like a dummy, up and after him, and he's still got the gun. Oy didn't even know about the knoife."

Kevin paused a moment to think about that, and went on. "Musta hurt him some cause he wasn't movin' too fast, and Oy took him down again."

He stopped and nudged Ralph. "Remember when Oy told ya I don't loike wearing gravel on my face?" He chuckled. "Well, look at me now." Kevin's skin was cratered and raw from his face-plant in the parking lot.

Harrison wanted to push the recital along so he'd have something to work with before the FBI reduced him to errand boy status.

"Ralph, where do you come into this?"

"I was driving past when I saw Kevin and some guy fighting in the parking lot. So I stopped and got out. Kevin's yelling that the guy's a bank robber, and so when he tried to run past me I chopped him. Then I grabbed the gun that had slid across the lot while they were fighting. I ordered him to stop and hit the ground, but he kept coming at me with a knife, so I kicked him in the kneecap. That's when your Officer Benoit skidded into the lot, just ahead of the rest of the department, and I gave him the weapon after I safed it. Then I went over to see if Kevin was okay, and he was, except for the new paving job on his face. I don't know, Kevin, it might turn out to be an improvement."

With the tension off, they were laughing at that when the conference room suddenly filled with suits and badges.

"Who's in charge here?" demanded the leading suit, a fortyish man with receding dark hair cut short.

"I am," said Harrison, taking his boots off the table. "Who wants to know? And how did you get in here past my men?" That last question, Ralph thought, was meant to irritate, and it seemed to work.

"Richard J. Shelton, Special Agent, FBI. Special Agent Brown and Special Agent Simmons. This is a Federal crime scene and I'm taking jurisdiction. What have you done with the victim?"

"Victim!" Kevin was astonished. "Mister, that fuck, sorry Marine. That "victim" troyed to rob the bank and foired two shots at the teller! She's the victim here."

"Who are you?" Shelton asked in his abrupt way.

"Kevin," said Kevin, and Suit Three wrote in a small notebook. Shelton looked Kevin over and was not impressed. "What are you doing here?"

"He interrupted the robbery," said Chief Harrison.

"When I interview you, Officer, you can speak. Now you, what are you doing here?"

"Oy don't loike you, bud," said Kevin.

Shelton didn't like being called out in front of his men. "Answer the question, or I'll have you arrested for impeding a Federal investigation," he threatened.

"I don't think you want to do that." said Ralph. "I can see the headline now. You guys like headlines, don't you? Well, try this one. *FBI arrests hero who stopped bank robbery.* Don't they teach you any manners at J. Edgar Hoover High School? You really don't have much to do here. The robber is in custody, and the locals prevented him from taking any money."

"And just who are you?" Shelton was still belligerent.

"Randolph Montgomery the Third. I've never been barked at by an FBI agent before, but I've been chewed on by admirals who are really good at it. You're not. So why don't we start over again, with you dropping the notion that you know everything, and that we're all idiots. Now this is Chief Jerry Harrison of the Nilesburgh Police Department, and this is Kevin Beaujolais, who tackled the robber, and this is Mrs. Maureen McGuckin, the teller who was victimized."

"All right, Mister Montgomery," the tone was slightly less bellicose. And how do you fit into all this?"

"I broke his leg, because I didn't want to shoot him," said Ralph. Suit Three scribbled furiously in his notebook, while Shelton stared bullets at Ralph, who looked relaxed.

"Maybe we should start from the beginning," Shelton said "But first where's the weapon?"

"It's an old Army issue .45 automatic. Had about half a clip in it when I safed it and surrendered it to Officer Benoit of the Nilesburgh Police, who accepted it by sticking a pencil into the barrel and placing it into an evidence bag."

Shelton glanced at Suit Two, who went outside in search of the gun. In a minute he was back, grousing that a local cop had taken it with him to the hospital.

"Go get it," said Shelton.

Harrison got on the phone to his office. "Julie, call Andy at the hospital in St. Albans, and tell him the FBI's coming, a guy named Brown, to get the gun." He looked at Shelton. "And tell him to get a receipt for it."

It took about two hours for them all to issue statements. The FBI was annoyed that Kevin had no permanent address, and unwilling to accept Chief Harrison's assurance that he could be found within an hour if need be.

Harrison was worried about Ralph. *He did deck the guy pretty hard. How come the FBI's not all over him? Wonder what's in his wallet that turned them around.* Harrison already knew that Ralph had been in a Coast Guard Special Operations unit. He did not know that Chief Petty Officers and above in that unit carried a card signed by the Secretary of Homeland Security. It gave the bearer sweeping Federal law enforcement powers in any jurisdiction, authority that was essentially a duplicate of the FBI's own powers. And that authority had no termination date. *Whatever it was, he didn't take any guff from this Shelton. Interesting man. If he's got the balls to whack that horse-turd Mangum, he's certainly capable of whacking Tourangeau.*

It was almost dark when they were allowed to leave. The man from the bank had tried to give Maureen the next day off, but she preferred to work than to be home alone, and said so.

"Maureen," said Ralph, handing her a card. "If your husband is away, call his cell phone and give him this number when you tell him what happened. You'll stay with Helene and me this evening, and we'll bring you back in the morning."

Kevin and Harrison were nodding agreement, and so she made only a token resistance. "I don't want to intrude."

"Look," said Chief Harrison. "If it were an intrusion, he wouldn't ask. You need company, and we'll know where you are if anything comes up."

Kevin just nodded, and grinned around the new scabs on his face.

Nugget

Maureen moved quickly through her house, gathering up what she'd need for an overnight, while Ralph waited in the car. He'd seen the neighbors peering out. *They can think what they want tonight. By tomorrow they'll get it figured out when they see the news.*

Helene Montgomery wrapped her in a hug when she came through the door, and the dam burst. Maureen could not, would not cry in front of all those men, but now…

"You've had quite a day, haven't you," Helene soothed, and Maureen sniffled into her shoulder. *Probably ruining the sweater she's wearing. Damn, I didn't expect this!*

Saying reassuring things, Helene led her into the kitchen, and asked for some help peeling veggies.

She doesn't need the help, she's just giving me something to do. That's really nice. "Here," Maureen said, hoisting a bottle of white wine out of a tote-bag. "This is for your kindness."

"No," Helene said. "This is for your nerves. Here, Ralph, open it."

She pulled three stemmed crystal glasses off a high shelf, and led the way to a huge sofa that faced the fireplace.

"Mmm," Maureen said, sinking into the cushions. "Perfect."

"Do you want to talk about it?" the blonde woman asked, handing her a glass of wine.

This is chilled, and mine wasn't. He must have switched bottles. "Well, you deserve to know," Maureen said.

"Helene," Ralph said. "Your secret admirer was right in the middle of this."

"Who do you mean?"

"Kevin."

"Oh, Kevin," she said, looking at Maureen. "Do you know him?"

"Yes, a little. He comes into the bank, and always comes to my line. Judy, that's one of the other tellers, teases me a lot about him, says this Kevin has a crush on me."

Helene laughed. "Ralph says he has a crush on me, but he's too shy to look me in the eye."

Ralph wasn't laughing. "Maureen, I think the only reason Kevin risked his neck by tackling an armed man is because he thought you were in danger. Otherwise he would have done the smart thing, and stay in the bathroom until the guy was gone."

Maureen sipped her wine and thought about that. "He was really brave, but I don't know about why he did it." She gazed into the fire.

"Hey, no replays," said Helene. "Come on, let's have dinner."

The Nilesburgh Nugget was all over the attempted robbery, in a report cobbled together hastily to meet its deadline.

BANK ROBBER FOILED BY LOCAL HEROES
Violent crimes still plague Nilesburgh
By William J. Demetrius
Staff Reporter

Two brave Nilesburgh residents and a plucky bank teller combined on Tuesday to stymie an attempted bank robbery.

As teller Maureen McGuckin, 25, was about to lock the North Country Bank's doors on Tuesday, a would-be robber burst into the branch bank firing an automatic pistol and demanding money.

Ms. McGuckin said she was complying with the bandit's orders when he was tackled by a local man, causing another discharge of the powerful pistol, and that the robber then fled, chased by "that very brave man."

Police say the two fought in the parking lot, and that the robber was brought down when another local resident kicked him after the robber tried to cut him with a knife.

FBI Special Agent Richard J. Shelton, in charge of the investigation, told this reporter that the suspect, who was treated for his injuries at the hospital in St. Albans, has been identified as Travis H. Mangum, 20, of West Alton St. in Nilesburgh.

The bank customer who tackled him, according to authorities, was Kevin Beaujolais, age and address unknown, of Nilesburgh. And the man who captured the robber was Randolph E. Montgomery III, 43, of Grist Mill Road in Nilesburgh.

Special Agent Shelton said the investigation was continuing, and that the suspect Mangum faced a number of Federal charges stemming from the incident. "I'm not going to talk now about the details of this case," he said.

Montgomery declined to answer questions about the incident, and efforts to reach Beaujolais were unsuccessful. Ms. McGuckin said both men were heroes in her mind, and that she was unharmed during the ordeal.

Coincidentally, all three are members of the special study commission on violent crime and drugs that the Town launched last month.

Ms. McGuckin is a recently-arrived resident, coming here last year with her husband Eugene, an IBM employee. She allegedly grew up in Philadelphia, Pennsylvania.

The Nilesburgh Nugget has learned that Montgomery, who told police he owns no weapons, is a recently retired Senior Chief Petty Officer in the United States Coast Guard. The FBI's Shelton would not comment on the incident, but Nilesburgh Police Chief Gerald Harrison suggested that Montgomery was quite familiar with the type of pistol used, a .45 caliber automatic, a type of side-arm once widely carried by military officers.

Suspect Mangum was unemployed, and had worked only sporadically since dropping out of high school here three years ago. He was said to be an avid player of computer games.

Sources at the hospital say Mangum shattered his kneecap in the brawl at the bank, and that he may face permanent impairment of function in his left leg. Mangum was also treated for three broken ribs, allegedly suffered when Beaujolais tackled him inside the bank.

He will be arraigned in Franklin County District Court on Monday, and the charges are said to include attempted bank robbery.

St. Albans attorney Francis X. Forgan, Jr. said he'd been retained by the Mangum family to represent their son, and that Travis was likely to plead "not guilty" to all charges at his arraignment.

Sources familiar with Courthouse procedures have said the case will be transferred to Federal Court in Burlington, where a trial date will be set within a few weeks.

See additional pictures and read more about the statutes governing bank robbery at our website, www.nilesburgh-nugget.com."

In the morning, Sgt. Jacobs had a new assignment. "See what you can find out about this Mangum kid. I know the Feds are going to be askin', but maybe you can get better answers."

It didn't take long. Travis Mangum should have been in the class of '96 at the Nilesburgh High School, but left a year early, saying he was bored. Nobody seemed to miss him, according to the overworked man who was listed as his guidance counselor. "Hardly ever saw him. He never came in to ask about college, or to complain about his teachers, or to report any kind of trouble with other students. I asked around this morning, and the kids told me he just stayed pretty much to himself. Liked computer games, and would hang around with other kids who were into that stuff too."

That assessment was confirmed by a neighbor. "Nice young fella, used to cut my grass. Always polite, never noticed him much to tell the truth. Stayed pretty much to himself. No, not a lot of friends came to the house."

Travis Mangum's parents were supportive. "He's a good boy, he's never been in any trouble, he just plays computer games. Work? Well, not so much lately, he says his employers don't understand him."

"Work! Hell, the kid don't know what work is. Mostly late, too good to do his share, just sorta dreamed his way through the day. I didn't ask him to run the place, I just wanted a day's work, and I never got it."

Harrison read the report and dropped it on his desk. "Cooney, did you ever notice that every time somebody does something really rotten, there's always them that step up and say, 'I just don't understand it. He's such a peaceful man, wouldn't hurt a fly'."

Jacobs grunted. "Chief, I've heard women say that about their men, while the blood drips down their faces from where the guy hit them."

"Yeah, why do the courts even bother with character witnesses? Actions speak louder than words, they say."

Dude

Four miles west of Stockbridge, Massachusetts, a pinprick hole developed in the big rig's hydraulic system, and a hose under the hood began spraying a mist of vaporized fluid. Some of it found its way into a flaw in the intake system that circulated fresh air through the Peterbilt's cab.

Homer "Dude" Potter was tired. His tractor-trailer unit had sat for a long time at a loading dock in Worcester, while the shipper tried to repair a broken-down forklift and complete the loading. Dude had spent the time reviewing his highway options.

Some of the guys like 90 to 88 to Binghamton, then 81 south. Not much traffic on 88, but the road's in shitty condition. At least the toll roads are pretty well maintained. I may not gain much time going south on 87 to 84 and then west to 81, all the way down to 77 in southwestern Virginia, and then it's less than three hours to Charlotte. Still, I'll probably want to do an overnight, tired as I am. Let's see, there's four or five places down in the Shenandoah Valley where I-64 crosses 81. Exit 205, I think. That's probably a realistic target point. Five hours to 81, three more to get into Virginia, and two more to the truck stops. Should be able to do that by daylight.

Dude was feeling pretty good as he slid up through the gears, southbound from the toll booth and into the dusk. Old Lucy had just gotten a clean bill of health at the Peterbilt shop in Tewksbury, and was running a lot younger than a '91 really should. Some of the guys along the road thought maybe Old Lucy was named for a girlfriend, and Dude let them think so. Some of those new guys wouldn't understand if he told them that Old Lucy had whelped more than twenty of the best coon hounds in all of South Carolina.

He slipped a fresh CD into the slot, and went out walking after midnight with Patsy Cline, as the mile-markers slid past.

Southbound now on I-87, the New York Thruway.

Damn, the four-wheelers are wild tonight. Sumbitches got no clue what's goin' on around 'em on the road. Worst thing, they get in my blind spot and never even know they're there. He'd bought one of those signs that say "If you can't see my mirrors, I can't see you," but it hadn't helped much.

The mix of oil and hydraulic fluids was now in the range where he could smell it, so he cracked a window and kicked the blower up a notch.

In combination, those air contaminants produce tunnel vision, but Dude Potter didn't notice that his peripheral vision had failed.

He fought off his tiredness with a technique he'd used before on roads where his was the only vehicle he could see. He swung into the passing lane on left curves and back to the right lane on right curves. He'd found that required a slightly elevated degree of concentration, and that he could counteract the soporific effects of the humming engine and the flashing road markers. He didn't care that any trooper who saw him lane-swapping would pull him over.

Left turn. Ole Dale would get that number three right on the inside line and sweep right through, gaining maybe a half-second. Here goes. Shit, where did that come from?

The small car was passing as Dude swung into the passing lane. It was forced off the road, though the two vehicles never touched, and struck a bridge support in the median strip, bursting into flame.

Dude hit his brakes hard, and pulled onto the right shoulder. He got off an emergency 911 call, set his flashers, grabbed a fire extinguisher, and ran back to the burning car.

Shit, nobody's getting outa that. I just hope the fucker died on impact. Vermont plates. That green's still visible through the smoke.

The driver's side of the car was crumpled as far as the back seat. Dude didn't even turn on his fire extinguisher.

He walked slowly back to his truck and put his logbook and

papers onto a clipboard, because the cops would want to see them. There were no skid marks except for his own, and they started in the left lane, moving quickly to the right shoulder. The cops assumed he was simply the first vehicle along after the accident, and Dude didn't change their minds. A few minutes in the open air had cleared up his vision, but he didn't notice the difference.

"You gotta look closely at these one-car crashes into bridges," the New York State Trooper told him. "Lotta times it turns out to be suicide by bridge abutment."

The cops let him go before he learned the victim's name. It took a little longer when they had to call another state to run the plates. Maybe he wouldn't try to push all the way through to Virginia tonight.

The trooper got the left lane shut down and waved an ambulance onto the shoulder. "We got us a crispy critter in there," he told the crew. "Hafta wait for the fire guys to cut him out when the car cools down enough."

The phone rang late at the McGuckin residence, but no one answered because Maureen was staying the night with the Montgomerys.

The next morning, she was surprised to see a personnel specialist from IBM come into the bank and speak to her manager. *I wonder if she has anything to do with the robbery yesterday.*

"Maureen, can you come in for a moment?" He sounded grave.

The woman stood as Maureen entered the office. "I'm Louise Maddox from the human resources team at IBM," she said.

What's this? Gene said everything was going really well there. What's she doing here?

"Please sit down, Maureen. We're waiting for a couple of other people." Before she could ask about that, they came in. Father Durand from St. Gabriel's and old Ruby Mongeon with him.

"It's about Gene, isn't it?" she blurted, the horror rising in her eyes as she blinked from face to face. "Isn't it!" she demanded.

"Yes," the old priest said, as the women shifted to sit next to her. "There was a traffic accident on the New York Thruway, and it looks as if your husband's car struck a bridge support at high speed."

"He's dead, isn't he? That's what you're all here for, to tell me my husband is dead."

"Yes," came the soft answer again, and hands reached out to touch her, hands she didn't want. *Don't throw up. I will not throw up in front of all these people, but I feel so nauseous, so empty. Just yesterday I was mad at him cause he wasn't here to comfort me when the bank robber came, and now... Who will comfort me now?*

Helene

The short answer was, everyone.

Judy called Helene Montgomery while Maureen was still in the manager's office. Helene was there within fifteen minutes. "I was a military wife for a long time," she told Father Durand and Ruby Mongeon. "I know how to do this." The tall blonde woman had a command presence that moved everyone else into support roles.

"Judy," she said. "Can you follow us to Maureen's house?"

"Yes, Ma'am."

"I don't want to go there," Maureen said in a small voice.

"You have to, honey. It's your house, and you've got some tough phone calls to make. Judy and I will be there. And others will help."

"But what about the IBM lady? She wants to talk about insurance and stuff."

"I'll take care of that." *Damn the woman! "Hello, I'm from IBM. Your husband is dead, and by the way sign here for your survivor benefits." And she's in human resources? Disgusting.*

"I have to freshen up," Maureen said as they entered her home. *So empty!*

"Three minutes, Maureen. Those phone calls can't wait, and nobody else can make them. Judy, people will be bringing food as soon as they find out. I don't know why, it's just what people do when they hear of a death. So go into the fridge and make space. Toss all the leftovers if you have to. And when the man from the funeral home gets here, send him to me, not to her."

"Yes, Ma'am."

"Judy, don't call me that. It's Helene. Thanks for coming here. I wonder how the bank is going to get by without you two today?"

Judy giggled loudly. "Maybe the manager will have to remember how to run a cash drawer."

"Maybe so," said Helene. "By the way if I hear that awful giggle again I'll slap you hard. Control it."

"Yes Ma'am."

Helene sighed. "Look, Judy, I don't mean to be harsh. But we've got some rough days ahead of us, so let's concentrate on making this as smooth as possible for Maureen, all right? No discordant notes, so to speak."

I think she really would slap me. I gotta stay on her good side.

Maureen and Helene took the walkabout phone into the seldom-used living room. *I know I should call Grace and Gerald first, but I gotta talk to Mom first.*

"Mom?" Maureen didn't realize that her voice had regressed about fifteen years, and that she sounded like a little girl again.

"Hi, Sweetie, what's wrong?"

"Oh, Mom, just everything. Gene was in a car crash, and he's dead, Mom. Can you and Daddy come up here? I really need you!"

"Oh, Honey, I'm so sorry! Are you sure?"

"Yes. He was on the Thruway in New York and he hit a bridge support in the median strip. Oh, Mom, they said the car burned! The IBM people came into the bank this morning and told me." She stopped to blow her nose.

"Maureen, we can be on the road in an hour, and I'll call the McGuckins before we leave."

"Good, Mom, I'm calling them next. Do I have to tell them the car burned? It makes me shudder so. And I'm sorry I couldn't call earlier. But I wasn't home last night when the police tried to reach me. Why? Oh it's been a busy day, Mom." She was slowly shredding a tissue, but her mind was far away from her hands, and she didn't notice the growing pile of white scraps on the carpet. "Yesterday afternoon a man tried to rob the bank, and fired two shots, and I was scared, and I was mad at Gene for not being there to hold me.

133

I was too nervous to go home alone, and so I stayed with some friends. Helene's been wonderful, you'll meet her tonight. And my friend Judy from the bank, too."

Maureen saw Judy motioning Helene out of the room.

"Honey," her mom was saying. "I'm so, so sorry. We'll be there a couple of hours after dark. Can we stay with you?"

"Mom you have to stay with me. And I've got lots of empty beds." *Empty beds. Empty beds. Empty years.* Then she knew she couldn't talk any more, and put the phone down, tossing another crumpled tissue into the waste basket.

Well, I guess I got through that one, more or less, I guess I can do the next one too.

"Hello, Grace? It's Maureen. I'm afraid I have some terrible news..."

"Mrs. Montgomery, you have to tell her this can't be an open-casket wake." Arthur Curtin exuded sadness in his black suit. He held a black hat in both hands, rotating it slowly. He was short, and trying hard not to become round. His eyes looked like timid little brown animals, darting around in their cages in the middle of his face. "New York is doing an autopsy, and we're on the way to recover the body. It was a high-speed impact, and I'm almost certain the coroner will rule that Eugene was dead before the fire ever started. Let's see, this is Wednesday, and we'll be ready for visiting hours Friday afternoon and evening, and then the funeral Mass and burial on Saturday, unless they want the body taken back to Philadelphia."

"I'll call you when those decisions are made," Helene said.

The couple from next door, Marie and Danny Macon came over and said they'd do whatever they could. Danny said he'd put "park here" signs on his driveway.

Maureen came out of the living room, traces of weeping fading from her face. Helene poured her a glass of wine, and asked if the extra beds were made up or needed sheets. Judy said she'd check. Maureen felt the adrenaline rush ebbing, and said she was tired. And when the doorbell rang, she barely noticed.

"Maureen, can you come to the door?" Marie asked. "There's a man here to see you."

"Tell him to come in," Helene called.

"He won't."

Maureen stepped to the door.

"Oy'm so very sorry," Kevin said, and handed her a clutch of wildflowers he had obviously picked on his way. The baseball cap was in his other hand, and he had tried hard to comb his hair.

Maureen felt fresh hot tears sliding down her cheeks. She took the flowers, and impulsively leaned forward and kissed him on the forehead. Kevin blushed and stood there with his mouth open.

"Thank you," she said quietly, and watched him walk back to the bike he'd propped against a tree.

"Who was that scruffy little man?" Marie asked in a voice that suggested dismissal and disapproval.

"That was Kevin," she said with a small smile. "He's full of surprises." She walked back to where Helene was taking inventory in the kitchen.

"Look what Kevin brought," she said. "Can you reach one of those vases on the top shelf? I'll put them in the hall near the door."

"You're going to get lots of flowers, Maureen, and these won't keep very long."

"I know, but those will all be commercial flowers. These are somehow much more personal because I know they came from the heart, and I cried again when he gave them to me."

Maureen's parents arrived in a flurry of hugs and bags and tears that night and told her the McGuckins had said they wanted Gene buried in Philadelphia, in the family plot bought a hundred years ago by the immigrant great-grandfather.

"Mom, I don't want to do that. I want to stay here, and I want to keep Gene here too. I'd hate to fight with them, but Gene's not going back. I hope you and Daddy can help when they get here tomorrow."

Grace McGuckin gave in first. *She's a lot more confident than she was when they were married. An even better choice than I had imagined.*

And she is, after all, now his closest relative. Besides, it's clear that she has embraced Vermont, and this little town, and she's not coming back.

Gerald McGuckin was harder to sway. "For four generations, all the McGuckins have been buried in Philadelphia, including my uncle, who was killed in France during the war and was brought back, and my cousin who died in Vietnam, and was brought home too."

Maureen didn't even blink. "For us, this is home, this small town in northern Vermont. Besides, when Patrick McGuckin went from Ireland to Philadelphia he broke a chain of burials in County Tyrone that went back, what, forty generations? Come on," she said. "I'd like to show you a lovely spot we'll all see again on Saturday."

They drove in two cars, eight miles out of the village, then left on a dirt road. A half-mile down that road, a waist-level dry-stone wall enclosed a square half-acre cemetery.

Maureen took her mother-in-law by the hand and walked her past the old stones and huge trees to a grassy area by the back wall. Grace McGuckin looked over the wall at a cornfield, green and rustling in a light breeze. The cemetery faced a wooded slope on one side, and on the other side a pasture where black and white cows stared at them briefly, and then went back to cropping grass and chewing.

"We found this when we were looking for a place to have a picnic," Maureen said. "And Gene said that he'd like to rest in as peaceful a place as this, and so I made the arrangements yesterday."

She didn't see Grace McGuckin catch her husband's eye and nod, but her mother did, and felt some of the tension slip sway. Gerald McGuckin said only, "It is peaceful here," and turned back toward his car. Maureen caught her mother's eye and allowed herself the smallest smile. On her way to the car she spotted a small stone she had not seen on her first trip.

REJEAN BEAUJOLAIS   LISETTE BEAUJOLAIS

1924–1971   1931–1979

There was a small bronze World War II emblem lying on its back next to the left side of the stone. Maureen bent and stood it up.

I wonder…

Oscar

The wake wasn't as bad as she'd anticipated. It was only a receiving line at the funeral home, and she stood just beyond the closed casket, which had the best photo of Gene she could find propped up on the top.

Judy and Helene had combed through her scrapbooks, building an easel-mounted montage of photos hinting at the brief, vibrant life of Eugene McGuckin, whose ancestors had been princes in County Tyrone, and who had been rising toward equivalent rank at IBM.

Father Durand was ruffled about the cemetery. "We have a perfectly good Catholic cemetery at the church, my dear. That's where he should really rest and await the Lord."

Maureen was serene, and that surprised her. She stood by her parents, sleek in the black dress, and suddenly quite sure of herself.

"Gene was a faithful man, Father. But he didn't believe that people laid to rest in other cemeteries would miss the call on Judgment Day, just because the ground they lay in wasn't blessed properly. Oh, my cousin, Father Denis McQuade, will be here to help celebrate the Mass. He's a bit stuffy. You'll like him."

She was grateful that local custom required all the passing well-wishers to say their names, even those she knew. She hugged, and touched cheeks, and kissed air, and shook hands in something of a haze as they passed by, some from IBM, some from the bank, some from the neighborhood, and every one of the crime study commission members. They included a small man in a bad suit. The legs were so short she could see white socks under brightly polished old shoes.

"Thank you for coming, Kevin. Mom, this is my friend Kevin Beaujolais. We're on the crime study committee together, and he's a customer at the bank."

Susan O'Rourke smiled warmly, caught the innate shyness, and realized this man must have overcome some big uncertainties to attend. She took his hand in both of hers and smiled into his eyes. "Thanks for being here, Kevin. Maureen really needs friends right now. Ken, would you introduce Kevin Beaujolais to the McGuckins, please?"

St. Gabriel's was small by Philadelphia standards, and not quite full when Maureen and the older women entered. The fathers were pall-bearers, along with Gene's brother from Texas, Ralph Montgomery and two of Gene's co-workers from IBM.

The casket sat on rollers in that wide spot where the pews were a little farther apart at the front of the church. It was nested in flowers, and Helene thought some of the arrangements were a bit gaudy. She sat in the second row with Judy and the Macons.

Father Durand had been difficult, citing a tradition that there were no eulogies at Catholic funeral Masses, but Ruby Mongeon had spoken up for Maureen.

"These people are from Away, Father Oscar, And they have their own traditions. I can't imagine that Irish Catholics would be any less respectful of the dead than French Catholics like us. Besides, if she wants to speak, it's part of the grieving process."

The priest subsided. Ruby was a force when she got started, and he seldom argued with her.

"I want to thank Father Durand for allowing me to reflect on Gene's life," Maureen began. She had chosen not to use the pulpit, but simply to stand in her front-row pew and face the congregation. Her glossy black hair and black dress set off her pale skin, only lightly touched by make-up.

"Gene was a light," she said. "He made everyone around him glad he was there, a big red-headed guy with a sharp sense of humor and a sharp mind. He honored everyone and belittled no one, and when I met him, I couldn't believe two things. One that he was for real, and two that he was available." She dabbed with a tissue, while the congregation smiled.

"Gene didn't think he was available, but I changed his mind. Her name was Kitty Walker, and I walked him out of her life. It took a while," she admitted.

"He was such a good companion, such a good friend. I'm sorry that so many of you never got a chance to know him. Gene and I decided shortly after we came to Nilesburgh that this was to be our home. We found the community, we found you gathered here, to be friendly and welcoming, and we thought we'd be putting down deep roots in this town. *Don't get caught in "deep." Don't think about the interment.*

"You know that Gene was Irish, even more than I am. You have to go back to the middle of the 19th Century, to the arrival in Philadelphia of an immigrant teamster named Patrick McGuckin from County Tyrone in the north of Ireland. That's when his family arrived. I think there must have been a sorrowful parting, when that man left a place where his distant ancestors had been chiefs and princes. I think there was a woman who wept in the knowledge that she would never again see the young Patrick." She couldn't see Gene's father from where she stood, but she thought she heard him snuffle.

"Gene loved a song that reflects that sorrow of parting as well as it can be done in words. I don't think the words were there to comfort Gene's great-great grandmother when her son left; they hadn't yet been written. But they are available to me, and they soften Gene's departure, a little. I'd like you to listen with me, and when it's over I won't be able to speak, so thank you all for coming today."

Cousin Denis pushed a button on a C-D player near the pulpit, and the full, rich voice of the late Kate Smith filled the sanctuary.

Oh Danny Boy, the pipes, the pipes are calling
From glen to glen and down the mountainside.
The summer's gone, and all the flowers dying.
It's you, it's you must go and I must 'bide.

But come ye back when summer's in the meadow,
Or when the valley's hushed and white with snow.
It's I'll be here in sunlight or in shadow.
Oh, Danny boy, oh Danny boy, I love you so.

But when ye come, and all the flowers are dying,
If I am dead, as dead I well may be.
You'll come and find the place where I am lying,
And kneel and say an Ave there for me.

And I shall hear, though soft you tread above me,
And all my grave shall warmer, sweeter be.
For you will bend and tell me that you love me,
And I shall sleep in peace, until you come to me.

The sound of sniffling over-rode the fading notes of the orchestra. Father Durand rose to continue the Mass. *Now I remember why I don't like these eulogies. When somebody gets it right, they run away with the congregation, and it's so hard to get them all back.*

Grace McGuckin, riding in the second car behind the hearse, noticed that cars pulled over to let the cortege pass, and that people on the sidewalks even stopped and stood still while they passed. *How nice. They don't even know who's in the hearse, they just do it out of respect. Maybe the kids did find something rare here. But it sure is different. Imagine not being able to bury anyone between November and April, because the ground's frozen four feet deep. I guess they just put people in freezers. I don't think I'd like that.*

As they crossed the river on the new bridge, she noticed a man pedaling an old bicycle along the route they were taking. He was wearing a suit that didn't fit very well.

At the brief graveside service, Maureen sat flanked by her parents, her in-laws and Gene's brother, while friends stood in a knot behind their chairs. There was prayer and holy water and incense, and then an "Amen." *How sanitized this all is. The widow is whisked away before they lower the casket, so I don't have to hear the sound of a shovelful of dirt landing on that partially hollow box. It's more like a stage pageant than it should be. It should have some hint of the starkness and finality of putting your life into the ground forever. Somehow it's wrong to just walk away with the burial unfinished.*

I wonder why I'm not crying more. Here, Gene, here's the C-D with Kate Smith's Danny Boy on it. Too bad I can't put it inside the casket. Poor Grace, she's having a tough time, and yet in a way, Gene left her long ago, for me. What can I do to help her? I'll ask Mom.

Kevin leaned his bike against the biggest tree in the cemetery and watched from a small distance as the clutch of mourners moved slowly back to the cars. Then he walked to a small stone with two names on it, and stood looking at it. *It woulda been nice if somebody besides the funeral guys had been here when my folks were put down.*

He did not see one of the gravediggers pocket the C-D before lowering the mortal remains of Eugene McGuckin of Philadelphia, into the sandy earth of Nilesburgh, Vermont.

Jeffrey

On the first Saturday morning after Gene McGuckin's funeral Ralph and Helene had breakfast at the Iron Skillet. As always, heads turned when they walked in, but for the first time, hands waved them to seats along the center row of tables. Ralph recognized several of the regulars, but didn't know all their names. There were smiles and nods, but no introductions.

Funny thing; they all know who we are, and so they think we ought to know who they are, by now. I guess at some point, it just becomes uncool to say "I'm so-and-so" when you think someone should already know that. That won't bother Helene.

"Good morning, I'm Helene," she said, offering a hand and a smile to Hatman. He returned the smile and said, "Good morning, how you folks doin'," without offering a name.

"The home fries are always good here, dear," said a woman down the table. She wore lots of metal bracelets and they chinged when she moved her arms. Ralph was fascinated. *I wonder if she moves her arms when she talks just to attract more attention, or whether she doesn't even notice the connection. I think it's a deliberate affectation, a nice bit of stagecraft so she doesn't get left out.*

Ralph got up and poured coffee for himself and Helene. *I've never seen Ralph do that before, and the others do it too. I wonder why the waitress doesn't bring coffee to the tables, like they do everywhere else.*

A young woman with an order pad came to the table, showing some cleavage under a tired face. Helene understood. *Work it, girl.*

In that stillness after the arrival of orange juice and before the scrambled eggs and sausage (with a side of home fries) Jeffrey Adams spoke up.

"You still got yer uniform?"

"Yes," Ralph said. *By now, they all know about my career, but they're not going to ask me about that, and they're not going to talk about the robbery, or the capture. Let's see where this goes.*

"I don't think I ever seen a Coast Guard dress uniform," Adams said. "Anyways, we got Memorial Day comin' up, and there's always some speechin' to do at Town Hall, where the memorials are set up in a little garden out front. I'm sorta puttin' together the program for that morning for the VFW, and I wonder if you'd feel like sayin' a few words about what the day should mean to us. I mean, you bein' recently on active duty and all, not like the rest of us who have been out of uniform for decades. You may have a different take on what the day should signify. Bill Ayres from the Selectboard will speak, and somebody from the Vietnam Vets, and an officer from the Air National Guard. But there's room for another speech, if you want to do it."

Ralph tried to imagine the portly Adams in a Vietnam-era uniform, and had to look out the window to keep from grinning.

I guess we've arrived. Center table and now this. He clearly wants me to do this, and he's afraid I'll refuse. Wonder if this is his idea alone, or did these Iron Skillet guys get together and cook this up over breakfast some morning after they read the newspaper?

"Who will the audience be?" he asked.

"Oh, there's a big range, from an old man who fought in North Africa during War Two, all the way down to the widow and kids of a Guard sergeant who was killed in Iraq a couple years back. Mostly vets and families. Mostly Army and Air Force, and the Vermont National Guard is active, both air and ground. There's a few Marines and a Navy guy or two, one of em's Ed Crocker. You see him in here a lot, or you used to, before he got sick. Ed's doin' chemo for the second time, and I don't think he's winnin'."

"Are there any Coasties?" Ralph asked.

"Coasties? Is that what you guys call yourselves? No, I don't think I even know one, at least until now."

"I'll have to think about it," Ralph said. "Can I let you know in a week?"

"Sure, I'll be here, probably in this same chair, unless Suzie finally throws me out for bein' obnoxious."

Helene waited until they were on their way home. "Well, that was different. Do you think it's because you stopped that robber?"

"Partly," he answered. "You know that I don't like to talk about myself very much. For almost a year, even you thought I was an only-child orphan. And I would have been okay if those people only knew me as some kind of business consultant. To most of 'em that means somebody who gets paid pretty well for doing not very much. But partly I think it's because, on a scale that matters to them, I'm not that much different. I think they value the ability to make a decision and act, and be willing to stand behind the consequences of that action."

"I don't know about all that," she said. "I think they just decided they like you."

"I think that's what I just said."

"Well, you tried."

Judy

"Good mornin', Marine," Kevin almost sang the greeting, sounding like that weather guy on Vermont Public Radio as he walked up to her window in the bank's newly repaired lobby. Six weeks after Travis Mangum's short career in crime ended, there was a new ceiling tile with no bullet hole in it, and the drive-up window had been replaced. "How ya doin'?"

"Hi, Kevin." She didn't want to add his usual responses, "Gettn' by," or "Not too bad," because she thought neither was dark enough to express her mood, and she didn't want to say, "I feel empty," because it was true.

Kevin noticed. He handed her five twenty dollar bills, and she gave him back two fifties. He lingered at the window.

"Marine, ya know Oy'm a pretty handy guy, and Oy ain't pushy. But back when a man Oy knew died, his wife was needful of some-body to do chores, and so Oy done 'em." Kevin paused as if he feared his own next words, and then plunged on. "Oy mean, if ya need mowin' or plantin', now that it's comin' inta garden season, or if ya need gutter cleanin' or any a them chores that come up around the place, Oy'd be happy if ya ask me. And just so ya know, it ain't fer money, it's just cause there's a need. That's when folks do their best work."

What a lovely spirit lives in this man. One that he's just learning how to expose. "Kevin, how nice of you. I have a kid from the neighborhood helping with the grass, but there may be other things to be done. I'll make a list and call you."

He shrugged with unconscious Gallic grace. "Oy ain't got no phone,"

"Then how do I get in touch with you when I need something done?"

Kevin smiled, and the lines around his eyes deepened. "Maybe we do it like them spoys in the movies. Go buy one a them greetin' cards that's got red flowers on the front, and then stick it in the bank's front window, and when Oy'm roidin' by, Oy'll see it."

He looks really proud of himself. "So, it'll be a secret signal, right?"

"Secret, roight, and nobody else will know what it means. Nobody will know it means anything at all." And the grin widened.

Maureen smiled back, caught up in the launching of a conspiracy. "But I can't have you doing work for no money."

The grin vanished. "Marine, Oy thought you was beginnin' to figure out how Vemawnt works." Kevin turned quickly and marched out of the bank, leaving her confused.

At the next window Judy had been aware of the conversation, without exactly hearing the words. She'd been dealing with an ancient customer who'd left his teeth home again, and as he worked his jaws, his nose and chin got together. She thought of him, very privately, as Mister Pliers.

When the bank was empty, Maureen sought help. "Judy, I did something that made Kevin mad, and he stalked out of here as cold as can be."

"Well, let's see. I'm guessin' that Kevin offered to do some chores for you, and you mentioned money, didn't you?"

"How do you know that?"

Judy grinned, but didn't giggle. "Well, I had a little head start. Kevin asked me if it would be pushy of him to offer to help, and I said no, it would be fine. And then you talked about payin' him."

"Judy, he brought it up first!"

"What did he say, exactly?"

"I don't think I remember every word, but he said something like it wasn't about money, but about 'cause there's a need', I think he said."

"Maureen, Kevin made that proposal after he thought about

it a lot, and after he checked it with me. He did it in spite of the shyness that made it hard for him. He did it as a way of saying he's sorry about Gene, and he's sorry you're hurtin', which still shows, by the way, and because he wants to do somethin' to help, and chores is all he could think of."

Judy stopped for a deep breath, looking as serious as Maureen had even seen her.

"I'm afraid you insulted him by mentioning money, by not just accepting his offer as a gift of friendship. Kevin doesn't reach out very easily, and now he thinks you've snubbed the whole idea that he could be a friend when you're in need. You don't pay for favors from the heart, Maureen. It's just like when he brought those wild-flowers to your house, the ones he'd picked. He did that because he wanted to, and imagine how crushed he'd have been if you had offered him five dollars for those posies. In his mind, it's the same thing."

Maureen stood looking out the bank's windows, but seeing Kevin on her doorstep with a handful of wild flowers in his hand and a blush on his face. *Well, I sure screwed that up. I knew he was shy, but he's like a man with no immune system. Everything gets to him. Or is it me? Am I not getting what Judy told me? Did Kevin overdo his reaction, or did I undervalue his gesture. I don't know. I just don't know.*

"Hey Dreamygirl! Here comes Mrs. Averill, and if you don't get back here from wherever you're having dark thoughts, I'll just get really busy and you'll have to deal with her."

Maureen was surprised how many greeting cards had red flowers on their front panels. She chose an anniversary card with what she thought of as a mooshy-gooshy sentimental message. She tried to mount it on the window without anyone noticing, but of course, Judy noticed.

"What's that, and why is it backwards, and how come you're sneakin' around to put it there. Something's going on here, Maureen McGuckin, and I want to know what it is."

I should have known. She would have made a good crime scene investigator. She never misses a clue. "Kevin doesn't have a phone," she said.

"I know that. Oh, I see. How clever. Like in *All the President's Men*, when somebody put a potted plant on a balcony. So what's he supposed to do when he sees it?"

"Come in, of course. He said I should do it if I have work for him, but I have to apologize for insulting him. You know, in a lot of ways, he's like a junior high kid trying to figure out to talk to the girl who grew boobs over the summer."

"Maureen, Kevin's social development got arrested somewhere back around then. He dropped out of school and worked mostly on farms with older people, so he doesn't know much about the way boys and girls talk and tease each other when they're teens. Kevin was on his own before he was sixteen, and has been ever since. In fact he's come closer to getting past the 'hello' phase with you, than with anyone I've seen. I don't know what's driving that. Must be the boobs."

"Judy, yours are bigger than mine," Maureen protested over a blush.

"Yeah, but you wear yours perkier. I'd say they're pretty good bait." Judy bit back the front edge of a giggle.

"Judy, behave yourself, I'm not fishing!"

"Yeah, right."

"Come on, it's only been six weeks. I still have his clothes in the closet, and when I'm really low I go over and sniff them. They still smell like Gene, and I don't know whether that helps or not. Was it like that when you were divorced?"

Judy got a rueful expression on her face, and the black curls on her neck trembled as she shook her head. "Hardly. The bastard just walked out and said if I ever found happiness it would be with another jack-hammer. He said he hated the way I laughed. And I got mad and told him I laughed a lot more before we were married than after, and things just went downhill from there."

"Come to think of it, I haven't heard that giggle much lately. Where'd you put it?"

"Oh, talk about scary. When you were on the phone to Philadelphia the day you found out about Gene, Helene Montgomery glared at me and told me she'd slap me hard if she ever heard it again. I think she would have done it too. I told my step-mom, and she had this tape recorder thingy, and she let me hear how it sounded. Ooh! I think I'm weaned, but if I ever do it again around you, just say Helene Montgomery, and that'll stop it. Now, she's a nice lady, and really elegant, but I haven't been slapped by another female since 6th grade, and I think she'd be good at it."

She really did take over, didn't she? Worked stuff out with the funeral guys, ripped into that IBM woman for being an insensitive bitch, managed the visitors until Mom got there, and this too. Maureen, be grateful for not-so-small favors. I'll have to figure out how to do something nice for her, and for Judy too.

On the 17th of May, Archie Tourangeau was indicted on a string of charges, including aggravated assault on a minor, attempted manslaughter through negligence, possession of controlled substances with intent to sell, possession of an unregistered weapon, operating a motor vehicle while his license was suspended, and a variety of parole violations.

His lawyer told reporters that Archie was a victim of torture, and that the charges had been made up by the cops to divert attention from the fact that his client was a victim of violence, and that, by the way, he would be proven innocent of all charges against him.

Walter Tourangeau told the same reporters in a lot of short unprintable words that the bleepin' Nilesburgh police had it in for Archie, and that if he ever found the bleep who cut off Archie's ear, that bleep would be bleepin' dead, man, as bleepin' dead as Abraham bleepin' Lincoln, that bleep.

One of the reporters wondered idly how a President martyred almost 150 years ago could have gotten into Tourangeau's rant, and then decided she didn't want to know.

The TV cameraman snickered while loading his gear. "You think we can get anything outa that? We can always bleep the rough stuff."

His reporter shook off that notion. "We'll stay with the smarmy lawyer. Besides, there wouldn't be anything left of the old man. But it sure as hell goes into our blooper file."

On the 18th of May, an arraignment was held in Federal District Court in Burlington, and Travis Mangum of Nilesburgh was formally charged with attempted bank robbery, and possession and use of a stolen weapon in that attempt. Francis X. Forgan Jr. argued that the charges should be dropped because his client had been illegally assaulted by an illegal vigilante, and had suffered life-changing injuries in the process. Forgan said an elusive and shadowy man called Kevin Beaujolais was probably the real robber, and that his client just happened to be in the wrong place at the wrong time.

Courthouse reporters awarded him an A for effort, a B for imagination, and an F for effectiveness.

On the 19th of May, a gravestone was placed in the back corner of the West Nilesburgh cemetery, and it was like no other stone on any of the rows of graves.

It was a gift from the McGuckin family of Philadelphia, a white marble cross about six feet high. There was a circle connecting each arm of the cross. It was patterned on the ancient high crosses of Ireland, some of them a thousand years old. This one had no carving on it, just the clean and simple lines of the 13 crosses placed in a cemetery just outside the walled city of Derry in Northern Ireland. They marked the graves of the Irish victims of the Bloody Sunday massacre blamed on British troops, early in 1972.

The stone carver would come later to chisel in the appropriate name and dates. Maureen wanted to add "The Day Innocence Died," a popular slogan from the incident that had intensified "The Troubles" in Ulster, but her mother talked her out of it. "Gene wasn't murdered," she said.

Two women stood and watched as a crane lifted the stone into place. One was a tall blonde just passing out of her youth. The other was younger, very pale, with dark hair. She stood quite still and clutched a tissue she was determined not to need.

When the workers were finished the younger woman walked over to the cemetery wall and picked four tulips growing untended there. She placed one in each of the open spaces where cross and circle intersected.

"Do you think it was all right to do that?" she asked.

"Perfect" she was told. "Why else would those flowers be growing here?"

Roger

Ralph liked the way Howard Eppley ran the Crime Committee meeting on the evening of May 19th. He was sure-handed in moving through the agenda items, but quite patient when necessary.

"This is not on the printed agenda," Eppley was saying. "And it doesn't touch directly on our charge from the Selectboard, but we've got an unusual situation here. We haven't met since that bank robbery attempt. Now that was a drama with four actors. One of them is in jail, but we just happen to have the other three here as members of this panel, and I know we'd all like a bit of insight into what happened that day. Maureen, would you like to start?"

She shifted her feet under the uncomfortable chair. "It was late on a Tuesday afternoon," she started. "And I was about to close when Kevin came in and asked to use the bathroom. While he was there this Mangum came in, I didn't know who he was at the time, and fired that gun. He made me go back behind the counter and put money in one of those cash sacks we keep for the business people to use for their deposits. Then Kevin snuck up behind him and smashed him into the counter. They both fell down, and the gun went off again. The bullet went through the drive-by window. Then the man Mangum got up and ran out, and Kevin ran after him. I didn't see any more until I went outside when the police were there."

Maureen sat back, disturbed at how clear those images still were in her mind. She would always link the robbery with Gene's death a few hours later, even though she knew they were unrelated events. It was hard to recapture now how panicked she had felt when the man waved the gun around and fired it. After all, she'd been through much worse within the next few hours, and she'd thought she had most of the robbery memories safely fenced off behind a bigger hurt.

Eppley said something sympathetic and nodded toward Kevin.

"Ya know," Kevin said. "Oy still can't figure out why Oy didn't just stay in the bathroom until that fucker, Sorry Marine, sorry Ruby, until that punk, that's a safe word, ain't it? Until that punk finished his business and left. But there Oy was, chasin' him outa the bank and him with a gun. Oy tackled him in the parkin' lot and we was rolling around, and then Ralph was there, and Oy hollered, "He's a bank robber," and Ralph smacked him and he went down like a shot ox. And the gun skittered away so Ralph picked it up. And then that punk guy, he's up an' runnin' roight at Ralph with a knoife that looks as big as a sword, and Ralph yells for him to stop, but he didn't, so Ralph stops him, and then Benoit was there and the Chief, and a bunch of others. What Oy got outa all that was a face fulla gravel."

Ralph smiled. "I guess you'll want to hear from me next. I gave the weapon, which turned out to be a stolen .45 caliber automatic, to the cops, and then the Chief herded us inside to sort of debrief us on what had happened. After a few minutes the FBI came in and started being rude to everybody. Kevin eyeballed the lead agent, a man named Shelton, and said, 'I don't like you, Bud.' The agent threatened to arrest him, but changed his mind."

Billy Brophy and Sergeant Jacobs laughed out loud, relishing the notion of Kevin Beaujolais, the invisible man, telling off an FBI official.

"Well Oy didn't," said Kevin, misunderstanding the laughter. "He was snotty to me and treated Chief Harrison like he was a rat turd. Sorry ladies, Oy gotta watch myself."

"It's okay, Kevin," said Eppley. "I'm still trying to figure out how come they didn't arrest you, Ralph, for assaulting the suspect."

"Well, you know I was a senior enlisted man in the Coast Guard. It's a law enforcement agency as well as a military one, the smallest of the Armed Forces. We enforced maritime law and do a lot of drug intervention work. Anyway, as a Senior Chief, I have law enforcement credentials as good as Sheldon's, better in some circumstances. It was ruled as justifiable force, to capture an escaping suspect."

"Even though you're retired?" Jacobs hadn't heard this part and thought it was extremely interesting.

"Even though," Ralph said. "Although they'll probably change that, now that they've got a precedent. Look, folks, I wasn't trying to hurt the guy, just stop him. On the other hand, I'm not weeping for the man. If you bring a weapon to the party, you have to take responsibility for what happens when the party goes sour."

"You're not on trial here, Ralph," said Billy Brophy, and there were nods all around.

"In fact, you and Kevin ought to get a commendation," Ruby Mongeon said in her emphatic way.

"That's nice," Ralph said. "But let's don't overdo this. Both of us acted on impulse, and we're lucky the robber was so inept. Maybe we ought to get back to the real agenda."

"Roight," said Kevin.

"All right then." Howard Eppley began to re-focus the meeting. "I'm curious to know whether any of you have had a chance to talk to people about our project, and what you've been hearing."

Alvin Kester spoke up. "Do you think the bank thing has overshadowed the two drug-related beatings enough to stop people from thinking about them?" The manager tossed that question out to everyone.

"I hope not," said Sgt. Jacobs. "Long-term, those incidents are much more important to the town than the loser kid who hit the bank. But if we look closely enough, we may find another form of the same kind of social alienation that some criminologists believe contributes to driving up crime statistics."

Eppley was intrigued. "Are you saying that if we identify the misfits we can get a handle on this?"

"I don't think the connection is that clean." The statement came softly from Roger Helprin, the school counselor. "Boredom gets into the mix, and peer pressures are very strong in the early to mid teens. The Willard boy comes from a supportive family that tends to be a bit smothering, perhaps, and I think with him it was experimentation, both chemically and in terms of his individual freedom. I think the same is true for most of the other boys who were witnesses when young Gordie was attacked."

Billy Brophy wasn't expecting much in the way of participation from Helprin, but his ideas seemed to be on point. "I still think we need to look harder at the misfits though, the ones like Archie himself, who never got much encouragement in school, and kept falling behind his age group. Maybe one thing we should move to is a look at how we as a town can enfold these outcasts before they do things like deal drugs or try to rob banks."

"Well, Oy was just gonna lissen, but Oy can talk about gettin' behoinder in school. Oy was shavin' in fourth grade, and then they just pushed me through whether Oy learned anything or not, and mostly not." He looked sharply at Helprin. "Oy don't recall gettin' a helpin' hand from nobody at the school, except for Mrs. Conrad, the math teacher. She did tell me to keep on stroivin', as she put it. Hell, I didn't even know what *stroivin'* meant until Oy was outa school, and Oy got away from there as soon as they stopped chasin' me for truant. Truth is, mosta the people I knew were farmers and farm workers, and lotsa that crowd had a hard time readin' too. So this ain't a new problem, it's just that it's a lot harder to make a livin' now. They ain't so many manual jobs, and they don't pay very good."

Kevin suddenly stopped, aware that he'd talked a lot more than he had intended.

"I'm not sure that schooling itself is a big factor," Maureen said. "I mean, look at Kevin. Not much formal education, but his sense of right and wrong is better developed than anyone else we've talked about." She stopped, noticing that he was looking very, what was the word he had used to her once? Squitchy, that was it. Besides, there was still an awkwardness between them over Kevin's reaction to her offer to pay him for chores.

"Let's not look at Kevin," said Kevin. "Kevin don't loike bein' in the middle when folks is reachin' for the finger-food."

When Eppley proposed another meeting in the second week of June, Kevin quickly got out his little calendar, and said he was free on the 12th. Billy Brophy smiled. *I think Kevin's comin' in out of the cold, or maybe he's like a stray cat that'll accept food that's put out on the porch, but won't come through the door. Maybe Montgomery and that girl are having a good effect on him. Wonder how they can reach him, when people he's known all his life just accept that he's a weird loner.*

Cross

The last Monday in May was Memorial Day, and Maureen decided to go to the cemetery. She took a flowering plant in a ceramic pot, thinking it would look nice next to the gravestone. The florist said it was an annual, hardy enough to last into November, but would not survive the winter.

I know Memorial Day is supposed to be about fallen soldiers, but I don't think anyone will mind if I go see Gene.

She parked on the dirt road and walked quietly into the green space dotted with markers ranging from shale to marble to granite. The place was empty except for a man sitting cross-legged in front of a small stone, clipping away grass.

"Kevin? I didn't know you'd be here."

"Hi, Marine. Oy come out here sometoimes. Oy talk to moy Mom a little, but Oy don't talk to moy Dad, Oy hardly remember him. The war done somethin' to his head, and the government put him in the state hospital when Oy was really little. And then they put Mom away too, when she got TB. Oy was a teenager then, so Oy remember her better. She used to say, 'Never let the government run over you.'"

How sad. What do I say to that? No wonder he hides from the government, he's terrified they'll find him and clap him away in an awful place.

"Kevin, what was she like, Lisette Beaujolais?" Maureen sat in the grass and read the name on the stone.

"She was tough, and at the same toime, she got hurt easy. There was a lotta boyfriends after my dad was taken away, and some of 'em were mean. Oy told the last one Oy'd kill him if he ever laid

156

another hand on her. But by that toime, she was pretty sick, and thin. Oy think she needed those guys to help us get by, cause we was awful poor. Not that any of 'em was worth a rat's ass. Sorry, my language again."

"Hey, I work in a bank, I know what a rat's ass is worth; not very much, right?"

His face lightened into a small smile, and he tugged at some weeds growing over the World War II medallion on his father's side of the stone.

"Oy went over and stood by your husband's grave for a minute when Oy got here. That's quite a marker there, that big cross with the circle around it."

"It's an Irish thing," she said. "You should understand, being French Canadian, that sometimes immigrants to this country prefer to keep connected to the place they came from. That kind of cross is very old in Ireland, but now it has political meaning too. It's kind of anti-English."

"Well us French have been anti-English for most of our history. Even Oy know about Lafayette helping in the Revolution. But Oy don't know about any fancy gravestones, and some years the Town gets me to come and clean up, here and at the other little country cemeteries too. Yours is the only stone loike that anywhere in town."

"Kevin," she said, leaning back a little. "I want to apologize for hurting your feelings at the bank. Judy explained to me how hard it was for you to offer your help, and how foolish it was of me not to understand that offer. I never meant to offend you, and I'm sorry I did."

"It's all roight," he said, coloring up a little. "Oy was hasty, stompin' out loike Oy did. It's hard for me to foind folks Oy can talk to, and the last thing Oy want is to chase one a them away." He stood up suddenly and walked over to the stone fence, looking toward the woods.

My gosh, he's crying, or he's about to. How alone he must be.

"Hey, I brought a plant to put beside Gene's grave. It's a bit heavy for me, could you move it over there for me?"

"Sure," he said. "Told ya Oy'm around to help, and that's still true." The sadness was out of his face now.

"Marine," Kevin said when they had the plant placed just so. "You gonna wanta rest here too, some day?"

"I think so. I've decided to stay in Nilesburgh even though my family wants me to go back to Philadelphia. But who knows what life will bring? Three months ago, if you told me I'd be standing by my husband's grave on Memorial Day, I would have said you're crazy."

"Three months ago Oy was too shoy to say anything to you."

"I know," she said with a small smile, remembering the mixture of deer-in-the-headlights confusion, caution and aggression that had marked his first meeting with her in the bank. "What changed, Kevin?"

"Not sure," he said, reaching out to tweak one of the branches on the small plant. "Mostly it gets better after Oy know folks for a while. Loike them guys at the Iron Skillet, Oy feel pretty good in there, cause Oy know all them guys, most of 'em for a lotta years. But loike on that crime committee, Oy still feel squitchy, ya know? Outa place, maybe."

"But you know everybody there."

He started ticking off names on his fingers. "Oy know Billy a long toime and Eppley and Jim Shipley, and Ruby. But you and Ralph is still new, and Oy don't know the school guy or that Keester fella at all."

She grinned. *Better not laugh, or he'll retreat.* "Kevin, make sure you say Kester. Keester means ass in some places."

"Marine, you shouldn't say words like that!" He looked stunned.

I can't tell if he's serious or not. If he is, he's got me on a pedestal I'll have to climb off of. If he's not, he's got a sense of humor I haven't suspected. Look at him. His eyes are squinching up, trying not to laugh. He's teasing! After all, he heard me say "rat's ass" a few minutes ago.

"Kevin, if I were to say "nose," would you be offended? Of course not, everybody has one. Well everybody has an ass too, and you'd better not think I got to be 25 years old without noticing that, or learning a dozen words for it. One of them is keester, but I suspect our manager friend may not take kindly to hearing it."

He was openly grinning now. "Oy'll just hold out on that one, an' drop a K-bomb on him if he needs it in one a them meetings."

As she drove away, Maureen's rear-view mirror showed her the image of Kevin that arose in the minds of most people in Nilesburgh if they thought of him at all. Green bike and green clothes, under a faded Red Sox baseball cap.

Two conflicting thoughts came to mind. *"Clothes make the man,"* and *"You can't tell a book by its cover." I don't think clothes make the man at all in Kevin's case, I think he'd look odd in a Brooks Brothers suit, and would hate it. And anyway, I don't think he's ever heard of Brooks Brothers. No, I think I like the other one better for Kevin. You can't tell a book by its cover. There is surely more to him than meets the eye. Damn, another cliché.*

As she made the turn onto the paved road, she did not see him wave from a quarter of a mile back.

Jacob

A small brook runs past the modest Nilesburgh Town Hall. At the edge of that mini-stream a huge eastern cottonwood tree sips from the stream and lifts its rough-barked limbs high above the town's municipal center, a white clapboard structure that still resembles the schoolhouse it once was.

A schoolboy named Jacob Harvey planted that tree on a sunny spring morning in 1865 to honor the memory of Abraham Lincoln, assassinated three weeks earlier in Washington.

Four of Jacob Harvey's remote descendants were among the crowd that gathered for Memorial Day services on the Town Hall lawn more than 140 years later. Not one of them knew who planted the tree, or that it was meant to be an icon of remembrance.

On the fourth Monday of May the Harvey cottonwood was shedding. It stood 85 feet tall and had a trunk diameter of more than three feet. A light breeze pulled fluffies off its newly greening twigs and snowed them down on the floral displays and military uniforms below.

Jeffrey Adams encouraged his fellow Viet vets to wear their fatigues to the ceremony because he thought the informal uniform was kinder to his distinctly unmilitary figure. *Besides, most guys ain't got their showier uniforms after all these years, and most of 'em wouldn't fit anyways.*

Helene Montgomery was surprised to see old Father Durand there in the well-tailored uniform of an army major, with a chaplain's cross on his tunic. An Iraq service medal rode prominently above the left breast pocket. *His face is a little sour, like there ought to be more glitter on that uniform. I'll give him credit for going off to Baghdad and Fallujah when the call came. And he's standing up straight. Doesn't do that in his priest suit.* Helene was not a big fan of organized religions, and she thought none of them were as organized and rigid as the Roman Catholics.

Major Durand was outranked by a light colonel from the Air National Guard, who carried his speech under his arm, and spent a lot of time whisking cottonwood fluff off his uniform.

"Shall I wear the medals?" Ralph had asked while getting dressed. She had replied, "Just the ribbons, dear, you don't want to overdo it."

Coast Guard blue is darker than Air Force blue and a lot lighter than Navy blue.

"I am honored to be here, and I must thank Jeffrey Adams and all the people whose work is reflected in the floral tributes and the honors paid to fallen companions. I'm told you've never had a Coast Guard speaker, and so let me brag a bit about my service. Just a few words, because as you know, Colonel Michaels is to be the day's main speaker." Ralph saw at a glance that Michaels was trying to nod and brush fluff at the same time.

"Most recently the Coast Guard was the only Federal Agency involved in the Katrina disaster that performed flawlessly. I believe I understand why that happened. The Coast Guard is the smallest of our Armed Forces, and is so widely dispersed that it's been forced to rely on its people on the ground to make good decisions."

He noticed some of the listeners nodding their heads, recalling the Coast Guard rescues and searches highlighted on TV coverage of the hurricane's aftermath. Helene had said they would find that incident an easy way to feel connected.

"When things went sour in New Orleans, it happened in a hurry, and every commander down to petty officers in charge of rescue boats simply did what had to be done. There was no checking back with a distant headquarters. That's not the way the Coast Guard operates. They just went out and saved lives." There was a ripple of applause through the audience, and Ralph was surprised.

"We don't expect applause," he said, "for performing our mission. But it's nice, and thank you all very much. Now, the name Alexander Hamilton probably means something to you, in part because he was a brilliant man, one of the Founding Fathers, and the first Secretary of the Treasury. Besides, he's on the ten-dollar bill. But as Secretary, Hamilton realized a need to enforce the laws on duties and tariffs in the new country, and to crack down on smuggling. One ancestor of the Coast Guard was the small fleet of revenue cutters that put to sea in the 1790s. I'm sure the name Hopley Yeaton means nothing to you, but he was the commander of the first revenue cutter. He had a crew of nine and was paid thirty dollars a month."

He paused to look over the crowd. "The pay scale has improved, a little," he said slowly, to smiles.

"The other half of our ancestry comes from the old Lifesaving Service established in the early 19th Century to save shipwreck victims along treacherous shores like the Outer Banks of North Carolina. To this day, there are members of the heroic Midgett family from that shore, serving proudly in the Coast Guard. Some of us have been astronauts. Some of us have won decorations for valor. All of us have served under an informal motto that's come down from those rescue efforts. It is, 'You have to go. You don't have to come back.'"

As he scanned the crowd, he thought he saw aging eyes focused on distant places where the long-stilled faces of absent companions yet lived.

"And some of us have not come back, which serves as a link between the Coast Guard and the rest of this nation's defenders. We're here today to make public the feelings we usually keep private. Those feelings include our intense pride in, and our sense of profound debt to, those who have paid the price, what Lincoln called the last full measure of devotion. We pay that price of liberty in every generation, sometimes in huge numbers, sometimes in small ones. And as long as we raise men and women who are willing to take up the responsibility of defending the rest of us, then I think this nation is as secure as it ever can be. And I don't see that spirit wilting, certainly not here in Nilesburgh. Thank you again for allowing me to express these thoughts."

Strange dogs get acquainted by sniffing each other's butts. Strange warriors are just a little more subtle. They scan each other's chests for clues to military careers.

Medals, or more commonly the ribbons representing those medals, are worn in rows of three on the left breast of the uniform tunic, with the most coveted decorations on top. The displays are sometimes called fruit salad, because the ribbons come in bright colors.

The uniform of Senior Chief Petty Officer Randolph E. Montgomery III, USCG (Ret.) had seven rows of ribbons, and a row of gold stripes marched down one of the sleeves.

"Can you read that stuff?" one Viet vet asked another during the applause that followed Ralph's speech. "Some of it," his friend answered. "Those black ones on the bottom are for rifle and pistol marksmanship, just, like the army, and he's got an 'E' for expert on both. There's a Bronze Star with a V for valor on the second row. That's a pretty big deal, so the ones above it must be even rarer. I don't know what they are but he's got a diver's helmet and aviation wings on the right side, and six of those gold service stripes on his sleeve means more than 24 years of active duty. Oh, there's the Iraq ribbon, I seen that on some of the younger Guard guys."

"Ya know," the other vet said. "I think our man's been up to a lot more than handin' out citations to drunken boaters."

Jeffrey Adams didn't speculate. He took a clear picture of Ralph's chest salad, and then went on line. Two days later he was telling the guys that those top row ribbons were the Defense Department and Coast Guard Distinguished Service awards, and that lifesaving and heroism awards preceded the Bronze Star on the second row. Below that he found the Coast Guard Meritorious Service medal, and a ribbon representing the Commandant's Letter of Commendation with two oak leaves, meaning three separate awards.

From that day on Ralph Montgomery was unable to pay for

coffee at the Iron Skillet, where he was invited to the center row of tables, and where he laughed at stories about a diner legend called Tough Thelma, who had died long before Ralph ever heard of Nilesburgh, Vermont. Nobody ever mentioned war, except to say that, in general, they were against it.

Edith

"Judy, the next time Mrs. Averill comes in, I'll take her if that's all right."

"All right? I'd love to pass her along to you, but why? She bites."

"No, she doesn't. She's just rude and lonely. Besides, I once promised myself I'd try to be nice to her, and I want to see if I can."

"Help yourself." Judy made a tossing motion as if she were passing a basketball. "But I'll keep some disinfectant under the counter, just in case."

Edith Averill came in three days later.

She's about one give-a-damn short of being well dressed, and about three short of being well groomed. That's a bad proportion. "Good morning, Mrs. Averill," Maureen called out while Judy disappeared into the vault. "I can help you over here."

"Who are you?"

"Maureen McGuckin. Judy has introduced us several times, if you recall. I'd be happy to look over your statement with you."

"Well." The customer moved briskly to the counter after scanning the bank for Judy. "Judy always knows how to explain all this to me."

"Let me have a look," said Maureen, reaching out on two levels. "I'll bet we can figure it out together."

"Why? The last girl ran for the loo when she saw me coming, why don't you?"

"Because you can't scare me." Maureen produced a big banker-in-training smile. She hoped it looked genuine. "May I speak candidly?"

The woman nodded, one eyebrow lifting a bit.

"You're a challenge, Mrs. Averill. You're rude and abusive, and you seem to like scaring people. You know what? I don't think you even need the help you come in here asking for. Every single entry in this statement is letter-perfect, so what I'm trying to find out is why you behave so badly."

"Where's Judy?" The lower jaw was out and the voice hardened. "Your manager is going to hear from me about how spiteful you are to good customers. Meanwhile, I don't want to talk to you, Missy."

"That's too bad, Mrs. Averill." Maureen showed concern and disappointment. "I was hoping that if we could get to where we can talk with each other rather than at each other, I was going to ask you for some advice." Edith Averill's mouth opened, twice, but no sound emerged. *She looks like a fish in a tank. Let me jiggle the bait a little bit.* "Are you surprised? You shouldn't be; you know a lot about a part of life that I need help with."

"And what could I teach you?" The old voice was laced with scorn and something else. Envy? "You're young and beautiful and happy, all the things I'm not." Maureen noticed that as she spoke, the sneer left the older woman's words and that curiosity was lifting the gray eyebrows.

"Mrs. Averill, we do have something in common, something so tragic that it's hard to discuss. You see, I don't know how to be a widow, and I was hoping you could help me."

Maureen had never heard the expression "gobsmacked." But when she learned it she would instantly apply the word to the way Mrs. Averill looked at the teller's window that morning.

Silence. Utter, stricken, statue-still silence. Finally Maureen dabbed at an unshed tear and stared into the Englishwoman's eyes, where she learned nothing.

"I see," came the slightly scratchy voice at last. "Widowhood has been a quite private thing for me, Missy."

"Maureen," said Maureen.

"I don't see why I should open my life up to you. We have nothing in common. I lived through the Great Depression and the Battle of Britain, and plenty of broken dreams. But you, the sun has shone on you all your life until now. You'll have to squeeze sympathy out of someone else, a softer cheese than me."

She was gone in a swirl of brown skirt and emphatic footsteps.

Well, that went very well. Good work, Maureen. So much for Rehab 101.

Two weeks later Mrs. Averill marched in with her account books and walked up to Maureen's window, looking grim.

"I'm still not sure I could share anything useful with you," She began, as if she had not stalked away on her last visit. "You did love him, I suppose."

Maybe she's interested. "Oh, yes, enormously. He was the centerpiece of my life, and he left such a huge hole in who I am." Maureen trailed off, realizing that she was telling this old woman more than she was willing to share.

The gray eyes across the counter showed a new brightness and Mrs. Averill leaned in, much as Kevin had done on his first visit to her counter. "This is no place for the chat-up we're to have. Can you come for tea tomorrow?"

Tea. I don't even have any. But I think she means more than just a cup. I'm being invited! Judy won't believe it.

"Mrs. Averill, I'd love to come, but you're assuming I know where and when. Don't forget I'm a new kid in town, just as you were all those years ago."

Those sharp eyes rested on Maureen's smile for a moment, and there was a subtle shifting of the lines on that old face. Maureen read it as a slide toward pleasant.

"Such a long time ago, oh well. That's for tomorrow. Four o'clock, dear, and that Judy, she knows where Jeremy's house, where my house is. Cheers, then."

"Wait! Didn't you want to go over your statement from the bank?"

"Oh, my, no, I'm much too busy for that. I've company coming!"

Wonder how long it's been since she said that? And didn't she bounce out of here!

"She what? Maureen, if I was a guy, I'd say yer shittin' me."

"Judy!"

"Well? I don't think anybody's ever been inside her house since Jeremy was killed, except to fix the plumbing and to wire up the satellite TV, and she was nasty to both of them."

There was a time when town officials named streets for trees and then planted those trees on that street. Nilesburgh had no more elms on Elm Street, and no more chestnuts on Chestnut Street, but as Maureen turned into Oak Street she could see a line of thick white oak trunks stretching away between curb and sidewalk. Their dark green foliage often met leaves from neighboring trees high overhead, providing an aerial mall for the squirrel population.

Edith Averill's house was a Victorian, three stories high with a steep slate roof. It was a muted yellow with a pea-green trim and multi-paned windows. A wide porch circled the north-facing front and swept down one side, ending in a door into the kitchen.

Maureen could see that the grass had been trimmed, but there were patches of last year's leaves here and there, and the bushes were growing unattended. Some of the gingerbread trim details, she saw, were hanging oddly, and many of them needed paint.

Maureen's car door closed at the same time the front door opened, and Mrs. Averill came out on the porch wearing an apron over what appeared to be her best clothes. Maureen was glad she had upped her own attire by a notch.

"Come in, come in," the scratchy voice called.

Those vocal cords need some WD-40, and some practice. I bet she doesn't even have a cat to talk to.

"I don't have a proper parlor, of course, but we'll manage in here." "Here" was a room that looked like what Maureen thought a parlor should be, but dustier. An upright piano with yellowed keys stood against one wall. A small ceramic vase on its top held plastic flowers that obscured an old wedding photo.

Afghans were folded over two heavy chairs upholstered in dark red velour, and dark wainscoting met faded wallpaper halfway up the walls. The windows were tall, but thick draperies allowed only a glimmer of light to enter.

It looks as if it's just been cleaned for the first time in years, and she missed a few spots.

There was a large silver tray on the coffee table between the chairs, and Mrs. Averill lifted it and went into the kitchen.

"Do you need any help?" Maureen asked.

"No, dear, you just make yourself comfortable and I'll be right back."

I don't know if it's possible to be comfortable in this room. I wonder what the rest of the house is like. All the other doors in the hallway were closed.

Maureen got up to look at the wedding photo. The bride wore white and a tense smile, and the groom wore the uniform of an American Army Air Corps sergeant. He looked happier than Edith did. The glass covering the photo had not been dusted.

There were prints of scenes from the English countryside, one over the fireplace and one between the windows on the outer wall.

"Do you like that scene? It's family land. That's supposed to be a view of the estate as it was about three-score years before I was born."

"Where is it, where in England, I mean," Maureen asked.

"Oh, it's in Kent," Mrs. Averill said. "Oh dear, I'd best be more specific. Kent is in the southeast of England, and that scene is near Ashford. It's a market town southwest of Canterbury and about 20 miles from Dover. Fifty miles, let's say, from London."

"Thanks," Maureen grinned. "My English geography isn't very good. But I know about Canterbury and the white cliffs of Dover, there are songs, aren't there, something about bluebirds?"

"Yes, that was popular when I met Jeremy. He was in the air wing of your army, and based near Ashford. He said the country around there looked like Vermont, only flatter." She looked out through the heavily draped window. "He said a lot of things that didn't stay true."

Maureen wasn't sure she was ready for more of that. "And this land in the print? It looks pretty rural."

"It is, or at least it used to be. It's called Mynx Hill, and it's a couple of miles east of Ashford. We had such a pretty house. I wish I could see it again."

"Why, you can," Maureen said. "We'll just go online and get a satellite photo. It shows things the size of cars, even smaller."

"Oh, my. You know, I've been so out of touch. At any rate, sit down, dear, and we'll have some tea."

She made a production of the pouring, and Maureen complimented her hostess on the china and freshly polished silver she brought out. "I don't think I've ever been asked to tea before," she smiled. "And I'm not quite sure how to behave."

A little glint appeared in the grey eyes. "You Irish don't still slurp from the saucer, do you?"

Maureen laughed. "Mostly we Irish don't have saucers. We drink liquids of this color, but they taste way different."

"Indeed they do," the old woman was smiling openly now, showing a slightly horsey set of front teeth.

"So how did it go?" Judy demanded when Maureen entered the bank the next morning.

"Pretty well. We're going shopping for clothes this weekend. I told her she's too nice a person to be trudging around in drab greys and browns, and wearing old-lady comfort shoes, you know the black ones that have laces."

"You told her she was a nice person? The last time I heard you talk to her, you were telling her she was behaving badly and she was staring lasers at you. Some turnaround!"

Maureen smiled. "Well, Judy, it didn't really take much. She's wearing this attitude like a self-inflicted wound, and she keeps picking at the scab. I think she is a nice person, and I'm trying to get her to think so too."

"Maureen the fixer! Next thing, you'll be talking Kevin into opening an account here and getting a driver's license too."

"I don't think so," she said. *Why don't I think so? What's the difference here between two wounded people who are trying to learn to stand in the sunlight, and feeling over-exposed. I suppose it's two different kinds of hurt. Kevin's fear of the government is probably deeper-seated than Mrs. A's sense of abandonment.* "By the way, Judy, you're invited to my house on Saturday night for dinner, about six. Don't bring anything except an appetite."

"Thanks, what's the occasion?"

"Oh, let's just say I've got some obligations to acknowledge."

Mead

Ralph thought he could figure out the guest list by the time he added his SUV to the variety of vehicles parked in and near the McGuckin driveway. There was a little red Honda Civic, an elderly Oldsmobile and an old green bike leaning on a bush.

"Hi, Ralph. Helene, this is Mrs. Edith Averill. I met her at the bank. And you know Judy Ploof, and Kevin Beaujolais. I think Judy and Kevin are related somehow. Please come in." *Kevin and Mrs. A aren't talking yet, I wonder how long that's going to take. At least with another couple here it's not quite so noticeable.*

Kevin circulated with trays full of this and that for the guests. *I hope nobody asks me what this stuff is. If they do I'll just smack my lips and say it's really good. This is a lot different from cookin' over propane at home. In fact, Marine's house makes my place look awful shabby.*

Edith Averill watched him carefully, and thanked him when she took a small scallop wrapped in bacon. *I suppose I'll have to talk to him, but I didn't know he was coming. He's so...unpolished, and I just know he had something to do with Jeremy's accident all those years ago.*

Helene watched the minuet. *This is Maureen's support system, but in two cases she's supporting them. That leaves us and Judy to prop her up, though she seems to be doing pretty well. Ah, I've got it. She's got two salvage projects now, Kevin and that old lady with the English accent, the one who's supposed to be so mean to people. Well, here goes.*

"Mrs. Averill, are you from the South of England?"

"Why yes, from Kent, umm..."

"Helene," said Helene.

"Yes. My husband was in the American Air Corps, and we met in a town called Ashford, near my family's home."

"Oh, I've been to Ashford. My sister and I got off the main road, the M-20, isn't it? Yes, and we had a lovely lunch at an inn called the Man of Kent on our way to Dover. Do you know the place?"

"Yes, of course. It was quite welcoming to Americans in uniform, and Jeremy and I had dinner there occasionally." She colored up a little, leading Helene to suspect that dinner wasn't the entire date.

Kevin was telling Ralph what he'd heard at the Skillet that morning. "They say the fucker's outa jail."

"Which fucker, Kevin?"

"It's Archie Tourangeau. Suzie's brother is a deputy sheriff at the Courthouse in St. Albans, and he called her this morning to get her to pass the word that Archie's lawyer got a judge to let him post bail, cause of excessive police force during the arrest. Turns out Benoit cuffed both his hands to the gurney when they carted Archie off to the hospital, and the judge thought that was excessive restraint."

"Shit. So that animal is loose on the street, and the first thing he'll do is try to find the Slicer and get some revenge. How will he do it, do you think."

"He'll go after Gordie Willard for sure and maybe the kids who seen the beating. He'll think Gordie gave him up to the Sloicer," Kevin said. "But they ain't to home, none of 'em. They're down in Boston, lookin' into some koind of cancer treatment for Leonard, and they got some Red Sox tickets to loighten up the trip. But Archie don't know that, and he's bound to turn up at the house."

"But if they're not home…" Ralph let the thought trail off.

"Then he'll trash the house and feel good about doin' it. He may have his old man or his brother with him. Ain't none of 'em worth a gobbet a snot."

"What about the cops," Ralph asked. "That Sergeant Jacobs seems like a pretty smart guy."

"Cooney? He is, but cops got their own boxes, Ralph. They're pretty good at dealin' with after, but not so hot at before."

"You mean prevention."

"Sure. Harrison ain't gonna stake out the Willard house, he's got a whole town to patrol. And anyways, if he's gonna put two and two together, he's gotta have at least one a them twos in his hand, and loike I said, he don't think that way."

"I think I get that," said Ralph. "You want to take a ride after supper?"

Kevin grinned. "Sure thing, Chief."

"I'm glad you could all be here," Maureen said when they'd all pushed their plates away. "I'm having to form my own social circle now, and look what I've got so far." She smiled around the room and held up what looked like a wine bottle. "Judy, would you pass around those little glasses behind you, please? This is mead, from Bunratty Castle in Ireland. Mead is a traditional Irish drink, and I'd like to use it to toast some very good friendships."

She walked around the table, filling the tiny stemmed glasses with a golden fluid. She lifted one of them, and five other glasses rose to meet it, while light from the chandelier danced through the mini-goblets and formed amber circles on the tablecloth.

"Slainte!" she said.

"Slantcha? What's that?" Judy asked, softening the question by taking a sip of the honey-laced drink. "Mm, this stuff is good."

"Careful, Judy," Helene said. "It's also deceptive. It's where the term honeymoon comes from. A man is supposed to give this to his wife for the first thirty days of their marriage."

"Yes," added Mrs. Averill. "And then she's supposed to announce that she's pregnant." She smiled. "I think I'd better confine myself to one glass."

"Slainte!" said Ralph, leading the chuckles. "Maureen, this has been excellent, good food, good company, good conversation. All you could want in an evening out. And it's a shame to break up the good times, but Kevin and I have an errand to run. Something that just came up. Maureen, could you run Helene home?" He hoped his smile took the sting out of his request. It didn't, he could see.

"I'll take her, Ralph," Judy said, and a minute later the two men were gone.

"Well, that was rude," said Mrs. Averill, looking indignant. "And I know about rude."

"Don't jump to conclusions, ladies," Judy cautioned. "I think I know what happened. Kevin told Ralph that Archie Tourangeau is out of jail, and probably looking for young Gordie. I think they've gone to persuade Archie not to do anything stupid."

"I don't like it." Maureen was frowning. "Not because they left, but because that's a dangerous man!"

"No, dear, that's a thug," Helene said. "Now Ralph *is* a dangerous man, and your Kevin has already tackled a bank robber."

"Wait a minute! He's not *my* Kevin! Where did you get that idea?"

"Figure of speech, Maureen, that's all. Now, maybe instead of being scared for those two, we should be feeling sorry for this Archie person. Meanwhile, *Ardu an gloine!*"

Maureen laughed at the puzzled faces. "It means, 'raise a glass.' and so we should. Helene, you surprise me."

"My grandmother had, shall we say, a firm hand in my raising. She was born Bridget Monaghan in the village of Doolin, on the coast of County Clare."

"Well," said Mrs. Averill, swirling the mead in her glass. "I'll drink to your grandmother, and to your husband and even to Kevin Beaujolais, but as for that Archie, a murrain upon him. Oh my, what a potent libation." She put her hand over her mouth.

"What's a murrain," asked Judy. *I never heard this kind of talk before, foreign words and all that stuff.*

"A pox, a plague, a damnation, a visitation of troubles. That's what I wish on that man!" And she shot such a jut-jawed fierce glare toward the door that Maureen and Helene caught each other trying not to laugh.

"Don't worry, Mrs. A," Judy said. "I think Archie Tourangeau will find trouble enough."

In another twenty minutes they were all gone, and Maureen stood in her driveway, waving at the last car. In the sudden silence she could hear the march of last year's leaves, hop-skitching across the asphalt under a light south wind that smelled of rain.

Archie

"How do you want to do this?" Ralph asked as they drove toward the Willard house.

"How do *Oy* want to do it? Oy thought this was your frickin' party."

"Kevin, why do you say frickin' and freakin? Why not just say fuckin'?"

"Man, that's a heavy word," Kevin said. "Ya hold back on that one till ya really need it, but them others got their place too. Freakin' is softer than frickin', and frickin' is way softer than fuckin'."

"I think I've got it," Ralph said. "Now, how do you want to do this?"

"Oy know where the key is. Drop me off, then go down and turn around while Oy get the garage door open. Just pull on in. Archie won't know what kind of car Leonard Willard drives. Then Oy'll change the loights in the house. They left on some a them 'Oy ain't here' loights, and if he's been cruisin' the house, he'll see a change and think they're home. Then we wait in the garage. We gotta take him down quick, cause he's a big fuck."

"Sounds like a plan to me."

"Ralph, is that you?"

"Yeah, sorry to wake you."

"It's okay, I was just dozing. So?"

"Oh, nothing much. That Kevin's a very interesting guy, would have made a good Coastie under other circumstances."

"Ralph, am I going to have to read the paper to find out what you've been up to?"

"Yup."

"Nilesburgh Police, Sergeant Jacobs."

"Good morning, this is Donna Garner on Hillside Street. My neighbor's garage door is wide open, and I know they're away, in Boston. Could you send somebody? I know it's probably nothing, but there's been some vandalism...."

"What's the neighbor's name, Ma'am."

"It's poor Leonard Willard, he's got cancer, and they went to Boston to talk to a specialist. There's no car in the garage, and I just thought... you know."

"Mrs. Garner, does this Willard have a teen-aged son?"

"Yes, Officer, his name is Gordon. He was injured in a fight not long ago, but he's going to be all right. He's such a nice boy, the whole family is nice people, and poor Joyce, with all she's got to cope with, I just pray to Jesus that nothing's missing."

"I'm on my way, Ma'am." *Shit! Those folks have had their share of trouble, all right, and then some. There has been some breaking and entering lately, but not around there, that neighborhood's pretty quiet.*

The police SUV turned into Hillside, and Jacobs saw a woman standing in her driveway, waving. *That'll be Mrs. Garner, she seems agitated.*

"Officer, there's noises coming out of the garage. Thumping sounds! You be careful in there."

"All right, Ma'am. You stay here, and I'll tell you what I find after a look around."

Now what? If I draw my weapon she'll think I'm being overly dramatic, and if I don't, I could get in trouble real quick. Okay, be safe, Cooney.

"Dispatch, 204."

"Go, Four."

"Julie, I'm on Hillside for a possible B&E, and the neighbor reports noises coming from the garage. Send me some backup, please, and have him bring the camera. No lights, no siren."

The woman was hovering and looking anxious. "Mrs. Garner, did you notice anything last night. Any activity over there at all?"

"Well, yes, now that I think of it. One of those boxy cars drove into the garage last night after dark, and I thought the Willards had come back. It was too late to go over there, so I thought I'd ask this morning how it went in Boston. But now I think it wasn't them at all, because the car's not there."

"204, Dispatch."

"Go, Julie."

"Sergeant, Harmon is your prime backup, and he's about two minutes away. Benoit's bringing the camera, he's about five minutes."

"10-4."

He looks as young as Gordie. Donna Garner watched the young officer get out of his cruiser and confer with the sergeant, who was using broad hand gestures to convey his plan.

"The garage opens to the side, so we can't see into it from here. Go the other way, around the house to the far side, and on my signal, weapons out, we go in fast."

Mrs. Garner watched as the young officer circled the house, staying below window level. Eventually she saw his head appear at the far side of the garage. The other one waved from the near side, and they both darted into the garage, with their guns out front. *It looks just like the TV, except it's very scary.*

She was very surprised to hear the sound of laughter drifting out of the garage.

"Well now, looky here. Timmy, didn't you haul this sack of shit off to jail once?"

"Sure did Sarge, by way of the hospital."

Jacobs reached down and jerked the electrician's tape away from the man's mouth, making no effort to be gentle about it. He also picked up an unloaded pistol, whose five bullets were standing on end in an arrow pointing toward the cocooned man.

"Okay Archie, what happened this time, or do I get to make it up again?"

"Fuck you, Jacobs."

"Come on, Archie, there must be a helluva story behind how you got to be trussed up like a Thanksgiving turkey, stretched out between two columns in a garage that belongs to the family of a kid you're charged with beating up. And you sure as hell don't have a permit for that gun. You got more gaffer's tape on you than Aubuchon's Hardware sells in a month."

"Hey, Sarge," Andy Benoit said, entering the garage. "Hey Archie, how come every time I see you, you're all tied up?"

"Fuck you, Asshole." Tourangeau twisted his head to the side.

Harmon twisted it back. "Sarge, look at his ear."

One side of Tourangeau's face held a somewhat dirty bandage where his ear should have been, and the other side was black.

"Archie, looks like somebody spray-painted your ear. Do you think that's a message, or is that too much for your mind to work on?"

Jacobs got a utility knife from the workbench, noting a half-empty box of rubber gloves. *So much for fingerprints.* He sliced away the layers of tape that bound their suspect, making sure to cuff him in the process. "Archie, you're going back to jail, and this time they'll keep you. No judge is going to let you out after you invade the home of a kid you beat up. So why don't you tell us how you got here?"

Tourangeau had had a long time to think about explaining his latest capture. "Oy come over here to apologoize to the kid, cause Oy felt really bad about what happened to him, ya know?"

"Well, why didn't you just go knock on the door?"

"Oy done that, and nobody came. So Oy come in through the garage, and was gonna knock on the kitchen door."

"Bullshit, Archie, the door's been forced. You broke in, and you were trying to force the Willard kid to tell you who the Slicer is."

"You can't prove that."

"I don't have to. Once the judge learns you came here, your bail is revoked, and your ass is in jail for a long time. Did you hear anything that might help us figure out who did this?"

"Not a word, just some grunts, and that was mostly when they done my ear."

"They? What makes you think there was more than one?"

"Lissen, Asshole, nobody takes me one on one. Besides, Oy think one sat on my head while the other one taped me up."

"Okay," Jacobs sighed. "From the beginning, Archie. Andy, take notes. Archie Tourangeau, you have the right to remain silent. Anything you say can and will be used against you in a court of law. You have the right to have an attorney present during questioning. If you cannot afford an attorney, one will be appointed for you. Do you understand all that?"

"Yeah, Oy've heard it before."

"I'm sure you have, and from me. Now, what happened here?"

"Oy come in through the small door, and Oy'm movin' along the soide of this car, and whap! The back seat door opens hard and knocks me down on moy face. And somebody holds my head down, and then they tape me up. Oy was foightin' but they kicked me in the balls when Oy went to raise up. Oy been here a long toime."

"204, Dispatch."

"Go, Julie," Jacobs answered.

"Sergeant, are you still on Hillside?

"10-4."

"Okay, we've got a call from over on the next street, Walnut Street. There's a truck parked there that the caller doesn't recognize. It's been there all night. The tags come back registered to Walter Tourangeau, but I haven't called him yet. Will you check it?"

"Sure thing, Julie." *Now we don't have to look for his car.* "Okay guys. Andy, you take Archie over to St. Albans and put him back where he belongs. The charge is breaking and entering, and make sure the prosecutor knows whose house he got into, plus the pistol, plus whatever they want to do about bail violations. It may be quite a list. Timmy, you go check the truck, and we'll have Aaron tow it. Archie ain't gonna need wheels for a really long time."

He walked back across the street to Mrs. Garner, who was standing on her sidewalk with two other neighbors, all of them watching the blue lights flicker on Andy Benoit's cruiser.

"It's all good, Ma'am," he said. "There was a man in there who didn't belong there, and one of my men is taking him to jail. I think it was an isolated case, and there's nothing more to worry about. Thanks for your call this morning, it helped us a lot." He tipped his cap to the other women, and drove off to have a chat with the Chief.

"He was probably free for about twelve hours," Harrison figured. "That is, until he got caught. Maybe we should have anticipated that the bastard would try to lean on the Willards."

"Well, somebody did," Jacobs pointed out, trying not to make it sound like a slip-up by the department.

"Okay, who do we know that keeps a closer eye on that rat-turd than we do?" Harrison asked, elevating his boots into thinking mode.

"Well, there's always the Slicer, except we don't know who that is, any more than we did the first day Archie got himself tied up."

"Well, is the tying a link or a coincidence?" Jacobs wondered. "What about spray-painting his other ear? The point is, he's been disabled very quickly in successive incidents, and he doesn't know who did it either time, but this time he thinks there was two of 'em."

"Jeezum, Cooney, if that's true, that complicates our case a lot. Now I can see the lawyers yelling that there's a conspiracy to deprive young Archie of his Constitutional right to pursue a criminal career."

"Chief, I know we talked about Kevin Beaujolais, only he's too little, and we got to thinkin' about that Ralph Montgomery, only he don't exactly run in Archie's social circle, but maybe I oughta check into where them guys was last night."

"Do it. But quietly. I don't wanta be raisin' flags I can't wave."

Zorro

Maureen put the red-rose greeting card in the bank's window on Monday morning, and Kevin came in after lunch.

"Hi, Marine." She examined the bright grin on his face and watched it fade under her stare.

She took him into the little conference room and closed the door.

"What have you been up to?" she demanded.

"Whoa! Nothin' that otter make you mad. What's up?"

"Kevin, the police are looking for you. They want to know where you were Friday night. They've already talked to Ralph and Helene and even Mrs. Averill. Judy too, and now me. I told them that you all had dinner at my house, and then you all went home. That is what happened, isn't it?"

He looked squarely at her. "Yeah, we had dinner, it was good too, and then Ralph dropped off me and the boike at the Skillet. It was pretty late when we left your house."

"No it wasn't. Ralph said he had to break off early, because you and he had an errand to run. You're holding out something, and you're not supposed to do that to friends." She wasn't quite waving her finger at him but her hands were in motion and her color was up. "I want to know where you went and what you did."

"And Oy ain't gonna tell you. Some things you don't need to know, and yer pickin' at me about stuff that don't concern you at all."

Maureen sat back in her chair. *Now I'm getting him worked up. Calm down, Maureen.* "Kevin, the cops think you and Ralph beat up that Tourangeau boy, the one that lost his ear. Helene told them that she and Ralph went home, but Mrs. Averill told them the two of you left together and that Judy drove Helene home. They could charge you with assault, and then where would you be?"

Jeezum, she's worried about me. Is that a good thing or not? "Marine, if they ask me did Oy beat up Archie, Oy can say no and be tellin' the truth. If they ask me did Oy see Archie last night Oy can tell 'em no and it's the truth." *Course it was too dark to see much of anything in that garage.*

"I know what you're doing, Kevin, and it's not quite honest. You're shading the truth. Suppose they ask you straight out, did you wrap the man in tape in that garage? Then what do you say?"

"Marine, first they ain't gonna ask. Second, they should give a medal to whoever done it. Somebody kept a house from bein' trashed and if that kid was there, Archie would have hurt him again, and his Dad's too weak to help. And the third thing is, don't be tellin' me what's honest. Oy know right from wrong, and Oy ain't stepped over."

"Look, let me put this in other words. I don't want to see you get your skinny ass in a sling, and when you start acting like a vigilante, I don't like it. It chips away at our friendship, cause that has to be based on trust."

Kevin caught glints of sorrow and pain in her eyes. *How did we get to this?* "Oy'd risk a lot to keep from losin' yer smoile. But Oy ain't a herd beast, and Oy don't steer very easy, and Oy ain't usta goin' by what other folks say. Whatever moighta happened that night was not supposed to be a wedge between two people that's learnin' to loike each other. This needs fixin', and Oy don't know how." He got up and went to stare out the window, pretending that an empty parking lot was fascinating. *Them parkin' loines is all straight. Life ain't got many straight loines, and mostly that's okay. But not now.*

Maureen saw a defensive stiffness in his posture as the silence became a layer of invisible insulation between them.

She got up and went to stand behind him at the window. "I know how," she said, and slid her arms around him. Kevin pulled his hands up to touch hers, while the silence evolved from confrontational to comfortable.

She's touching me, and not by accident.

Why did I need to hug him? Why do I keep thinking he's so vulnerable?

He disengaged and turned around. "Marine, we're in here with the door closed."

He was blushing, she saw. One corner of her mouth lifted as her eyes found his. "Are you concerned about your reputation?"

"Not moine," he blurted. "You don't want folks to link us up. Most folks don't think much of me, and they'll think less of you."

"Kevin, please let me worry about my reputation. It's intact. I choose my friends without regard to what 'folks' think, whoever they are. What I think is that you're like nobody I ever met, but please stop acting like Zorro before you get in real trouble."

"Zorro? Who's that?"

"He was a young man who seemed to be wasting his life. Nobody thought he was worth a jellybean, but at night he'd go out and fight the bad guys, secretly."

"And what happened to him?" Kevin asked.

"He cleaned up his town and won the girl," she admitted, sorry now that she'd brought up the old movie legend.

"Pretty good story," he grinned. "With a happy ending."

Here goes nothing. "Yeah, but in the end he had to give up his secret life to keep the girl and the respect of his community."

"Well, Oy ain't got no secrets."

"Kevin, your whole life is a secret. You hide from the authorities, nobody knows where you live, you don't have a phone, you don't have a job, I don't know what you *do* have." *He's doing that eye-smile thing again, with the lines on his face scrunching up. Why do I think that's cute?*

"Oy got freedom, and happiness, or at least Oy did until Oy started getting' hen-pecked."

"Hen-pecked! I'm just trying to keep you out of jail."

"Would you put up moy bail if they take me in?" *She's got this little thing going on with her face when she's being funny. Her eyes crinkle up a little.*

"I'd have to think about it. Would the town be safer with you in jail or out?"

"Well, think hard, cause Oy don't take to bein' locked up. Oy been there before, mostly for truant. Makes me fret, bein' closed in loike that."

He's not smiling now, and I can see how he'd hate being locked up. "Yes, Kevin, I'll go your bail if you go to jail. But try not to. By the way, Mrs. Averill wants you to come over and do some work around her house. My guess is it's been neglected for a long time, and there's some rot around the windows and some of that gingerbread trim is loose."

I guess we're not talking about us any more. "You sure about that, Marine? Mrs. A snoots whenever she sees me. She thinks Oy had to do with old Jeremy's dyin'."

"Just go over there, I think it'll be all right. She's changing, coming out of herself a little, and opening up a bit. You should try it," she added, flipping her hair out of her eyes and smiting him with a perky grin.

Jimmy

"We were out riding around." Ralph was filling his SUV when the sergeant found him at Michelle's.

"Look," Cooney Jacobs persisted. "You leave a dinner party early and drive off with Kevin Beaujolais instead of going home, as your wife said you did. Somebody sees a boxy car drive into the Willard's garage, and the next morning I find this Archie Tourangeau in there, trussed up like a caterpillar in duct tape. How about fillin' me in on where you were and what you did that night after you left Mrs. McGuckin's house."

"Am I a suspect in some criminal activity? Where are you going with this, Sergeant, you've implied that I participated in an act of violence."

"All I'm after is the truth. The truth has to fit into a pattern. Lies don't."

"All right," said Ralph. "But you've got to keep this confidential, because I gave my word that I wouldn't tell anybody. First of all, your man Kevin is a very confused guy right now. He's been alone most of his life, he didn't have much social contact as a teenager, he knows little or nothing about women, and now he's got this huge problem."

"What's all that got to do with Archie Tourangeau?"

"Nothing. I'm getting there. Kevin is trying to come out into the place where the rest of us live, to get over being a loner who doesn't trust anybody, especially the authorities. As you may know, that's because both his parents were taken away involuntarily by the government when he was quite young. But in hiding from the government, he's also been hiding from himself, and trying to turn these little acts of kindness that he does into a substitute for real interactions with other people. He was doing all right with that until Maureen came along."

"Maureen McGuckin, the widow?"

"Exactly. Maureen the widow. Kevin is in love for the first time in his life, and it's driving him crazy. He's afraid, on several levels. He's afraid he'll do something stupid and drive her away, he's afraid he'll be rejected, he's afraid to push, precisely because she's a widow, and he doesn't want anyone to think he's putting a move on a vulnerable woman. And on top of all that, he's deliriously happy because she's in his life. And she may not know any of that."

"And so where does all of that fit into last Friday night?" Jacobs asked, in a voice drenched in doubt.

"Sergeant, Kevin doesn't have any buddies. There's nobody close that he can talk to about important stuff, life stuff." Ralph paused. "You know the last few years I was in the Coast Guard, I wasn't diving as much as I was counseling the young Coasties. Emotionally, Kevin is younger than a lot of the kids I had in my shop the last time I was at sea. He needed to unload some heavy stuff on somebody, and I guess I was elected. I think sharing that business at the bank had something to do with his willingness to open up."

"Are you tellin' me that you just drove around in a confessional on wheels while Kevin Beaujolais poured out his lovesick soul? Is that it?"

Ralph could sense that Jacobs didn't want to believe him, but that his tale made enough sense to be plausible, and so he pushed a little. "Yeah, we even had a witness. There was an old man out on the Poor Farm Road, trying hard to walk home. Kevin recognized him, and asked me to stop. Old Jimmy Hanson, his name was, I didn't know the guy.'

"I do," said Jacobs, trying to recall how many times Old Jimmy had barfed in his police car while being taken in.

"Anyhow, Kevin told me how to take him home, and we dropped him off in a trailer park. Kevin no sooner got him out of the car than he threw up, and then this huge woman was there, dragging him inside and using language that would shame a bosun's mate."

186

"So you're tellin' me that Old Jimmy Hanson is your alibi, huh?" *Pretty slick. Old Jimmy won't remember anything, and as for Laura Jane, once she finds out the ones who brought her father home are under suspicion for anything, she'll testify as if they're being beatified. And she was probably sloshed too. Damn.*

"Sergeant, I don't need an alibi. But we did pick up an old drunk and take him home."

If Cooney Jacobs was disappointed that Montgomery batted aside his alibi suggestion, he didn't let it show. "And what did you say to Kevin, after all that."

"Listen, Arnie, I need to tell you one more thing that illustrates Kevin's thinking. After we dropped the old man off, he was quiet for a while and then he said, 'I don't wanta end up like that. At least Old Jimmy's got a daughter. I ain't got nobody.' It was pretty sad. I think Kevin was looking downstream at the rest of his life, and not liking what he saw there. Besides, what I told him is personal. But in general, people live best around other people that they respect. I might even have said no man is an island. I don't know if any of it helped."

Ralph put the nozzle back in its slot on the gas pump. *Can't remember the last time I fed this thirsty beast for less than thirty bucks.* "You know," he said. "The Willard family seems to have a pretty active guardian angel."

"You know Kevin's kin to that family, don't you?"

"Didn't know that. But come on, Sergeant, Kevin's not the hero warrior you'd like him to be. And besides, did any harm come to that shit-licker?"

Jacobs shifted his feet and hitched up his belt. "Well, somebody can be charged with assault," he said.

"And you want to charge Kevin Beaujolais with assault on an armed burglar who was caught breaking into the home of a kid he'd beaten up? So he got tied up and his ear got hosed down with Rust-oleum, what's the big deal? Seems to me somebody did you guys a favor, but the prosecutor is not going to go after the hero of the great Nilesburgh bank robbery."

It took about an hour for Ralph's mistake to sink into Jacobs' mind. *Son of a bitch! How did he know about the Rust-oleum? Those two guys done it, sure as Hell, but I'll never prove it, and the state's attorney will run away from the case, and frickin' Ralph was right. They covered the cops' ass, and put that cocksucker back on ice. It's hard to knock this vigilante stuff when it works.*

Thelma

She's gonna ask about Jeremy, sure as Hell, and I'm gonna lie, sure as Hell. Won't do no good now to have her thinkin' he fixed up his own death cause she was impossible to live with. And anyways, the truth would rip up years of not-trues that was built mostly to protect her from how ugly the truth was.

Kevin was replacing balusters on the front porch of the Averill house on Oak Street. He'd been nervous about knocking on the door, but Maureen had told him it would be all right. It was.

Mrs. Averill had been pleasant, but a guardedness continued to tilt their conversation toward polite and formal.

"Ma'am, there's a fair amount o' thisnthat on the list, but one a the most visible things would be the railing right here. These uprights are called balusters, and it don't take much to knock 'em loose. I'll go up to the hardware and get some new ones, and some paint that'll match the old ones. They'll call you to authorize a charge, if that's all right."

"Yes, of course, and thank you for doing this."

"This is what Oy do, ma'am, and besoides Marine said I should come to help you."

He saw the old lady peering intently at him. "Kevin, has it occurred to you that I'm a rehabilitation project for Maureen? She's trying to entice me out of an old bitterness and make me a more tolerant and sociable person, and it looks to me as if she's working on you, too."

Kevin stood up and leaned against the newell post at the bottom of the porch stairs. He made a mental note that it was loose. "She

189

thought Oy was gonna get arrested over that Archie business. Oy ain't usta havin' anybody fret over me."

"Neither am I," she said, and he saw a small smile creeping down from the grey eyes. "But look what she's done so far. She's got us talking to each other after how many years? It's been eight years, hasn't it, since Jeremy died?"

"Seven, Oy think. And when that happened, you know Oy was there."

"I've always wondered if I know everything that happened that day."

This is gonna be tricky. What is it they same in them court movies? The truth and nothing but the truth, but maybe not the whole truth.

"Mrs. Averill, here's what happened." He turned to face her squarely and looked her in the eye. "Oy was takin' a buncha New Jersey guys, four of 'em, out to Jeremy's hunting cabin, and into the woods the next morning. Oy put this one fella up in a tree stand, cause Oy thought he was reckless and had buck fever, and Oy didn't want him shootin' one a them other guys, or even me. Oy got the rest of 'em spread out along a hillside, driftin' on a south-facin' slope, and then Oy went back to check on this Jordan, not bein' sure he'd stay in his tree. And Oy'm just getting' there when there's a shot, and a falling body. Oy got into the clearing and told the hunter to stay put, and there was Jeremy on the ground, gunshot, and he died right in front of me."

He sat down on the top step and looked down the street where the oaks arched over the pavement.

"The one thing Oy never figgered out was what he was doin' out there in the dawn, wanderin' around in the woods. He was born here, Mrs. Averill, and he knew damn well that you don't go just walkin' around in the woods in deer season, even if it was his woods. It didn't make no sense to me back then, and it still don't to this day." He stopped talking and shook his head slightly, as if trying to clear his confusion by speaking it aloud.

Edith Averill walked slowly down the porch steps and turned to face him.

"I've always feared it was me," she said very softly. "You see, we'd been arguing almost all night, as we often did. And then he stormed out, yelling some very ugly things over his shoulder. Oh, I don't know why I'm opening all those old wounds... perhaps they never healed. Kevin, please have a seat on the porch whilst I fetch some lemonade. I've quite a lot to say, and I'd rather do it sitting."

A few minutes later she dropped into a wicker chair, and Kevin noted that it sagged more than a little. Probably not used for years.

"I was a war bride, you know, and six weeks pregnant when we were wed in Ashford. It was 1945, in the summer, and Jeremy was to be sent back to the States in a few more weeks. While I waited, I stayed at Mynx Hill, my family home, and there I had a miscarriage. My family never approved of the match, and were not supportive, in fact my father seemed to think the loss of the baby justified his opposition. They never said exactly why they opposed us, but I gathered that my family thought I was marrying down in social status, and that running off to America with a minor landowner from the back woods of New England was far from the dream they held for me. I was the only living child after my two brothers were killed in the war, and the rest of my family thought I should be bringing strong new blood into the family right there in Kent."

Now her eyes were also scanning the canopy of trees, and Kevin sat very still, watching her and listening.

"Jeremy would have none of it, of course. He was drafted out of Nilesburgh, and was a reluctant warrior at best. Not that he ever shirked his duty, but he was forever homesick, and he told such grand stories of this place. I was so impressed, I wanted to believe, and so I did. Jeremy left first on a troopship, and I had to get a cousin to take me to Southampton, where we'd booked second-class passage to New York. There were a lot of young British girls on that ship, all newly married or engaged, and about a third of them expecting. We clotted together, of course, speculating about what lay before us. I stayed in touch with some of them for a while, but not after I realized that they were all having a better time of it than I was."

She stopped and sipped at her lemonade. Kevin had questions, but thought asking would interrupt her, and perhaps divert her from sifting old memories and their attached emotions.

"Jeremy met me at the pier, and I was more glad to see him

than I was the Statue of Liberty in the harbor. We took the train to St. Albans, and then drove here, not to this house, his parents were living here then, but to an apartment he'd rented in here in the village. There was something strange and a little remote about him even then, and I can still only guess that something very basic had changed."

Kevin started to respond when she paused, but realized she was only taking a breath before reaching into an especially sore place in her mind.

"Kevin, did you ever know a Nilesburgh woman named Thelma something? Supposed to have red hair."

"Some years back there was an old droyed up woman named Thelma who worked as a waitress at the Iron Skillet. She usta brag about how she welcomed the boys back from the war, and hinted that moy daddy was one of 'em."

"That may be the one. Jeremy was here for about four weeks before I arrived, and I soon learned he'd been sleeping with this old girlfriend in the meantime. And somehow she got it into his head that I had faked the pregnancy and the miscarriage just for a chance to marry an American, and that I had trapped him into the wedding. Fact is I never even told him we were pregnant until after the ceremony was over. We had been sleeping together, at an inn in Ashford, and pretty dumb about it too. At any rate I think he believed that slander for the rest of his life, because our relationship soured from then on, and we concentrated on making each other miserable. Apparently, we were pretty good at it."

She stopped to drain her lemonade, sucking thoughtfully on a last cube of ice. There was a glistening in her left eye, and Kevin knew if she blinked it would turn into a tear. She did not blink.

"Marine, have ya got a boike?" Kevin shoved two fifties into his pocket and raised an eyebrow.

"Yes, we thought that would be a good way to explore Vermont, but I haven't used it since, since last spring."

"You mean since your husband died," he prompted.

"Yes."

"Marine there's no reason not to say that, ya know, unless it's just too hard to bring the words out."

"It's not too hard, but it's still a pot-hole for me, especially when the notion creeps up on me, as it just did."

"Well, Oy think yer doin' just foine. Couple weeks back you was chirpin' at me fer hidin' away, and that took hold pretty hard. Oy'm not the invisible man folks think Oy am, and Oy don't roost in a tree at night. Oy've got a place Oy'd loike to show ya, but ya can't get there in a car, not all the way, anyways."

"Is this going to be another secret between us, like the card in the window?"

She was smiling. *Good sign.* "Well, Judy figgered that one out roight quick, didn' she? But even she don't know this one, cause it's a bigger secret. Oy never took nobody there before, and Oy'm even a little squitchy about lettin' you in on it. Ya know trust don't come easy to me."

"You have to reach for it, Kevin, and trust grows as you nourish it. Now, when do you want to do this excursion?" She saw his eyes brighten as he read "yes" into her response.

"Ya know where the Squirrel Hill Road cuts off the 133 highway just outa town? Well ya take that for about a moile, and Oy'll meet you at noon on Saturday where a little track runs off into the woods."

"Should I bring anything?"

"Nope, but ya can leave somethin' home, a critical eye. Ya know yer not sposed to look a gift horse in the mouth? Well, don't stare too hard at this secret either, cause it may fray around the edges."

"Kevin, you're being very mysterious."

"Well, that's what Oy do best, banker-lady. See ya Saturday, and thanks for sayin' yes."

He's literally bouncing out of here. I think he just turned another coming-out corner, I just wish I could see around it.

Finulla

In the old Disney animated film classic *Fantasia*, a flock of Autumn Fairies flit through the branches of trees, touching them with colors far brighter than green.

In the off-screen world, those sprites are invisible, but they had been at work in the woods of Nilesburgh. On a bright mid-September morning a light breeze teased the changing leaves above an unpaved lane, while sunlight and shadow tussled for possession of the roadway below.

Maureen drove slowly, captured by the strobe effect of sunlight slanting down through the leaves.

The maples! No wonder Vermonters love them so much. Syrup and floors and furniture and these wild colors, all from one tree. And the show is just getting started.

She stopped to admire a huge maple near the road. Kevin would later say it was a wolf tree, dominating its immediate neighbors and casting seeds prolifically late in its life. She saw that its limbs were at different stages of coloring up, and the overall effect was that this one tree by itself embraced all the colors of the season.

She noticed Kevin a hundred yards away, standing in the middle of the road and waving. She followed his elaborate gestures into a small turnoff marked by no sign, a strip of grass separating the seldom-used tire lanes.

"I wasn't lost, Kevin, I was just looking at a tree."

"No trees in Philadeffya, then?" he teased.

"Of course, but not like this!"

There was something about the fresh fall air that enhanced the color in her face. He thought she'd never looked better and wanted to say so, but didn't. *Ralph said it's too easy to go from magic to tragic, and I'd hate for the wrong word to tip it over that way. I never thought she'd trust me enough to come out here. But here she is, and really enjoying herself.*

· Maureen had her bike off the car's rack. "Come on, let's ride back there and I'll show you."

"Marine, Oy see trees all the toime. Oy tap 'em in the spring and cut 'em in the fall."

"Come on, country boy, see this one through my eyes!" And she peddled off.

How could I ever say no? She's so full of life today. Right now I think she could talk me into anything. Good thing this is a short ride, I could get really distracted watching her work those pedals from behind. Jeezum, I don't know where this is going. I don't even know who's steering. Steady as she goes, boy. Oops, that's got a wiggly meaning in this case.

"Look, Kevin, it's magic!" She let the bike fall on its side, and Kevin gave her points for not trying to balance it on a kickstand. She laughed and leaped into the air to snag a low-hanging leaf. "Look!" She ran over and pushed it under his nose, almost too close to see. The big five-pointed sugar maple disc was about five inches across and tethered to a three-inch stem. In the center it was a rich dark green. But around the lobes, the colors of Maureen's "magic" pushed in against the central green, in concentric waves.

"See? There's yellow and a band of orange, and something in between, and even some red, all on the same leaf! Kevin, how can you see that, and not believe in magic, or in God?" She cradled the leaf in both hands and looked for a place to save it. *He says he sees maples all the time. Can he still see the wonder, or does he only see the tree and the floors or firewood it will become?*

"Marine, the woods was moy first friend. Oy could read animal tracks before Oy was shavin', and Oy knew the names of all the trees and what they're good for. Oy'd come out here after school, or when Oy was feelin' sad and skippin' school, and Oy always felt peaceful in the woods. To some folks a forest is just a lotta tress growin' close together, but for me it was the first example of a community that I recognoized. And if Oy had ta pick a favorite, it'd be the maple, cause it does so many things for folks.. Now, let's see yer trophy."

Jeezum Crow, she's most as tall as me! He cupped his palms to receive the leaf, and as she dropped it, her sharpened perception showed her his hands as she'd never bothered to see them. *There are little scars on his palms, and callouses, so different from Gene's. The hands of a working man. So different from Gene he is, and so shy. Well, so am I right now. Back off a bit, girl.*

"Kevin, can we collect some more? Look, they're all different!"

"Marine, Oy can't count hoigh enough to number the leaves on just one tree. Besoides, you don't need to jump around after these things, they come to you if you're patient." *Will she come to me if I'm patient? What will I do if she does?*

He stuck the leaf stem into a buttonhole on his shirt and climbed back on his bike. "Let's go put this in yer car. Ya can shut it between pages of yer owners' manual, and Oy'll troy to save it. Maybe we can fix the colors the way they are by pourin' some polyurethane over it. That's just a maybe, Oy can't remember seein' it done, but Oy'm thinkin' about how to troy." *Can you flash-freeze magic? Is there some way to preserve Maureen as alive as she is right now? I don't know, but I'm thinking about how to try.*

He smiled when she locked her car with the multi-colored leaf inside it. "Now get back on yer bike and let's go see the real reason Oy asked you here."

Where is he taking me? This is a trail, not a road. There's no hint of parallel tracks, just one not-quite-straight pathway through the trees. But it looks somehow as if it's used frequently, if not constantly. She grinned as Kevin turned his head every fifty yards or so, clearly checking to be sure she was still there, pedaling along a few feet behind him.

He pulled over and stopped, waving her up beside him. "Oy want you to lead from here on. It's not far now."

Look at him! He's hiding a secret. He's trying not to look excited, but if he were a puppy, his tail would be wagging hard enough to thump him in the ribs.

Maureen rode ahead, beginning to hear moving water, stream sounds reaching her above the small ticking noise of drying oak leaves, clinging to their branches and rubbing together in the light breeze that filtered through the woods.

After fifty yards, the pathway swung left and ended in a tiny meadow spangled with clumps of blue asters on a background of high grasses, goldenrod and bright yellow heleniums. But it was what lay beyond that drew her eye and her breath.

"Oh, Kevin, it's beautiful!"

Water fell less than six feet, in a shimmering curtain maybe twenty feet wide, dropping into a circular pool that seemed to be forty feet across, from the waterfall to a small beach of shale stones at the meadow's edge. The stream resumed at one edge of the pool, and chuckled away downhill. In the early afternoon sunshine, light struck the falling water and spun up little diamond-bright reflections among the concentric ripples.

Maureen was enchanted. She dropped at the edge of the meadow and sent shoes and socks flying, then waded in until she got her shorts wet.

"Come on, Kevin, you have to try this!"

"Oy was in it an hour ago," he said behind a huge grin, watching her delight animate her face.

"What do you mean?"

"Marine, this is moy bathtub, in warm weather anyways. Oy come here to get clean after a day's work, and to soak in the magic. Sometimes Oy think there's a stream fairy in charge here, cause this place is always so perfect. It just makes me feel better for bein' here, and when Oy'm soakin' in it, it just ain't possible for the world to be a better place." Kevin stopped suddenly. *I gotta install a filter between what I think and what I say. Why is that only a problem when I talk to Maureen?*

She clapped her hands in glee. "A naiad! Kevin, a naiad lives here! How wonderful!"

"Marine, Oy ain't sure what one a them is. But if it's a spirit that's in charge of good feelin's, then it's here, all right."

"Do you know that naiads are always female? Is it all right with you that a female guardian looks out for this pool?"

He was grinning again. "It's okay, Marine, in fact Oy think Oy can see her roight in front of me." He stopped again and blushed.

"Kevin, that's sweet, but I can't be a naiad, I'm wearing clothes!" He blushed again, and she knew he was imagining her standing there in water up to her knees, wearing nothing. *Oops, I didn't mean to invite that vision.*

"Have you got a name for this magic creature?" she asked, stepping out of the water and then standing statue-still. "Kevin, what have you done?"

He's squirming with happiness. Either that or he has to pee.

"Oy brought you here for a picnic, cause you said Oy didn't have any place of moy own. Well, this is moine, and here's the picnic."

She hadn't noticed the quilt spread on a patch of mowed grass, nor the hampers that held down two of its corners. The neck of a bottle poked out of one of them. "Are you hungry?" he asked, opening the other hamper.

"Yes, but mostly I'm stunned! What a lovely gesture."

They laid out plates and glasses and sat cross-legged on the quilt and ate chicken sandwiches and chips with a French onion dip. Kevin struggled with the bottle, and Maureen was pleased to see it was mead, just like the one she had served at her own dinner a few weeks back.

That proves how carefully he planned all this and how much trouble he went to, to get it right. Now, how should I react? Clearly, he wants to please me, and he has, but now what? Okay, back to the name thing, that's probably safe. No, dammit, let's face this for what it is.

"Kevin, is this a date?"

"Ooh, boy. Oy don't know, and that's the truth. Look, Oy want it ta be a date. Oy want ta impress you, cause yer smoile loights me up in ways that are strange to me. But the other truth is, Oy don't want ta push moyself on you, Oy don't want ta hurt you, and Oy don't want ta hurt moyself either. Oy never been so confused, and yet never so happy as watchin' you jump around this meadow loike a young deer in the summer sunshoine. So it could be a date, or it could just be a chance to share moy special place with a friend. Oy guess you hafta answer yer own question." He leaned back and raised a paper cup containing mead. "What is it you say? Sloncha!"

198

"That's pretty close," she smiled, and took a sip herself. *How do I manage this? Or can I? And do I want to? It's less than a year since Gene died, and I could never explain Kevin to his parents, and maybe not even to mine. Come to think of it, I'm not sure I can explain Kevin to me, but there really is something there, something strong. And this may be entirely the wrong place to think about all this. Whatever spirit rules here, it operates on emotions, not on logic. What an odd couple we are, if couple we are. He can set wonderful stages like this, but I think his own fears keep him from taking a truly overt step. If I'm going to be kissed, I'll have to start it myself. Is that what I want? Maureen, be honest with yourself, you don't want to be alone, and you see a good man here, way different from Gene, but with sensitivities even he didn't have.*

She got to her feet and drew him up beside her.

"Yes, this is a date. And a very, very nice one." She put her hands on either side of his face, and kissed him squarely on the lips. Kevin jerked and trembled, but he did not pull away. Eventually his hands went behind her waist and pulled her close.

He's not much of a kisser, judging by technique, but judging by enthusiasm, he's pretty good, and getting better by the second.

She broke the kiss and tucked her face into his shoulder, feeling those rough hands floating up and down her back, calluses snagging on the fabric of her shirt.

"Marine, Oy…"

"Shhh. Don't say anything. This is very fragile right now. Just hold me."

She twisted around within the circle of his arms, to face the waterfall. *He's so tense. He doesn't know whether to hold on or to let go.* Kevin's hands were folded across her beltline, and she moved her own hands over his as she leaned back into his chest. *He's so nervous, I can feel his Adam's apple wiggle. Good thing mine doesn't show.*

"Kevin, does this magic place of yours have a name?"

"Not yet. Do ya think we should name the pool and this naiad thing of yours separately, or should the place and the spirit be the same name?"

She looked at the pool, at how it shimmered and threw reflective sparkles into their eyes, and she could almost feel it tugging at her. *Almost? Not almost, definitely. I should be in it, I should bathe in the peace of it. I must. If he weren't here, I would. But he is here, he brought me here. This is not about sex, or is it?*

"Kevin, I have to go in the water." She pulled his hands apart, leaned her head back and kissed him on the cheek. "Close your eyes."

She didn't watch to see if he obeyed. Quickly, her shirt and bra fell away and she shimmied out of her shorts and the thong beneath it. As she entered the pool she called back over her shoulder, "You can join me if you'd like." *Finulla.* The word flowed into her mind as her body sank into the pool.

As the water reached her waist, she heard splashing noises behind her. With a brilliant smile, Maureen turned and held out her arms.

"She says her name is Finulla," Maureen called, as the naked and visibly aroused Kevin blushed and dropped into the shallow water to hide himself, duck-walking into deeper water. *Jeezum, she didn't even seem to notice! What does that mean?*

When the water was deep enough, he stood and faced her with an uncertain grin on his face. *What do I do now?* "Now, yer a naiad."

"Kevin, forget about being bare. Can't you just feel the peace and perfection?" She was glowing and wet from the neck down. Kevin, feeling more confident by the second, reached out with his left hand, his fingers curling behind her neck, and the side of his thumb tracing the line of her cheekbone. He reached out with his right forefinger, plucked a droplet of water from the tip of her breast and tasted it, while she giggled over his exaggerated lip-smacking.

Finulla ramped up the pool magic, swirling around their legs like a lazy cat. Maureen and Kevin stood entwined in the water, cheek to cheek from head to toe, and stopped thinking.

She rode alone back to her car, the bra, the thong and the socks tucked into a basket on her bike. And on her way home, she reflected on their last hour at the pond.

We sure got out of that pool in a hurry when we realized we couldn't finish what we'd started in the water.

They tumbled onto the quilt and embraced, the tension high between them. "Kevin, are you all right with this?" she asked, tracing the scar on his stomach. It didn't seem like the right time to ask about it.

"Yes, more than all right. Oy'm holdin' moy breath cause Oy'm scared that if Oy breathe, you'll melt away, and Oy'll be alone again."

"Silly, I won't melt, and I won't break if you hold me hard, and you don't have to be alone unless you want to be."

She reached down and touched him, marveling at the soft-hard heat of him, and how he reacted to the small movements of her fingers.

She rolled onto her back and pulled him on top of her. "I was going to tell you that I wasn't ready to have you inside me yet, but I think I am now."

Later, sweaty and spent, they went back into the pool to rinse and to hold each other in a rush of sweetness their rising passions had denied them earlier. Then, lying side by side to dry, they held hands, all shyness leached out of them.

"Ya know, everything changes now," he whispered, his breath shivering her ear.

"I know. We have to figure out how to deal with this new reality, because it's not going to be easy. We're the classic example of opposites attracting each other. We still don't know that we're compatible on all the levels that matter. I'd hate to think we've done this just because we got all steamed up by the pond-spirit."

"Oy think she had a hand in it," he grinned. "But yer roight, there's a lotta space between us in ways a livin'. Oy hope ya believe Oy done this in spoite a them difference, and not because of 'em."

"Kevin, it would be easy to say we did this because Finulla the naiad reduced our inhibitions and fanned our passions. But I don't believe that."

He propped himself up on one elbow and smiled down at her. *She's so beautiful, with her hair fanned out around her.* He moved to cup her breast gently, sliding her nipple into the hollow between his thumb and forefinger.

"Moy hand will never ferget the warmth and softness of you, but Oy don't want it ta be just a memory. Oy'm scared, Marine. We're loike a couple a bar magnets. At one end we attract each other strongly. But if ya switch ends, those two magnets don't wanta touch, and foight off bein' pushed together. Oy don't know which end is stronger, but if moy fears win Oy'll be alone again, and that's hard. But if you and yer Finulla spirit win, moy loife will change big-toime."

He took both her hands in his and smiled into her eyes. "Oy just don't know if Oy can manage them changes, when all moy loife experience is tellin' me ta run away, ta hoide from the loight. Can Oy be the new me that you think Oy am?"

That question lingered as Maureen drove home, having promised to meet Kevin at the pond again the next day.

Am I being selfish? Am I dragging Kevin out of his comfort zone just because I don't want to be alone? If we have a future, does it have to be on my terms only, or is there a middle way? Do I have to insist on a Kevin who has a bank account and a social security card and a real job?

I think he'll try that if I ask, but will the effort destroy him, will he morph into another kind of person who lacks the things I'm drawn to? Oh, crap, I'm just as confused as he is. Maybe more so.

Carl

Eldon pounced when the phone rang. "Yes, he's here, just a minute. Dad, it's for you," he called, managing to sound disappointed.

Is he waiting for a girl to call? He's not old enough, he's still playing with toy bulldozers, isn't he? No, not any more. Damn!

"Hello? Hi, Kevin, what's up? Yeah, I can get loose. Michelle's? Okay, give me twenty minutes. Yeah, see you then. Bye."

"Was that your project?" Helene asked.

"Honey, he's not a project. He's a friend who needs to talk. It sounds serious."

"Yeah, well the two of you are probably plotting your next macho vigilante stunt." Her voice went into announcer-mode as she continued: "In the never-ending fight against evil, crime and corruption in the metropolis of Nilesburgh, the Dynamic Duo, the Chief and the Invisible Man prepare to lash out against the dark side of human nature, and woe unto him whose criminal scheming falls afoul of their home-grown brand of Justice!"

"Very funny, Helene. But I think Kevin's got girl-friend trouble, nothing more complex than that."

"Honey, you dolt, there is nothing more complex than that. Is it about Maureen?"

"I'll tell you when I get back," he said. "But I think it is. I've never seen anyone so moony over a girl."

"I have," she smiled. "And you don't recall your own silly antics when you met me, do you? I'd be happy to refresh your memory."

"No thanks. Do you need anything while I'm out?" When it was eight miles to milk, no trip to the village was made without that question.

"Yes, a quart of whole milk, the one with the red cap on it, and a bunch of bananas. Get 'em a little on the green side, we still have a few left. Bye. Oh, and a ream of paper for the printer."

Kevin was sitting at one of Michelle's rickety deli tables, nursing a soft drink, and twirling a salt shaker absently in the circle of his palms. He was as animated as old Carl Cole was stony, staring morosely into his ever-present coffee. *Michelle says he looks like a smaller, sadder version of Jack Palance, with those high cheekbones, and that nose shaped by a fist. But how different Kevin is. He looks happy and confused at the same time. That girl has quite an effect on him.* "Hi Kev."

The weathered face split open in a huge grin, and Kevin jumped up and shook hands. "Thanks for comin. Yawnta drink?"

"Yeah, but I'll get it, you sit back down and relax."

Kevin twiddled the salt shaker some more, managing to tip it over.

"All right, my friend, what's all this about?"

He grinned, but a little furrow remained in his sun-creased brow. "It's about Marine," he said softly with a remarkably Gallic shrug. "Moy whole loife is about Marine these days. Remember me? Oy'm the guy who used to say a simple loife is a better one. That ain't true any more. A loife with Marine in it is a way better one, but man, it ain't simple."

Ralph leaned back and watched emotions scuffle for primacy on Kevin's face. There were no emotions at all on the face of a man staring into a coffee cup at another table.

"When we talked the night of Maureen's dinner, I thought you had decided to take it slow and easy, and see what developed."

"Oy did, but man, it developed loike one a them old Polaroids, ya know? All blank, and then in a minute, all colored up."

"Go on."

"Today me and Marine went boikin' to a secret place Oy know." He looked Ralph in the eye, and his face reddened. *Well, well! Look at that. Even now, he's wondering how to tell me whatever it is he wants to say.* After a little more salt-shaker twisting, Kevin took a deep breath and went on. "And now we ain't strangers no more, in any way."

"Kevin, I'm cheering for you, and for Maureen too, but is this a case of 'be careful what you wish for, because you may get it'?"

"Jeezum Crow, man, Oy don't know. I wanta make a loife with Marine, but loike Oy told her today, Oy don't know if Oy can be the me that she sees when she looks at me."

Ralph nodded. "I think I've got the idea. You don't want her to become the invisible woman, but you're not sure you can become the visible man." He glanced at Kevin for confirmation, and got it in a nod. "So why don't you take one step, and see what happens. How about getting a driver's license? Then you won't have to use that bike, it must be as old as you are."

Kevin's eyes crinkled into a grin. "It's older. Noineteen fifty-two, the boike service guy said the last time Oy bent the frame. That boike is me, in a lotta ways. But yeah, Oy could start with a droiver's loicense."

"What will you do about an address?"

"There's a post office box number for the trust that pays moy land taxes. Did ya know about that? Oy don't tell nobody about that, cause Billy told me not to." He looked over at Cole, but the old man was lost in whatever far place his thoughts took him.

Ralph was flabbergasted. "You have a trust fund? And Billy Brophy knows about it?"

"Yeah, he writes the checks, but ya can't tell."

"Well, I'll be damned."

"Yain't done nothin' that bad, have ya?"

Dinner

In the late afternoon Maureen walked around her house, nursing a tiny glass of mead.

It reminds me of him, of how sweet he was today, and I guess from now on it always will. Oh, this is too good to keep secret, but who can I tell? I'm sure he doesn't want the word to get around, and I suppose I don't either, so that lets Judy out, she might as well be a radio station.

And I can't call Mom, it's too soon. You need a big sister, kiddo. How about Helene? No, she's not the secret-sharing type, not the real secret secrets, anyway.

She snapped her fingers and smiled, doing a little swirl step on her way to the phone.

"Edith? Hi, it's Maureen. Listen, Edith, do you ever do anything on the spur of the moment, just give in to a whimsy?"

"Not often enough, I'd say. My, child, you sound all atwitter. Is something wrong?"

"Wrong?" she almost sang. "Oh, far from wrong. I'll tell you about it over supper. May I pick you up in twenty minutes?"

"Well, I don't know," the older woman said.

That's just pro forma. She's intrigued, as I would be. "Whimsy now, spur-of-the-moment, remember?"

"Make it half five, dearie. Thirty minutes to get these old bones moving, and to change. I've not been out to dinner in such a long time."

Maureen navigated both the traffic and Edith Averill's questions without crashing, all the way to St. Albans. But she couldn't hide from the twinkling gaze the old woman focused on her as they settled into a booth in the city's best restaurant.

"It's a celebration, then. And I know what you're marking. I may be old, but I'm not dead."

"I have no idea what you're talking about," Maureen said, trying to meet those eyes.

"Rubbish, dearie, rubbish I say. I know the look on your face, I used to wear it myself when I'd sneak back home after a tryst with Jeremy. You've been out snogging and shagging, haven't you?"

"I don't know those words." *But I have a pretty good idea what they mean. And oh, boy, have I ever!*

"I don't know the American slang for it, and those words are probably crude anyway, but you've had your knickers pulled off you, and you enjoyed every minute of it," Mrs. Averill said with unshakeable certainty.

Maureen blushed a little. "Actually, I pulled them off myself." She went on to explain how on a perfect day, she'd found the perfect place, describing the pond below the waterfall, and the tiny meadow that faced it.

"Oh, my good Lord!" The old woman gasped, and took a quick sip of wine, her face pale and then flushed.

"Edith, what's the matter?" Maureen was concerned that the old lady might have a seizure right in front of her.

"It's all right, Maureen. It's just that an old memory came flooding back and hit me in the face, something I haven't thought about in decades."

She leaned forward and took both of Maureen's hands in hers, in a very strong grip. And there was something vulnerable in the gray eyes that stared out way beyond where Maureen was sitting in the booth. "I've been there," she said, remembering as a small smile lifted the corners of her mouth. "Larking about starkers all over that meadow like a wanton doxy, and jumping in the water with Jeremy. We only went there once, and I think it was as close as we ever got to a true reconciliation. Ah, it was wonderful, a noble effort. But the poison between us was stronger." She clutched Maureen's hands even tighter. "I even thought there was a spell on that pond, one that reduced inhibitions, because I've surely never acted that way before or since. My, my, you talk about spontaneous and spur-of-the-moment, it's almost as if a benign fairy rules the place, like in Shakespeare's plays. Did you feel anything like that?" She whispered the last words.

"Her name is Finulla," Maureen whispered back. She didn't think Edith Averill's eyes could open as wide as they did then.

"So, it wasn't just me!" She gasped, and thrust out her famous chin.

"How did you learn her name, when I never got a clue?"

"I don't know. I was in the water up to my waist, and the word just came into my mind. I turned to tell him, but I think he was so embarrassed that I could see his penis that he never heard a word I said." She grinned at the memory of the mortified Kevin dunking himself.

"But I still can't figure out why you got such a clear signal, and I got only the emotional stimulus."

Maureen reached across the table and recaptured the hands that had just gripped hers. "I may be way off, here, Edith, but perhaps it's because Kevin and I were building something, while you were trying to repair something that was essentially broken."

"Could be, my dear, but I just realized something. That's the first time I've heard the word Kevin in this entire conversation. I've heard "we," and you've said "he," and "us," but never a name. Now what should we think about that?"

Maureen's face showed the arrival of clouds, not very heavy ones, but clouds nonetheless. "Oh," she breathed. "Is that evasion? I don't mean it to be. Am I ashamed that it's Kevin instead of a more polished person? Oh, I hope not. I do hope not." She gazed back into her day, and then leaned forward with a smirk. "You know, Edith, I'm glad I don't have that condition, what is it? Oh, short term memory loss. Because my short-term memories are so good!"

"You're hugging yourself, you shameless woman! Let me tell you, my long-term memories are pretty good too, when I allow myself to isolate them. Especially the ones about a magical afternoon at the waterfall."

They both looked at each other, noting the high color in the other's face, and laughed in the furtive manner of conspirators everywhere.

"Now, my girl," said Maureen as they clinked glasses. "We've got to find you a boyfriend. You're already dressing better and looking better, and getting out a bit. Actually, Edith, you make pretty good bait for the right kind of guy."

There was that jaw, and there was that wagging finger. "You stay out of my space, I think that's what they say here. I'll live vicariously and in delight through what's happening to you, but don't you dare try to drag me along. There aren't any Kevins for me, and the sooner you come to terms with that, the better."

"Oh, my," Maureen said in a mock-fearful voice. "You know you can't scare me like you used to scare Judy, so stop growling. By the way, Judy is seeing that nice young sergeant on the police force. Do you know him? Cooney Jacobs? Actually his name is Arnold, or Arnie, but Kevin says he hardly answers to that because almost everybody calls him Cooney. He has these dark smudges under his eyes, you see, like a raccoon. Tell you what. Come with me to the next Crime Commission meeting. It'll get you out of your house, and I'd enjoy having you there. I'd like to know what you think of the work we're trying to do."

"No promises, and why do I think you're trying to Shanghai me into doing something I'll regret?"

Billy

"Billy, Oy need some help."

"Well, you don't say that very often, Kevin, what's up"

Kevin squirmed a bit on the not-very comfortable chair Billy kept in his office for visitors. The clerk had learned that if you made visitors comfortable, they stayed, and you didn't get much done.

"This is not easy for me, Billy. You know Oy've been keepin' moy head down for a long toime. But now Oy'm thinkin' about some changes. One a the ways to do that is to get a droiver's loicense, and Ralph said that would be a good place to start. Well, Oy can't get one. Can't prove Oy exist. No birth certificate, no passport, nothin' the DMV will accept as proof of identity. Oy don't know how to look for what's missin'."

Billy Brophy leaned back in his own comfortable chair, and looked hard at Kevin. "Does this have anything to do with that widow, Maureen?"

He saw agitation and "gotcha" in Kevin's face, and didn't push the issue. "Kevin, what happened when you went to the DMV? I gotta know that before I can say if I can help you."

"Well, Oy roide over there, and it takes more than an hour, and Oy get in with this lady that does that stuff, and she says, where's your current license? And Oy says Oy ain't got one. And she says, well where's your passport? And Oy says Oy ain't got one. And she says, well, where's your birth certificate? And Oy says, well my mama told the school people we never got no paper from the county."

Billy saw his face reflecting disgust and frustration.

"And she says, well, Mister Beaujolais, if you can't prove you exist, we can't issue you a license. And she starts pushin' papers around on her desk, and so Oy give it up and came here." He leaned forward and looked as agitated as Billy had ever seen him. "Jeezum Crow, Billy, prove Oy exist? Sumbitch, Oy'm sitting roight in front a this lady, and Oy'm thinkin', if Oy smack you, you'll know Oy exist. But Oy never. Oy just folded up and come back here. Oy just don't know what to do next."

Jeezum, he spends thirty years hiding from the daylight, and now when he tries to get out in it, the bureaucracy won't let him, That's kind of ironic. "Let's see if we can find a starting place. Tell me what you know."

"Mama always said Oy was born on May 5, 1964. You remember the old birthin' woman, Shirley Cota? Yeah, well she was there, and she phoned it in to the County."

Billy was making notes. "What was your father's name, and your mother's maiden name?"

Kevin pulled up an image of the small gravestone in the country cemetery. "Rejean Beaujolais, and Lisette Paquette. Mama said they got married in 1956."

"Well," said Billy. "I make no promises, but I hafta go over there tomorrow, and I'll get into the Vital Records office and see what I can find. The best hope is that if the county screwed up, we can get a court to fix it, and the DMV will accept a court order that certifies a person's identity. I should know something in a week or so."

Billy was looking up Vermont's identity document regulations when he was interrupted.

"You've got a long distance call, very long," said Alice. Alice fended off the trivial stuff, so Billy picked up the phone with his usual gruff "Billy."

"Mr. Brophy?" The very British voice had what Billy thought was a snooty undertone that suggested a hope that he wasn't really Mr. Brophy.

"Speaking," he said, curiosity rising.

"Mortimer Sloan-Watson, here. I'm senior clerk for a firm of solicitors in Ashford, a city in Kent, in the southeast of England. I'm engaged in tying up the loose ends in an inheritance case. One of the potential heirs has gone missing, and there are little indicators that you might have the records of her death. The name was Edith Wellington, and she left here for the States in late 1945."

"I see," said Billy, who didn't. "And why do you think I should know something about this woman?"

"Well, sir, there are records of a civil marriage here, a marriage the family never condoned or recognized, you know, and the alleged groom was one Jeremy Averill of your, what, village?"

Snotty little turd. Don't you slime that British superiority all over me, asshole. "There is an Edith Averill living here, Mr. Sloan, a widow. And by the way, I've seen the marriage document, and it is binding, no matter what her family may say."

"I say, it's Sloan-Watson, old boy." *Prick!* "Are you telling me," the prick went on, "that there is a living heiress to the Mynx Hill property, and that she's a resident of your community?"

"Yup, that's what Oy'm sayin'," Billy said, allowing his accent to thicken up in the hope that it would annoy the man on the other end of the line.

"Mr, ahh, Brophy, is it? I say, you've complicated a routine transfer of assets to one of the collateral descendants. Are you certain you are correct, sir?"

Billy had had about enough. "Lissen, clerk, Oy'm a Clerk too, a duly elected official put in office by noine thousand people to moind a part a the public business of this Town. Now foind yer pen and write this down, Jack. Edith Averill is aloive and well and living in Noilesburgh, and if you stop actin' loike a foireplug, Oy'll tell you how to reach her."

"A foreplug. I fail to understand, Mr. Brophy."

"Foireplug, Mortimer, foireplug. One a them foire hose connection things that dogs love to piss on."

Two minutes later, after some spluttering on the other end of the line, Billy put down the phone and yelled out to the room where lawyers ran down land records. "You know, Alice, some days are better than other days. Remind me I said that the next time I have a bad one. No wonder we won the freakin' Revolutionary War. I hope that bastard's as ugly as an old bulldog chewin' on a wasp!"

Maureen caught herself making mistakes at the bank, seeing Kevin's face in Andrew Jackson's on the twenty dollar bills that moved across her counter. *Judy's giving me funny looks, and she's so perceptive about personal things, she'll guess before noon why I'm so chirpy and moony. Oh, well, there may have been a better day in my life than Saturday, but I can't think of one, unless it was Sunday.*

"Oh, yes, Mrs. Archer, that was twenties and fifties you wanted? Certainly. *Twenties and fifties. Fifties for twenties. Stop it, Maureen.* There you go, and thanks for coming in." *What a long day this is.*

"Maureen, Maureen, you'll never guess! Never!" Edith Averill was dancing across the floor toward her window, bad knees and all.

"Guess what?" *I've never seen her so animated before. Something pretty nice must have happened, and I think I'm about to find out.*

"I'm the heir to Mynx Hill! I've just heard from the family solicitors that I've inherited the family estate in Ashford. Imagine that, after all those years of being cut off, I out-lived all of them and the land is mine! The man said they were doing due diligence. What's that, Maureen?"

"It's tying up loose ends, dotting Is and crossing Ts. I suspect you were an oops to them, my friend. Now they'll have to deal with someone who is inconveniently alive."

"Serves 'em right." Maureen smiled to see the chin jut out, and a combative look in the old woman's eyes. "I didn't like the way they spoke to me on the phone. They were rude, and I know something about rude, in fact I'm an expert, or I used to be." Her smile was a bit rueful.

"Don't you knuckle under an inch. What do you do now? I hear the British inheritance taxes are ferocious," Maureen asked.

"Well, when I finally got the senior partner on the phone, he said that some of the estate would have to be sold off to meet those taxes, but that there's a firm of developers sniffing around, and a lot of the land is better suited to housing than to agriculture. Things have changed there since I left, and there are now leases for commercial concerns, and other rentals. The man said the property is producing quite a nice income. As to what happens now, I have to go over there and sign some papers." She put her old pocketbook on the counter at Maureen's window and leaned forward. "Oh, Maureen, come with me! I'll need a sharp set of eyes and a good mind for all those details. And I'd love to show you my old home."

"Edith, I can't just up and leave. What about the bank? What about Kevin? I couldn't possibly…" *Yes you can, silly goose. You never took any bereavement leave, and you've been here long enough to qualify for some vacation. Besides, there's the robbery.*

Maureen nearly laughed out loud when she realized she was shoving her lower jaw out in a gesture reminiscent of Mrs. Averill in battle mode.

"Wait here," she said. "I'll be right back."

"It's a done deal," Judy told the old woman, as she watched Maureen stride into the manager's office.

Two minutes later, without having sat down, she was back.

"You have to come with me to tell Kevin," she grinned. I've got three weeks whenever I want it. When do we leave, Edith?"

"Whee!' Edith chirped, and then clapped a hand to her mouth. "Oh, my, do people still say that? Come on, Kevin's repairing my porch railing this morning, we can catch him now. Judy, I'm borrowing your colleague for a half hour. Tell the manager it's lunch, if he has the courage to inquire. Come on dear, grab your hat. Oh, bother, there I go again, women don't wear hats any more. Half of life is adjusting to change, isn't it, and the most awkward changes are the little ones."

Maureen laughed. "Judy, I'll be out with this philosopher for a short time. I'll have my cell phone."

"Maureen," Judy called as they went through the door. "Tell Kevin I said he's for this."

Calvin

Amy Shipley had occasional days on which the down side of library management was eclipsed in a glow of professional satisfaction.

This was one of those days. She didn't care, for a few minutes, that there were chronic vacancies on the Library Advisory Board, that the Town Manager was nickeling her budget to death, or that bodice-ripper novels were growing wings in rising numbers and flying off the paperback shelf.

That funny little bicycle man had come in when the library was empty. *Did he time it that way, or is it just that the place is empty often enough so that he just lucked into a lull?*

"Oy'm pretty good with the numbers," the man had begun.

Kevin, that's his name, what's his other name? Jim will know, they're on that crime committee together.

"But Oy ain't so good with letters. Oy sorta outgrew school, and some a that stuff was just off moy path in them days. But not now." The man, Kevin, glanced around with a wary look.

Is he scared of the books, or is he scared that someone may see him in here?

"Oy want ta learn ta read," he whispered.

He's so uncomfortable. It must take a lot of motivation for him to come in here as a full-grown man, and admit to such a basic weakness.

She put on a professional smile that Kevin recognized. *It's just like the lady at the DMV in St. Albans, she's not going to help.*

"First," the woman was saying, "we have to figure out where

you are on the scale of read/not-read. How far did you get with reading in school?"

Kevin shuffled a bit and looked ill at ease. *Right. Find the perfect pigeonhole, lady.*

Amy led the way into a separate alcove, where the book covers were bright and the print was large.

"There's Dick and Jane," he smiled, pointing at some frayed books that probably should have been thrown out years ago. If the budget for purchases had been adequate, they'd be gone. "Oy got them pretty good, but then things got hard at home, and Oy got lost a little." He looked at her and shrugged. "Maybe more than a little."

He's just stating a fact. He's not expressing shame for having this problem, only regret. How interesting!

The librarian smiled, a better one this time. "Listen, Mr., ahhh…"

"Kevin," said Kevin.

"Well, Kevin, this is a lot easier when you're six or seven, because then we just toss you in and you flail around until one day, Bingo! You get it. In your case, I think we can start with patterns that little kids can't yet see, and go from there." The smile was back again, looking really genuine this time. "Don't be discouraged if this seems a little basic. It'll be a good refresher, and will oil up some old memories that may be a bit rusty. I'll give you a dictionary so you can work out the ideas that are held in the words you don't know. Remember that a word has to make sense in the sentence where it lives. So most of the guesses you'll make will be the right ones, Just sound out the letters, and see if they sound like a word you've heard."

She plunked down three books on the counter, and swallowed hard when she got no address, no phone number, and go through Billy Brophy to find him, or maybe leave word at the Iron Skillet.

Kevin walked out with the unfamilar weight of books in under his arm, promising himself that he would work hard.

"Hey, Billy, ya gotta minute?"

Well, when you have a gas pump nozzle stuck in your truck, you have time, a little anyway. "Yeah, what's up, Kevin?"

"Oy wanta put electric in that house that Uncle and Hannah left me. How do we do that?"

"Well, Kevin, you may have to have to expose yourself a little to get that done. Let me talk to the CVPS guys, and you know Charlie O'Malley, don't you from down at the Iron Skillet?"

"Round-faced guy, laughs a lot?"

"Yeah, well he's a master electrician, and he may be able to wire it without tearing everything out. I'll get back to you." *Jeezum, the more he comes out of the shadows, the more work it is for me. How the Hell did that happen?*

Billy Brophy walked into the Vital Records office in the Franklin County Courthouse.

"Hey, Billy. Long time," said the Assistant Clerk in charge of births, deaths and marriages.

"Hey, Margo, how ya doin'?"

"Not too bad. What brings you to my little backwater?"

Billy hesitated. File clerks were a protective bunch, and he needed unruffled feathers on this one. "Margo, I hope you can help me straighten out a very tangled life. I've got a guy in my town in his thirties, who can't get a driver's license because the state wants to see documents that prove his identity, and he can't produce the right ones. So I need to look into a birth record from May of 1964."

Without batting an eye, she said, "Oh, you're likely to find all kinds of oddities from back then. That's back in old Frankie Forgan, Senior's time. Frankie once entered a death record that showed the woman was 237 years old. We find that stuff every month or so, until he finally had a heart attack in 1968.

"Well, try this one," said Billy, feeling somewhat encouraged. At least the incumbent clerk was accustomed to finding old errors. "Calvin Beaujolais, May 5, 1964. Son of Rejean Beaujolais and Lisette Paquette. Can you look that up?"

"Sure, let's have a look. '64 wasn't one of Frankie's better years, especially after he was rejected as a delegate to the Democratic convention."

Billy watched as the long file drawers slid open. The clerk was fast.

"Okay, nothing on the 5th. But Frankie was notoriously imprecise about dates. I think you're going to like the 6th. Calvin Roosevelt Baudelaire, white male, Nilesburgh, born to Ray John Beaudelaire and Lisa Parquet, husband and wife."

"Jeezum," Billy breathed. "No wonder the poor bastard couldn't be found. Old Frankie gave him the wrong date, the wrong name and the wrong parents. Pretty much a clean sweep," he said, shaking his head.

"Well, it was before my time, of course, but the old clerks used to tell me, when I found stuff like this, that Frankie Forgan was only reliable on Thursdays when he was broke."

"Does this mean Oy can get a loicense?" Kevin asked, when Billy told him.

"I don't know, Calvin," said Billy, trying out the sound of it, and deciding it didn't fit. So did Kevin.

"Billy, Oy remember bein' called Calvin when Oy was too young fer school. But Oy been Kevin for a long toime, and besoides that's how Marine knows me. Just call me Kevin. Now, how about the loicense?"

"Well, you'll have to get a lawyer to ask the Superior Court for an order that establishes your identity legally. Have you got a lawyer?"

"Billy, yer kiddin' me, roight? Oy can't even name one. It's loike askin' me if Oy know any serial killers."

Billy laughed. "Most of 'em aren't that bad, and I know just the guy. I think he'll do it for free as a matter of family honor." He watched relief shine through the furrows on Kevin's face. "Now, what have you heard from Maureen?"

"She gave me a cell phone before she left, and she calls every day to say she misses me, and Oy say some mushy stuff right back."

It's amazing how transparent he is. His face shows everything he's thinking. I guess I always knew that, but this Maureen thing is hitting him like nothing ever has. I hope she doesn't hurt him, cause right now he's all bare wires and no insulation.

"They're havin' a great toime," Kevin was saying, "and they'll be home in a week. "Marine says the legal stuff is going well for Mrs. Averill, but she says she can't wait to get back to me and Finulla."

"Who's Finulla?" *There he goes again, coloring up. I've never seen him like this.*

"Oh, just a friend that's taken a big loikin' to Marine in the last few weeks. Oy think she spends the winters away, like a lotta folks from here."

Marine

At the airport in Burlington, some of the passengers who emerge from planes walk along a corridor that makes a left after the security screens. That's as far as meeters and greeters can go toward the planes, and that's where a man sat alone, positioned so he could see as far down that corridor as possible.

He wasn't a patient waiter, rising frequently to check out a partial sighting behind other passengers, and then sitting again in disappointment.

They'll be last, I'm sure. Helene said the law of averages doesn't work at airports. Baggage or people, whatever you wait for is always last.

But they weren't. This time, the figures he spotted behind people who were simply in the way did not turn out to be unwanted unknowns.

"Marine!" he shouted, not caring that he looked just like those idiots who jump up and down on the outdoor set of the *Today Show*. Kevin didn't know anything about the *Today Show*.

What he did know was that he'd been waiting for weeks for this moment and here she was, running toward him.

If they'd been explosive the force of their collision would have wrecked the terminal. He swung her in circles, while she hugged his neck, and anyplace would do to plant a kiss.

"Well," the acerbic voice penetrated their effort to lock out the world.

"Don't you dare greet me that way, young man, or parts of me would just come off and fly all over this airport."

"Would ya settle for a hug?" Kevin grinned, releasing Maureen and reaching for Edith Averill.

"If you must," she said, failing to make it sound grumbly. "My goodness, that was chaste, what a contrast," she twittered as they moved toward the baggage claim.

"Kevin, I've missed you so," Maureen said, her fingers entwined in his. "What are you doing here, I mean I know why you're here, but how did you get here?"

"Ralph and Helene drove me down here, and Oy'm going to droive you back."

Maureen stopped in the middle of the concourse and stared at him. "But Kevin, you don't have a license. You can't do that!"

"Aha!" he crowed. "But Oy got a learner's permit. Look! Oy can droive in the company of a loicensed droiver, and that's you. Really, I been droivin' since Oy was eleven, maybe a bit before on tractors."

"But how…."

"You'll hear all about it on the way home. You think Oy just been sittin' on moy keester since you been gone? Now let's get those bags and get on the shuttle to the parkin' lot."

Maureen and Kevin insisted on putting Edith Averill in the right front seat, but before they reached the highway she made him stop, and changed seats with Maureen.

"It's bad enough that he looks at you more than he looks at the road, but it's worse when he turns right the way round to do it."

She's got harder to understand since she went back home. I hope it's not catchin', I'd hate to hear Maureen start talkin' like that."

The women spent the rest of the drive chattering about their adventures in Ashford, most of which Kevin had already heard on the phone. He didn't want to think about how big that cell phone's bill would be for twenty days of lengthy conversations.

The late afternoon sun was slanting down onto Oak Street when they carried Edith Averill's bags, including some new ones bought on the trip, upstairs and into the house. More hugs, and even a tentative peck on the cheek for Kevin. *Well, I did shave today, but not for her.*

"Kevin, I want to go to Finulla."

"Roight now? Marine, it's gettin' dark soon, and it may be chilly in that water."

"Oh, come on, I've missed it so much, and I've missed you so much, I just can't wait."

"Ya may hafta wait a little, we can't get there by car, ya know. We'll have to walk in."

Maureen grinned, her face as alive as he'd seen it in his memory.

"I won't be walking, silly, I'll be running, and I don't think you can keep up with me."

"Is that a dare? Do you really think you can outrun me in moy own woods?"

"Maybe, maybe not. After all, you will have an advantage. I'm going to be dropping stuff on the way in!" She gave him a saucy look and started with her sweater, long before they reached the turnoff on the back road.

She won, plunging headlong into the pool ahead of Kevin, who was still struggling with his pants.

"Ooh, you were right. It's biting cold. My ankles feel like they're in a vice. I need you to warm me up."

"You can see Oy always rise to a challenge," Kevin grinned and went into the water with a series of not very Kevin-like squeaks, as the cold water chilled him. Then he reached for her, and the cold went away.

Later, their skins shaking with goosebumps, they stood in the little meadow as the cold renewed its hold on them.

"I guess that was pretty dumb," she said. "I should have at least brought my clothes with me, but most of 'em are scattered back there for a quarter of a mile. Funny how easy it is to get carried away around you."

Kevin took one of her hands between his two and chafed it. She didn't tell him that the friction from his calluses was somewhat less than helpful.

"Marine, Oy got another surprise for you. Just come with me."

"But Kevin, we're naked."

His laugh echoed off the waterfall. "That didn't bother you much a few minutes ago. Now come on, it's not far." They walked along a path she hadn't seen before, one very much like the one that led to the pond.

Maureen saw lights between the trees and shrank back. "Kevin, somebody lives here! Suppose they see us?"

He laughed again, wiping spilled glee out of his eyes. "Marine, Oy can already see you, and a lovely soight you are, too. Now come on, we don't have to freeze."

Her mouth hung open and she gasped, but not from the cold. "You mean you live here? How come I didn't know that?" She pounded on his arm until he winced.

"Hey, wild woman, beat me up later. In the meantoime," he said, still leading her toward the house, "Step up on the porch, and sink yer cute little ass into that."

"Kevin, it's a hot tub!"

"Yup."

"But how did you do it?"

He sank into the churning water beside her, letting the jets massage the cold out of his skin.

"There's some changes goin' on, Marine, ever since you left. If you recall there wasn't much fuss from me about you goin', cause Oy needed the toime. No, just lissen for a few minutes, and then we'll get somethin' to eat. By the way, you're not goin' to yer house tonoight, if all goes well."

He took her hand while the bubbling water murmured around them.

He's got that cute crinkle-eye thing going on, but he's so quiet.

"We been thinkin' that our new relationship would force me outa moy proivacy, and wonderin' whether that could work. Or at least that's the way Oy was thinkin'. But Oy spent the last three weeks learnin' the difference between alone and lonely. Oy was always alone, but Oy didn't know Oy was lonely until Oy'd get up every mornin', knowin' it would be a Marineless day. And waitin' empty until that phone would ring at noight."

She started to speak and he hushed her with a fingertip and pulled her into the hollow of his shoulder.

"It only took me a few days to figure out that fallin' in love with you, Jeezum, did Oy really say that? Yes Oy did, Oy love you,

Marine, for now and for always, shhh, just lissen. So the thing is, these changes are not forcing me to come into the loight, they're allowing me. It's loike you're a springboard to a new loife for me. Oy hope you understand, you're givin' me a powerful reason to stop hoidin' and stand in the loight next to you. Now that means sluffin' off some a the things Oy usta do to stay outa soight. It koinda started with the loicense. Ralph told me before you left that it was one step Oy could take towards the dayloight. Then they wouldn't give me one, cause they said Oy can't prove Oy'm aloive. So Billy Brophy, you know him, the Town Clerk. Good man, Billy. So he went over there to St. Albans and found out that the old record clerk had screwed up recordin' moy birth. What would you think of Calvin Beaujolais? That's moy real name."

Maureen nestled closer and said, "Hmm. Calvin. Calvin Beaujolais. Kevin Beaujolais. Okay, Calvin, do you mind if I call you Kevin anyway? It just seems more like you. I don't know who Calvin is, but I know Kevin, and the more I do, the more I want to."

"Good, cause that's the way Oy think about it too. And one more thing. Oy know your name is Mow-reen, and that's what other folks call you. But Oy first heard Marine, and to me that's yer name. Not quoite roight but there it is. Besoides, Oy connect it to water, not to a military force."

Maureen, don't get mushy. How lucky you are! Sometimes you don't want to pull the lid off a garbage can, because you know what you reveal will stink. But when Kevin's lid comes off, the more he reveals the sweeter. And I have a feeling there are still a few surprises.

"I like being called Marine, but only by you."

"Good. So Kevin and Marine go on into whatever waits for us, is that it?"

"Yes, and what an adventure, even looking back from here."

"Well, there's a couple more things. When we get insoide, Oy'm gonna show ya the books Oy got outa the town library. Sit still and lissen. The lady in charge there is Jim Shipley's woife, and she says Oy'm devourin' her remedial readin' books. Oy looked it up. Devourin' means eatin' somethin' up, and with a good appetite. So the news is, Oy'm readin' up to Grade Foive now, and she says by next week Oy could be six or seven."

"Oh, Kevin, that's wonderful!" She squirmed around until she got him in a full body hug.

"Careful, Oy pumped this water outa the pond, There's some Finulla in it. Now before we get carried away, here's the only two promises Oy'm gonna make. One, Oy will love and cherish you forever. Oy looked up cherish too. Two, when Aiee am around you, Aiee will tryee to trade Oy for Aiee."

Maureen knew she was crying, but it didn't seem important, maybe just another symptom of the flood tide of emotions pouring through her. "Kevin, you don't have to do that. If I were put off by the way you talk, it would have showed up long ago, not now."

"It ain't fer you, Marine, it's fer me. Sometoimes folks look down on people that talk in the old Vemawnt country way, and Aiee don't want anybody lookin' down on the man you're with."

After that, words didn't matter very much, and not all the ripples in the hot tub were caused by the jets.

Epilogue

THE NILESBURGH NUGGET, APRIL 14, 1999
Homeowner Kills Armed Burglar

(Nilesburgh) Convicted felon Archibald Tourangeau, 27, of Nilesburgh, was shot to death last night during his second break-in at a home on Hillside Street in Nilesburgh.

Tourangeau had been released from prison on parole three days earlier, after serving time for drug dealing, aggravated assault, and a prior armed burglary at the same address.

"We picked this guy up here several years ago, and we think he was trying to intimidate the family that lived here back then," said Acting Nilesburgh Police Chief Arnold Jacobs.

"Apparently he believed the Willard family still lived here, but then Archie never was very good at the headwork. He blamed young Gordon Willard for an altercation that led to the loss of his ear.

"But after Leonard died, his wife sold the house and moved to Fairfax, and young Gordie joined the Air Force. I hear he's serving in Kuwait."

Homeowner William H. McGreevy said he was watching television when he heard his dog fighting in the next room. McGreevy said he took a shotgun out of a cabinet.

"I loaded up and went in there, and this guy had a gun out and was aiming at my dog, so I shot him."

The dog, a 95-pound Golden Retriever named Guinness, was unhurt.

Tourangeau was pronounced dead at the scene of massive head trauma. Acting Chief Jacobs said the State's Attorney would review the evidence in the case, but that it was unlikely that McGreevy would be prosecuted.

A source close to the investigation who requested anonymity put it this way to *The Nilesburgh Nugget*: "The chances that a jury in this county would convict anyone of murder for shooting a man who breaks into his house with a gun, are just too small to measure."

The next day, police removed Walter Tourangeau from Hillside Street after he threatened to emasculate McGreevy with a linoleum knife.

That same night, police arrested the senior Tourangeau for attempting to set fire to McGreevy's house.

"This is a very troubled family," said Acting Chief Jacobs.

THE NILESBURGH NUGGET, MAY 3, 2000
Beaujolais-McGuckin Vows

(Nilesburgh) Calvin (Kevin) Beaujolais and Maureen O'Rourke McGuckin, both of Nilesburgh, were united in matrimony Saturday in a civil ceremony held at the home of Nilesburgh Selectboard Chairman Randolph E. Montgomery, III.

The bride's attendants were Mrs. Judy Jacobs and Mrs. Helene Montgomery, both of Nilesburgh, and Mrs. Edith Averill of Mynx Hill, Ashford, Kent, England, and Nilesburgh.

Groomsmen were Billy Brophy, Chief Arnold Jacobs of the Nilesburgh Police Department, and the Best Man, Randolph Montgomery.

The double-ring ceremony was conducted on the lawn by Justice of the Peace Steve Delaney, a distant relative of the bride.

Mrs. Beaujolais is employed by the North Country

Bank, where she serves as loan officer in the Nilesburgh branch. Her husband is employed by the Nilesburgh Town School District, where he serves as Buildings and Grounds supervisor.

After a honeymoon trip to an undisclosed location, the couple will make their home in Nilesburgh.

THE NILESBURGH NUGGET, MARCH 27, 2001
Landmark restaurant sold

(Nilesburgh)) The Iron Skillet Diner, long a gathering place for working Nilesburghers, has been sold to a group headed by local contractor Albert Jackson. Retiring owners Al and Millie Harmon said they were sure the new management would retain the Skillet's unique role in the town.

Jackson said the kitchen staff will not change, but that he'll need a new morning waitress, since Suzie Cassell is being promoted to manager. When asked about rumors that he and Cassell are romantically linked, Jackson said, "Suzie and I have been friends for years. Just good friends."

THE NILESBURGH NUGGET, MAY 6, 2001
Nilesburgh woman inherits British Estate

(Nilesburgh) The late Edith Averill of Nilesbburgh and Ashford, Kent, England, whose death in England was reported last month in this newspaper, has left her entire estate to Nilesburgh resident Maureen McGuckin Beaujolais.

Mrs. Beaujolais, who said Mrs. Averill was a very special friend, told this reporter she was gobsmacked by the news. The British word apparently means flabbergasted or astonished.

The British property, called Mynx Hill, now consists of 600 acres of English countryside, part of which is under long-term lease, developed as commercial enterprises or residential neighborhoods.

Mrs. Beaujolais said that when she went to England with Mrs. Averill several years ago as the older woman claimed her family holdings, she co-signed a document for the lawyers. Mrs. Beaujolais said she thought she was signing as a witness, but has now learned that by that signature she became a co-owner of the property, and is now sole owner, with no additional legal steps necessary.

"She never told me, and I know that somehow she's aware of my amazement and shock."

In addition to the British holdings, Mrs. Beaujolais' new inheritance includes a home on Oak Street, and three hundred wooded acres north of the village. She said she and her husband have always liked the wooded property, which includes a hunting camp and is traversed by a small stream she calls Finulla Brook.

The second file drawer in Chief Arnold Jacobs' desk holds a yellowing folder marked "Slicer." About once a year Jacobs gets it out and goes over the facts of an assault against a dead drug dealer. He envisions a playground seesaw with Kevin Beaujolais on one end of the board and Ralph Montgomery on the other. When the seesaw morphs into the Scales of Justice, he closes the folder and puts it away among the unsolved cases.

ABOUT THE AUTHOR

STEVE DELANEY is the middle link in a five-generation family love affair with Lake Champlain and Vermont.

A Vermonter since 1988, and a summer kid since 1947, he classifies himself as a Recovering Flatlander.

Delaney is a fifty-year broadcast journalist who has covered politics and other petty crime in Washington, finance and other felonies in New York, and wars on three continents.

He has won national honors for two NBC White Paper television documentaries, and for radio documentaries and news programs produced for Vermont Public Radio, where his distinctive voice has been heard for a decade.

He is also the author of *Vermont Seasonings: Reflections on the Rhythms of a Vermont Year*.